Dear Reader,

Love at first sight ca[n be wonderful, but] sometimes second chances can be even sweeter. This month, four breathtaking new romances from Bouquet prove it!

Veteran author Colleen Faulkner starts us off with the first in the new Bachelors, Inc. miniseries, **Marrying Owen,** the story of an estranged couple forced into close quarters by a sudden storm—and ready to give love another try. Next up is the final installment in Vivian Leiber's the Men of Sugar Mountain trilogy, **Three Wishes.** When a man from her past returns to her small town, one woman wonders if he's now the key to the future she's always hoped for.

Sometimes romance blooms in the most unexpected places. That's what happens when the heroine of Wendy Morgan's **Ask Me Again** finds herself in a wedding party with the most boring guy she knew in college—and discovers he's become a fascinating and sexy man. Finally, Susan Hardy proves that every cloud really does have a **Silver Lining** when an accident that threatens everything one woman has leads her into the arms of a man who becomes the one thing she really wants.

Laughter, tears, desire, and most of all, love—Bouquet delivers them all. Why not give one a chance today?

Kate Duffy
Editorial Director

# OPPOSITES ATTRACT

Patience pulled Jace through the crowd toward the door behind the bandstand, and they slipped out onto the quiet pier behind the club.

It was deserted and dark even in the light of the three-quarter September moon. The air was chilly, and Patience shivered as soon as the breeze off the water hit her.

"I'll warm you up." Jace had pulled her into his arms. She'd leaned her cheek against his chest and listened to his heart racing before she tentatively pulled back and looked up at him.

He was watching her, his eyes so black and opaque that she couldn't read their expression. She held her breath, watching him, wondering how he could look so composed when her whole body was electrified with wanting him.

After a long moment, he finally leaned down toward her and she released a sigh, closing her eyes in the instant before she felt him gently cupping her face. He held her like that, his hands warm on her cheeks, while his lips came down over hers in a kiss that was at first gently searching, almost tentative. But within moments, she was leaning back against the splintered wood railing of the pier and he was leaning over her, brushing her lips repeatedly with his fervent, probing mouth, stroking her face, her hair, her neck with his hands.

Never before had Patience been kissed this way—thoroughly, passionately . . .

# ASK ME AGAIN

# Wendy Morgan

**ZEBRA BOOKS**
Kensington Publishing Corp.
http://www.zebrabooks.com

ZEBRA BOOKS are published by

Kensington Publishing Corp.
850 Third Avenue
New York, NY 10022

Copyright © 2000 by Wendy Corsi Staub

All rights reserved. No part of this book may be reproduced in any form or by any means without the prior written consent of the Publisher, excepting brief quotes used in reviews.

If you purchased this book without a cover you should be aware that this book is stolen property. It was reported as "unsold and destroyed" to the Publisher and neither the Author nor the Publisher has received any payment for this "stripped book."

Zebra and the Z logo Reg. U.S. Pat. & TM Off.

First Printing: August, 2000
10 9 8 7 6 5 4 3 2 1

Printed in the United States of America

*For my new sister, Mari, and for my newborn
nephew, Rick Payton . . .
And for my dear brother Rick, who brought them both
into our lives.*

*And, as always, for Mark, Morgan, and Brody,
with love.*

# Prologue

*1995, Barnbury College*

It wasn't so much the shouting that woke Jace Hoffman from a sound sleep in the middle of the night.

It was the pounding on his door that had rapidly progressed from plain old knocking to the splintering sound of something being repeatedly heaved against it—either a battering ram or the five-foot-eight frame of one fuming twenty-two-year-old female.

Somehow, Jace suspected the latter.

He reached for his glasses, made sure his flannel pajama top and bottoms were buttoned and snapped, and got out of bed. He felt his way through the darkness around his roommate's empty bed, two desks, and two dressers.

He flicked on the light and opened the door, apparently just as Patience Magee was hurling herself against it again.

Jace barely had time to wince before he was on the floor with Patience sprawled on top of him.

"Where is he?" she hollered, literally collaring Jace. "I want the truth . . . where is he?"

Jace blinked and grunted.

"Come on, spill it, Jace," Patience said, shaking him a little. "Where's Bryan?"

"If you'll get *off* of my *chest*"—he gave her a shove and tried to sit up—"maybe I'll tell you."

"What? Tell me what? Where is he?" In one agile move, Patience was on her feet and glaring down on him with her hands on her hips.

"I have no idea." Jace straightened his glasses and gingerly felt his ribs.

"You're his roommate," she said in a don't-give-me-that tone. "His best friend. Of *course* you know where he is."

"I don't."

"You're lying."

"I'm not." Jace regarded her calmly. "You have pine needles stuck in your hair. And there's dirt on your face."

Patience reached up and raked her fingers through her glossy black curls. A pitter-patter of green needles rained onto the functional gray dorm carpet. She shrugged, her chin set stubbornly as she watched Jace, waiting.

He stood and dusted off his pajama bottoms. "You still have dirt on your face."

She sighed and ran an impatient hand over her cheeks and chin. She looked Jace in the eye, and he saw a flicker of something besides irritation in their flashing green depths.

Pain?

Vulnerability?

Nah . . . not Patience Magee. Everyone knew she was as tough and sassy as they come.

Jace glanced at the smudge of—what was that, soot?—on the tip of her impudent nose. For some strange reason, he was gripped by the sudden overpowering urge to reach out and gently wipe it off.

*Give it a minute. It'll pass,* he advised himself.

Lord knew he wasn't about to risk touching Patience

Magee. Considering the state she was in, she'd probably snarl and nip his fingers right off.

"Try your nose," he instructed her.

Without removing her eyes from his, she reached into the pocket of her blue corduroy coat and produced a handkerchief.

Jace blinked. She wasn't the kind of girl he'd expect to carry one of those. It was pastel linen, with lace edges and tiny embroidered flowers.

*Well, if that doesn't beat—*

Patience lifted the handkerchief to her mouth and spit noisily into it. Then she rubbed it over her nose, crumpled it into a soggy, dirt-smeared wad, and shoved it back into her pocket.

"I'm waiting," she reminded Jace, giving him a level gaze.

"I told you, Patience, I have no idea where Bryan—you have a giant rip in your knee, did you know that?"

She glanced down at her Levis. The tattered, gaping hole on the right leg was caked with what looked like mud.

Patience shrugged.

"Geez, where the heck have you been? Crawling through the underbrush?"

"That's *exactly* where I've been," she said, poking Jace in the chest with her index finger for emphasis.

He took a step backward.

"And do you want to know *why* I was crawling through the underbrush?" She gave him another poke.

He took another step backward. "Why?"

"Because *your* roommate left the library with another girl, that's why!"

Jace retreated before she could poke him again. His back was against Bryan's dresser. He held up a hand like a traffic cop to ward off Patience.

"We have one little fight in the dining hall today," she said, shaking her head. A twig dropped out of her hair and landed on Jace's bare big toe. "And what does he do? He takes off with some girl from Brown. What was that little S.B. doing in the library at B.C., anyway?"

B.C. stood for Barnbury College. Jace had no idea what an S.B. was, and he wasn't about to ask.

Patience raged on. "After four years, you'd think Bryan would know better than to think I meant it when I said to get lost for good. Oh, yeah, right—like I really meant it when I told him to go out with anyone he wanted."

"You told him that?"

"Yeah."

"What did you expect him to think?"

Patience scowled. "Look, Jace, this is none of your business. Why don't you just stay out of it?"

"I *was* out of it," he pointed out, trying not to raise his voice, "until you came barging in here at"—he glanced at the digital clock on the dresser—"12:23 A.M. and dragged me *into* it. On the night before finals start, besides!"

"Oh, finals." Patience waved an airy hand. "That *would* be all you care about."

Jace chose not to respond to that. He knew she—and everyone else at Barnbury—thought he was a hopeless brainiac.

*Well, let's see where the rest of them wind up in a few weeks, after graduation.* Jace thought. He'd already lined up a prime position on Wall Street.

He focused on Patience again. "You still haven't told me why you were crawling through the underbrush."

"Why do you think? I was following Bryan and Miss Brown University across the campus. And they came back to *this* dorm. Now where are you hiding them?"

Jace just shrugged.

Actually, he knew exactly where Bryan must have taken the girl. There was an empty single on the first floor at the end of the hall. Anyone who had a roommate and brought a girl back to the dorm could "rent" the room for the night by slipping the R.A. a few bucks.

There was only one rule: You couldn't bring girls who went to Barnbury there, or even tell them about it. No one in the all-male dorm wanted to risk letting word get out on campus.

"You know where Bryan is," Patience announced, watching Jace's face carefully. Her expression was lethal. "I can tell."

"I do not." He forced his eyes to stay steady on hers. No way was he telling her. If he let it slip, Bryan would be a dead man.

Not that this was the first time Patience and Bryan had had a raging battle. And somehow, he'd always managed to survive the wrath of Patience before.

But as far as Jace knew, this was the first time she'd caught Bryan cheating.

And this time, there was an especially deadly gleam in her eyes.

Patience regarded Jace narrowly for another long moment, then shrugged abruptly. "I guess you don't know after all," she said. "Okay, thanks anyway. I'll get going now."

Jace frowned. The suddenly amiable creature who left the room quietly bore no resemblance to the Patience Magee he'd known for the past four years.

Shaking his head, he turned off the light and climbed back into bed.

If it hadn't been so late and if he hadn't been worried about exams the next morning, he might have noticed that her footsteps didn't retreat back down the hall.

# One

Patience Magee did a double take.

The guy who'd just snuck into the back of the empty church was good-looking.

Great looking, in fact.

A gentle nudge in her ribs alerted her that her friend and fellow bridesmaid Beth had noticed him, too.

Patience fought the urge to crane her neck and squint as the newcomer started walking up the long aisle toward the altar, where the wedding party was gathered. They were listening to Father Bianco's instructions about what would happen tomorrow after Anne, the bride, and Ned, the groom, finished lighting the unity candle.

Patience, half-listening, squinted at the approaching male.

Too bad she'd forgotten to put her contacts back on after returning from the beach this afternoon.

Still, she could tell that he was handsome—tall, dark-haired, and very tanned. He wore khaki shorts, a short-sleeved J. Crew polo shirt, and white-soled brown leather deck shoes without socks—practically a uniform in Newport in late August.

Hmm.

There was something familiar about that walk—the kind of shuffling action around the feet . . .

Patience glanced over at the row of guys lined up on the altar alongside Ned. There were six, including Ned's brother Barrett, the best man. And seven bridesmaids, including herself and Anne's sister Mary, the maid of honor.

That meant this was the missing usher.

And that meant he was . . .

No way!

Unless . . .

The way he was raising his left arm to look at his watch, tilting his head in that unruffled, annoyingly familiar way, clinched it.

Patience tapped Beth urgently and hissed, "See that guy? The one who just walked in?"

Beth nodded, keeping her gaze politely focused on Father Bianco.

"You'll never in a million years *guess* who he is."

"Matt Lauer?"

Patience rolled her eyes. "Matt Lauer? You mean, the guy who does the "Today" show with Katie Couric?"

"It looks just like him from here, and I read that he's—"

"Beth, trust me. It's *not* Matt Lauer. Guess again." Then, because she couldn't contain herself, she blurted, "Jace Hoffman—that's who he is."

She had the satisfaction of watching Beth's jaw drop.

Just then Father Bianco halted the rehearsal to say, "You must be our missing usher."

Everyone else on the altar turned and Jace gave a little wave.

"Hey, buddy," Ned called cheerfully. "Glad you could make it."

Jace nodded. "Glad to be here. Congratulations," he added in his quiet, composed way.

"Hi, Jace," Anne said. "You belong on the end, next to Bryan."

Patience, Father Bianco, and the rest of the wedding party watched as Jace stepped up onto the altar to join the line of ushers. Bryan reached out and slapped his former roommate on the back in an old-buddy-old-pal-o'mine gesture. Jace grinned. The next usher down the line, Henry Farnham, reached across Bryan to offer Jace a handshake.

"Looks like we're all old friends here," Father Bianco remarked. "Don't worry—there'll be plenty of time for getting reacquainted after the rehearsal. For now, though, let's get back down to business. Mary, you'll want to take Anne's bouquet again when . . ."

As the priest droned on, giving instructions, Patience snuck another look at the opposite side of the altar.

There was Ned, looking glad and a little stunned to be finally marrying Anne.

*They've only been going out for five years,* Patience thought wryly. *It's about time.*

She still remembered the night, senior year, when Anne had come rushing back from the campus center to tell her suite-mates that Ned had asked her out.

Patience had said *it's about time* then, too. After all, she had always figured Anne and Ned would be perfect for each other. They both came from old Newport money. They were both blond-haired, blue-eyed, and athletic. They were both political science majors. They hung around with the same group of friends. And neither of them ever skipped a class or got the punch line to a dirty joke.

Patience scanned the line of men, past Ned's two prep school friends. She couldn't tell them apart; she just knew that one was John something-or-other the third and the other was Jack something-or-other the fourth. They wore identical madras shorts and had the same clench-jawed blue-blood speech patterns.

Next came Ira Swann, one of the partners in the law firm where Ned and Anne worked. He was surprisingly laid back, Patience had decided. She'd met him on the beach behind Anne's parents' house today after the bridesmaids' brunch.

Patience continued down the row. At this point, it was like traveling down memory lane. Henry, Bryan, and Jace rounded out the bunch—all three of them alumni of Barnbury College.

Henry was still the same old crew-cut, flask-in-the-hip-pocket good-time guy. Immature. Definitely. Patience had figured that out after talking to him for five minutes this morning. He'd been trying to find out where he could buy chalk to write "Help Me" on the bottoms of Ned's shoes tomorrow.

Bryan—*skip right over Bryan*.

Patience couldn't believe she'd ever gone out with a jerk like him. Her first thought upon seeing him again earlier had been *Good—he's gone bald*. Gleefully, she'd noted that Bryan's once thick, wavy dark hair had thinned considerably in the past five years. And he'd been looking pretty paunchy on the beach this afternoon, too.

Then there was Jace.

Patience still couldn't believe it was him.

Bryan's roommate had always been the pale, sickly, nerdy type. He'd had a passion for studying and a penchant for driving Patience crazy with his unruffled, matter-of-fact way of looking at everything. Never once had she seen him flustered, excited, or even angry. He'd always maintained an even keel that was maddening to someone like Patience.

Apparently, he hadn't changed much in that respect, she noted dryly. Jace was standing with his feet planted slightly apart, a bland expression on his face. He appeared to be listening intently to Father Bianco.

## ASK ME AGAIN 17

But boy, had he changed when it came to looks. Gone was any hint of the anemic, weak, bespectacled student Patience had known. In his place was someone she would have been extremely attracted to . . . if she hadn't known better.


"All right, now—let's practice the recessional," Father Bianco announced. "Anne and Ned, you'll walk out first, followed by the maid of honor and best man. Then the lines of ushers and bridesmaids move toward the center of the altar. As the lines converge, each gentleman will take the arm of the lady opposite and escort her out of the church. Shall we try it?"

There was a murmur of consent among the wedding party.

Bryan muttered to Jace, "Let's get this thing over with already."

As Jace looked over to see which bridesmaid he'd be matched up with, he was thinking, *same old impatient Bryan.*

Speaking of impatient . . .

It couldn't be.

But it was.

Patience Magee.

Jace would have recognized those shiny black ringlets anywhere. She looked exactly the same as she had the last time he'd seen her, five years ago, in college. Same tall, slender build, same intense green eyes, same nervous energy—he could tell that by the jittery, rhythmic way she was shaking one long, bare, sun-browned leg, obviously anxious to get moving.

Jace pitied the usher who ended up walking with her. She'd probably haul him back down the aisle at lightning speed. Patience didn't do anything slowly. She'd probably—

Wait a minute.

Patience was the last bridesmaid in line.

Jace was the last usher.

That meant *he* was her partner.

He barely had time to digest that unnerving information when the organist struck up a classical march and the lines began to move. Before he knew it, Bryan had taken the arm of the pretty blonde Jace remembered as Beth Stenner and Jace had arrived face to face with Patience.

She was too busy shooting a dirty look at Bryan's retreating back to acknowledge Jace at first. But when he reached out and took her arm, she looked up at him and winked. "Hey, Jace. Remember me?"

"How could I forget?"

"Long time no see, huh?" She grinned at him and started to take a step forward.

Father Bianco held up a hand that meant *wait*.

Patience sighed restlessly. Jace felt her whole body tensed and ready to spring into action. It made him incredibly nervous.

Hell, *she* made him incredibly nervous. She always had.

Father Bianco beckoned them at last, and they started down the aisle, following the plodding parade of ushers and bridesmaids.

Jace attempted to adapt the measured footsteps everyone else was using. But as he'd predicted, Patience was practically breaking into a trot, pulling on his arm.

"Stop dragging your legs!" she hissed at him.

"Will you slow down?" he returned in a low, reasonable voice. "We can't beat the bride and groom out of the church, you know. This isn't a race."

She giggled, her rippling laughter spilling over musically, just the way Jace remembered it. "Wouldn't it be something if it were?"

Jace frowned. "Were what?"

"A race!" Her voice was hushed, amused. "Can't you just see Anne tearing down the aisle in a long white gown, like Katherine Ross in *The Graduate*?"

Jace had to smile at that. "Yeah, well, if there were a race, you'd win, even though everyone else has a head start . . . unless you've changed an awful lot in the past five years."

He glanced down at her and their eyes collided. Hers were flashing, probing, intense. Jace quickly looked away.

"What'd you mean by that?" she asked sharply.

"I just meant that you never liked to be last in line for anything back when I knew you." He kept his gaze focused on Bryan's and Beth's backs.

"Yeah, well I still don't." She sighed. "But unfortunately, as the tallest bridesmaid, I get to be last. So do you."

"Bryan's taller than me." As Jace recalled, his former roommate was six-foot-four. He was only six-three.

"Oh, come on," she exclaimed incredulously. "I wasn't about to let Anne and Ned match me up with *him.*"

"Tell me you're not still nursing a grudge against him after all these years. You must be over him by now." He glanced at her.

Her jaw was stubbornly set. "I may be over him, but that doesn't mean I want him to touch me ever again. Even on the arm. That lousy, two-timing, son of—"

"Uh-uh," he cautioned. "You're in church, remember?"

She was silent, but he could feel her simmering.

Jace recalled how badly things had ended between his roommate and Patience at the end of senior year. She'd caught him cheating on her. Her wrath had been lethal. Jace hated to think what would have happened to Bryan if Patience had known that it wasn't the first time he'd been unfaithful.

Jace had never understood how Bryan had even had the energy to keep up with someone like Patience, let alone cheat on her. She was so demanding, so scattered, so utterly exhausting.

Jace had always been half-fascinated by her, and half-terrified.

Except for that one time . . .

That brief instant when he'd glimpsed a side of Patience he'd never expected to find.

It was the morning after she'd shown up at the dorm looking for Bryan, who was out with that other girl, the one from Brown. When Jace had opened the door at six-thirty A.M. on his way to the library to study more for his early exam, he'd nearly stepped on Patience.

She was curled up in a little ball, fast asleep on the rubber doormat. Obviously, she'd been lying in wait for Bryan, but he had never come home.

Jace had stared down at her peaceful, slumbering face. It was the first time he'd ever seen her that serene and quiet. Heck, it was the first time he'd ever seen her *motionless*.

He'd noticed how young she looked—young and utterly innocent.

And then he had seen that her cheeks were tear-stained.

And in that instant, something had stirred inside of Jace. Suddenly, his mind wasn't busily processing facts he'd need for the upcoming exam at all. It was filled with—*consumed by*—the image of Patience.

All he'd wanted to do was protect her.

Comfort her.

*Kiss her.*

Inexplicably, Jace had felt a sudden, overwhelming

urge to lean over and brush his lips against Patience's soft, full, pink mouth.

He'd never know whether he would have actually done it, because just then, her eyes had snapped open.

His only thought then had been, *uh-oh*.

She immediately came wide awake, consumed by fury as she realized it was morning and Bryan had never come home.

Spurred by an urgent instinct of self-preservation, Jace had hurried off down the hall to his exam, leaving her to storm and rage alone.

And that was the last time he had ever seen her.

Until now.

Back at the waterfront hotel where she was sharing a room with Beth, Patience stood in front of the mirror in her black french-cut panties and matching bra.

She used a Q-Tip to smudge the smoky charcoal pencil around her green eyes. Then she curled her lashes and began liberally applying black mascara, the tip of her pink tongue poking from the corner of her mouth as she concentrated.

Beth edged her own reflection into the mirror. She was clad in a white satin slip, her long pale hair wound around hot rollers. "What I wouldn't give for your naturally curly hair," she told Patience wistfully.

"What I wouldn't give for your straight blond hair," Patience returned. "What time is it?"

Beth checked her watch as she strapped it onto her wrist. "Five after seven.

"We're late."

"I know."

The rehearsal dinner hosted by Ned's parents had started at seven o'clock in the restaurant downstairs.

"Are you almost ready?" Patience asked Beth, tossing a lipstick onto the counter and blotting her mouth with a tissue.

"Do I look almost ready?"

"We're bridesmaids. We can't walk in there at seven-thirty." Patience went over to the closet and yanked open the door.

"Just give me five minutes. Besides, you're not even dressed yourself."

"I am now." Patience's voice was muffled beneath the folds of fabric of the dress she was pulling over her head. She tugged it down, raised the zipper in one swift motion, and shook her head vigorously. Her tousled curls bounced back into place.

She examined herself critically in the full-length mirror as she stepped into her low black pumps. She loved this dress. It was black and simple, with boxy shoulders, a scoop neck, and a long, tapered skirt.

"Great outfit," Beth said over her shoulder. "Where'd you get it?"

"At the Antique Boutique."

"That's a second-hand dress?"

"It's from, like, the forties or something." Patience knew Beth, who was strictly Saks Fifth Avenue, would never wear something someone else had worn. She hadn't even liked to borrow or lend clothes back in the old dorm days.

A bland "wow" was Beth's reply.

The two had been friends ever since their first day of their first semester nearly ten years ago. They'd been roommates all four years, and then they'd moved to New York together. Now Patience lived in a studio apartment on the sixth floor of a Village walkup and Beth lived in a two-bedroom duplex with a terrace in an Upper East Side high-rise, and they met every Sunday afternoon in midtown for brunch.

Patience put on her dangly silver-and-onyx earrings

and fastened an antique locket around her neck. Then she picked up the small vintage cigarette case she used as an evening bag and looked over at Beth. "All set?"

Beth, still in her slip, just rolled her eyes and unwound another roller.

Patience paced across the floor, then to the door, then back again. She picked up the *Welcome to Newport* booklet from the telephone table, ruffled through the pages at lightning speed, checked her watch, and looked at Beth again.

"Beth? . . ."

"Hold on." Tossing the last roller on the counter, Beth reached for her brush as Patience resumed her pacing. "Why are you so anxious to get down there, anyway? Afraid one of the other bridesmaids has already snagged Jace Hoffman?"

Patience stopped dead and snorted. "Jace Hoffman? Don't be ridiculous."

"If I'm not mistaken, less than one hour ago, you were drooling when he showed up at the church."

"That was before I found out who he was."

"That makes no sense. Drooling is drooling."

"And Jace Hoffman is Jace Hoffman." *Even if he does look like Matt Lauer.* "He's Bryan's old roommate, remember?"

"What does that have to do with anything? College was another lifetime. Anne told me he's single *and* he lives in New York."

"Oh, yeah? When did she tell you that?"

"When I asked her about him. After the rehearsal. While you were arguing with Father Bianco about not being able to throw rice tomorrow."

"Well, birdseed is ridiculous," Patience muttered, remembering. "Why would anyone want to be pelted with birdseed? With all the seagulls around here, that's just asking for trouble."

"Oh, come on."

"I'm serious. It'll get stuck in Anne's veil . . . I can just see a flock swooping down on her, pecking . . ." She shuddered.

"Patience, you have an amazing imagination. That would never happen."

"Oh, yeah? Ever see what happened to Tippi Hendren in *The Birds*?" she asked darkly. "Anyway, what else did Anne say?"

"About—?"

"Jace, what else? And why were you asking about him?"

Beth shrugged her delicate shoulders that were creamy white despite the afternoon on the beach. "I was curious."

Something flared inside of Patience. Taken aback, she paused to wonder what it was. It almost felt like jealousy, but of course that was ridiculous.

"You and Jace would make a perfect couple," she told Beth. "You're both levelheaded, logical, rational . . ."

"Exactly what I was thinking," Beth said with a demure smile. "And Anne said he has a great job on Wall Street."

"Figures," Patience muttered. "He always said he'd make his first million before he turned thirty."

"I don't know about that, but . . ." Beth shrugged. She finished with her hair. It hung in smooth blond waves down her back. She walked over to the closet and reached for a silk dress that was still in a Manhattan dry cleaner's plastic bag.

Patience looked in the mirror again. Her own cheeks were ruddy from today's sun, and a new crop of freckles was visible even beneath the layer of foundation makeup she wore. Her curls had a tousled, vaguely wild look. She tried to tame them with a few hasty swipes of one unmanicured hand. It didn't work.

She looked over at Beth, who was glowing in sunset tones, from her golden hair to her peach lipstick and nail polish to her soft coral dress. She was fastening a strand of pearls around her neck.

"Are you finally ready?" Patience asked, striding over to the door.

"Ready." Beth had added pearl drop earrings as a finishing touch. She picked up the small coral bag that exactly matched her dress. "Do you have your room key?"

"I don't know . . . don't you have yours?"

"I do, but you'd better find yours. We might not come back together, you know." Beth flashed her a small, meaningful smile.

Patience knew what she meant by that. Beth was hoping she and Jace might end up together later.

Feeling suddenly irritated with her friend for some strange reason, Patience stomped back across the floor and began rummaging through her beach bag for her key.

Jace noticed her as soon as she entered the restaurant.

"Look at that," one of Ned's prep-school-friend ushers, Jack or John, said low in Jace's ear. "She's gorgeous."

Jace just shrugged. Maybe she was, but she was also dangerous.

"Do you know her?" the other usher, John or Jack, asked in his other ear.

Jace nodded. "Stay away from her," he warned.

"Why? Is she married?"

"No. She's out of control. She'll eat you alive." Jace turned back to the bar and picked up his drink.

"That sweet, innocent little blonde?"

"Blonde?" Jace turned around again. Only then did he notice Beth at Patience's side. "Oh, you were talking about Beth?"

"Yeah, that's her name," John or Jack said. "What did you think? That we were talking about that wildcat with the crazy black hair?"

That was exactly what Jace had thought.

He'd never considered bland, blonde Beth to be gorgeous. Patience, on the other hand . . .

"Wildcat?" he commented, sipping his drink and watching Patience over the rim of his glass.

"Yeah. She flipped that guy Henry on the beach today."

Jace raised an eyebrow. "She . . . *flipped* . . . Henry?"

"Right over her shoulder. I guess he must have made a comment or something when she walked by us in that bikini of hers. The next thing he knew, he was face down in the sand."

Amusement flickered through Jace, who'd never been able to stand Henry. But he kept his face carefully passive. "How unfortunate."

"Yeah," Jack or John agreed with a shudder. "You couldn't pay me enough to get near that chick. It's almost ski season and I have no intention of spending the next few months in a body cast. But the blonde, on the other hand . . ."

Jace watched Patience saunter up to the opposite end of the bar. She seemed to have lost Beth. She ordered something, then stood tapping her fingers in a rapid staccato rhythm on the wooden counter while she waited.

"Excuse me for a second," Jace told the two ushers. "I'll be right back."

*You shouldn't be doing this.* he warned himself as he walked toward her. *You know better than to tangle with her.*

*But I'm not going to tangle with her,* the foolhardy side of him argued. *I'm just going to say a brief, polite hello like a civilized person.*

"Hello," he said, arriving at Patience's side just as her drink was placed in front of her.

She looked up at him, her eyes flashing their usual mixture of amusement, curiosity, and plain old intensity. "Hi."

"How's it going?"

"Fine." She sipped the amber liquid. "Aren't Ned and Anne here yet?"

"Ned's over there, talking to his dad and Father Bianco. I haven't seen Anne yet."

"She's never been on time. She'll probably show up late at the church tomorrow."

Jace nodded and swallowed some beer. What was it about Patience that had always made him faintly uneasy, even when she wasn't saying or doing anything the least bit threatening? Even after all these years?

"I heard you flipped Henry on the beach today."

She responded to that with her rippling laugh. "Right. He deserved it. He grabbed my—"

"Yeah, I'll bet he did deserve it," Jace cut in hastily. "Never could stand the guy."

Her eyes widened with surprise—and delight. "You're kidding. I thought you were friends."

"I was friends with Bryan and Ned. Henry happened to be Ned's roommate, so we all hung out together. But we weren't 'friends.' "

She contemplated that. "Neither were you and I," she said after a moment, in that direct way of hers.

Jace wasn't quite sure what to say to that. "I . . . uh . . . no, I guess we weren't."

She shrugged. "I don't blame you for not liking me.

I was pretty ridiculous back then, chasing after Bryan and trying to force him to be a good boyfriend."

"That's true." He paused. "But, you know, I didn't—*not* like you."

"Oh, come on, Jace, don't be so damned polite. Of course you didn't like me. I didn't like you, either."

He blinked. "Oh."

She laughed at his expression. "Don't take it personally."

"Why didn't you like me?"

She seemed to mull it over, as though sorting through the numerous reasons. For some reason that bothered him.

He was about to tell her to forget it and walk away when she said, looking earnest, "Because you took school so seriously, you know? And you always acted so . . . I don't know—superior? As if you thought the rest of us were just a bumbling bunch of idiots, or something."

Had he been that bad? He couldn't think of a response, so he raised the beer to his lips again.

Patience gulped her own drink.

"What is that?" Jace asked, pointing at her glass, for lack of anything else to say.

"Jack Daniel's and water."

"I should have guessed." It had been her drink of choice even back in college, when Anne and Beth and the other girls had been into wine spritzers and sloe gin fizzes.

"Why do you say that?"

"No reason, just . . . I guess you haven't changed much."

"You sound disappointed," Patience told him. "You haven't changed much either, have you? You're still planning to become a millionaire, I hear, if you haven't already."

He wasn't about to tell her that he had. "Yeah, I play around in the stock market a little. I'm an investment banker in New York."

"How nice," she said in a tone that told him she wasn't nearly as impressed as she would have been if he'd told her he'd dropped out of the corporate world to live in a vegetarian nudists' commune and make whale sculptures out of scrap metal.

"What are you doing now?" he asked her.

"I'm in New York, too. I'm an associate editor for *She* magazine. Ever heard of it?"

He nodded. "My ex-girlfriend used to read it."

She raised an eyebrow at him. "Ex-girlfriend?"

"Yeah." Then, because Patience was obviously expecting him to give more detail, he offered, "Her name was Sue."

"That's a nice name.

"Yeah." Jace cleared his throat.

She was still waiting, those green eyes focused on him expectantly.

"We broke up last spring."

"How come?"

"Because she wanted to get married."

A sly little grin lit Patience's face. "Ah, I see. And you're one of those always-an-usher, never-a-groom types."

"Not exactly. I mean, I, uh, I'll probably get married someday. I just—didn't want to marry . . . her."

Why was he telling Patience all of this? He hadn't spoken to anyone about Sue since the breakup. Talking about his personal life wasn't his style.

Patience sighed. "I know what you mean."

It was his turn to raise an eyebrow. "You do?"

"I was seeing this guy who wanted to get engaged last Christmas. He was into moving to Jersey—or, God forbid, to *Lawn Guyland*," she said with an exaggerated

Long Island accent, "and having kids, windowboxes, lawn mowers—the whole nine yards."

"And you weren't?"

"What, are you kidding? I'm too young to be tied down. I've got a great apartment in the Village. I travel every chance I get. I'm just getting started on my career—in another few months, I'll be promoted to editor with any luck. There's no way I'd chuck all that for some guy." She tilted her head back and downed another generous swallow of the whiskey.

"What was his name?" Jace asked.

"Whose name? Oh, you mean Crispin?"

*"Crispin?"*

"Crispin Nigel Broadhurst the Fifth, to be exact. He worked down on Wall Street, too."

"Is that a fact?"

"It is." She looked him in the eye. "I'd never get involved with that type ever again."

"What type?"

"Oh, you know. The dull type. Uncreative. Unspontaneous. Logical to the point of being no fun."

Just then, Ned's father turned on a mike that gave a long, high-pitched squeak before he tentatively said, "Testing . . . testing.

When the room had grown silent, he straightened his navy-and-maroon-striped tie and continued, "Please take your seats, now that my lovely daughter-in-law-to-be has arrived. You can find your table assignments listed on the sheet located near the door."

There was a murmur, and everyone began moving toward the tables.

Jace set his beer down on the bar. Ned's father hadn't interrupted a moment too soon. It would be a relief to get a break from Patience's probing questions and opinionated way of thinking. Of course, she was beautiful and smart and interesting, and Jace didn't mind her as much as he once had—not really. Not in small doses.

But it would be better to share dinner and conversation with someone who was less—complicated. Someone who wouldn't aggravate his chronic ulcer more than the beer probably was going to. Someone who was more . . . simple.

"Well, I guess I'd better go find out where I'm sitting," he told Patience. "See you later."

Jace turned to walk away, but a long arm swiftly reached out and strong fingers clamped around his wrist, stopping him in his tracks.

"I already know where you're sitting," Patience informed him sweetly. "You're at table three. With me."

# Two

Patience couldn't sleep.

According to the hotel digital alarm clock, it was 5:41 A.M., and she'd been awake ever since she'd crawled into bed at two. At this rate, she was going to be one exhausted bridesmaid tomorrow . . . make that today.

In just a few hours, Anne and Ned would be getting married.

And Patience would be seeing Jace again.

She flopped over onto her stomach and punched the typically flat foam hotel pillow into some semblance of fluffiness. In the next bed, Beth stirred and made an annoying staccato tongue-slapping-against-the-roof-of-her-mouth sound, then sighed softly.

Patience squeezed her eyes shut and prayed for sleep.

Please.

Sleep.

Please.

*Don't think about anything,* she instructed her racing mind.

Nothing.

Nothing but sleep.

What was the matter with her tonight? She *never* had trouble sleeping. Every single night of her whole life, she'd climbed into bed, closed her eyes, and conked

# ASK ME AGAIN

out immediately. She always slept straight through the night, too. Even when she was worried about a project for work or a boyfriend problem. Whenever anyone had told her they had insomnia, she'd always been bewildered. What in life could be simpler than falling asleep?

*At this point, everything.*

She realized she was clenching her fists and teeth and willed herself to relax. Why was she so keyed up? What was wrong with her tonight?

*Don't be stupid. You know what's wrong tonight.*

*Jace.*

There he was, intruding again on her consciousness, just as he had ever since she'd gotten into bed.

What had happened tonight after dinner was just too disconcerting to forget. Patience had been over it repeatedly, replaying exactly what he'd said, what she'd said, what she'd done, what he'd done. Sometimes she played it in slow motion, sometimes at high speed, skipping ahead to the good parts.

*Not the "good" parts,* she reminded herself. *The bad parts. The totally confusing, scary, big-mistake parts.*

She groaned and flipped restlessly onto her back.


Jace slipped out of bed and turned on the air-conditioner. Not that it was hot in the room. Actually, it was a cool night, even for the shore.

But maybe, if he were lucky, the steady hum would lull him to sleep.

If he didn't freeze to death first.

He padded back over to the bed and got in. The hotel sheets and blankets had that detached hotel smell, and the pillow was much too fluffy, the way hotel pillows always were. Jace punched it down to try to flatten it, then settled back in and closed his eyes.

*Now go to sleep.*

*Yeah, right.*

He looked at the glowing digital alarm clock on the telephone stand beside the bed. 5:41.

He was no stranger to insomnia. Nearly every night of his life, he spent a good half hour trying desperately to relax and stop thinking.

He was used to it.

Tonight was no different.

Except . . .

*Patience.*

This was all her fault. Everything was. Everything that had happened.

He couldn't stop thinking about it.

*Well, get over it,* he told himself, exasperated. *Get her out of your mind. Just forget about her.*

Patience was beginning to panic. It was almost six o'clock and she was still wide-eyed, not the least bit tired.

She knew she had to get up in less than an hour. Anne's parents were sending a limousine to pick up the bridesmaids at eight. They were all going to have their hair done by a stylist, then they would be brought over to Anne's for photographs.

Patience really hated this bridesmaid business.

This was her fourth time, counting her stint as maid of honor for her sister Hope. Actually, that hadn't been as bad, because Hope and Jermaine had been married barefoot on the beach, and the whole thing had been incredibly easy and informal. The bridal party had worn whatever they felt like wearing, and there had been no annoying posing for pictures, no required dancing. In fact, there hadn't even been a band—Jermaine's friend had just shown up with his

# ASK ME AGAIN

guitar, and everyone had sat around and sung old songs by America and Simon and Garfunkel.

There would be no such luck this time. Anne's parents had hired one of the best photographers on the east coast, and a full orchestra. That meant lots of pictures . . . and at least one bridal party dance. She would be expected to dance with Jace.

Jace, again.

Again she pushed her mental "rewind" and "play" buttons.

It had all started during dinner when Father Bianco stood up to say grace. He'd asked everyone to join hands.

Henry had been sitting on Patience's right. He'd muttered, "No way am I holding your hand. How do I know you won't flip me again?"

Patience had just smiled sweetly at him and turned to her left. Jace was there, looking expectantly at her. Bryan, on his other side, was clinging to some poor bridesmaid—Anne's cousin, who wore ashtray-thick glasses and had an overbite—with one hand. He was also kidding around, making a big show of pretending to hold Jace's hand.

Patience shot Bryan a dirty look, then glanced at Jace. He shrugged. Patience shrugged.

They both looked straight ahead, then simultaneously reached out.

The second they touched, something happened. Patience knew it was unbelievably cliché and corny to even think the word *electricity*, but she couldn't help it. Jace's hand was surprisingly strong and warm and masculine, and some kind of—*current*—was tingling its way from his skin to hers, all the way up her arm, to spread a quivery warmth through her whole body.

She'd looked over at him. As soon as their eyes collided she felt his grip on her hand tighten, just slightly, but enough to make her heart beat a little faster. She increased her own pressure on his hand, squeezing back as if they had some private signal.

Suddenly, holding hands with Jace Hoffman was the sexiest thing Patience could imagine.

She tried to focus on what Father Bianco was saying, but before she knew it, he'd finished with a hearty "Amen."

Was she only imagining that Jace had held her hand for a few extra seconds? When he did let go and they both sat down, Patience couldn't look at him. She grabbed her water glass and took several gulps, then noticed Beth, who was seated across from her. She raised her delicate blond eyebrows at Patience in a way that announced she knew exactly what had just happened between Patience and Jace.

Which seemed incredible, because Patience didn't even know what had happened . . .

Oh, whom was she kidding?

Of course she knew. She knew chemistry when she felt it.

She was wildly attracted to Jace, and judging by what she'd just felt in a simple handclasp, the feeling was mutual.

Jace burrowed further beneath the scratchy hotel blanket.

He couldn't seem to stop going over and over what had happened tonight. It had all started when he'd had to hold Patience's hand at dinner. There'd been no way out of it.

He didn't know what he'd expected when he'd reached out to take her hand. A joke buzzer, maybe. Or perhaps a karate grip.

Certainly not soft and feminine skin, or graceful, cool

fingers that he automatically entwined in his own, as if to warm them. He'd been surprised by her delicate touch, and something had made him want to keep holding that smooth, slender hand, to protect it—to protect *her*.

Which was ridiculous, Jace told himself, because if anyone needed to be protected, it was he—protected from the very likes of Patience Magee, in fact.

But in that quiet moment, as Father Bianco was saying grace and Jace was holding Patience's hand, he'd felt odd.

Oh, he'd always been nervous around Patience, though he'd learned long ago not to let her see it. But that was because she was so unpredictable, so opinionated and gutsy and direct. You never knew what she might do or say next.

Jace had always preferred people who were more subtle, more even-tempered, more dispassionate. People like him.

Now, however, Patience was making Jace jittery for an altogether different reason. A reason he didn't even want to contemplate.

So when the prayer had ended and he'd dropped her hand, he'd told himself that he'd only been rattled because of the prayer. Of course he was. He was Jewish; he wasn't used to Catholic priests or prayers before meals.

But deep down, Jace knew that wasn't the problem at all.

It had nothing to do with Father Bianco's saying grace, and everything to do with the hand-holding.

Patience had looked over at Jace. For an instant, she looked the way he felt—vaguely shaken up and confused.

And in that fleeting moment, Jace had again glimpsed something unexpected but undeniable in those green eyes. It was that same flash of softness, of utter vulnerability, and he'd only seen it once before, when she'd been asleep.

Then that familiar glint of confidence had danced back into her expression, and she'd looked like Patience again. Her eyes were their usual bold mixture of penetrating sharpness mingling with slightly amused detachment. You could practically see the way her mind worked just by looking at her. Of course, you didn't know what she was thinking—unless she wanted you to—but she clearly never missed anything that happened around her, and that clever, bright, intense brain was constantly busy processing all of it.

It was no wonder Jace only had to be in the same room with her to feel vaguely unsettled.

The waitress appeared and began setting salads down in front of everyone. The talk turned to the wedding the next day. Henry kept badgering Anne's cousin Marnie, who was a teacher, to break into the school where she worked and steal some chalk for him so he could write on Ned's shoes. The scary thing was, he was only half-kidding and everyone except Marnie knew it.

After a few minutes, Jace snuck a glance at Patience.

She was looking at Henry with a distinctly disgusted expression, rolling her green eyes at him. She stabbed a piece of lettuce with her fork, plucked it off with her teeth, and washed it down with a swig of bourbon.

No softness there. No vulnerability.

He must have been imagining it before.


Patience skipped ahead in her mental video, passing over the whole boring part about the rehearsal dinner, which had concluded with countless toasts, and then Anne and Ned handing out their gifts for the wedding party—pearl earrings for the bridesmaids and leather portfolios for the groomsmen.

Afterward, everyone had decided to go out to a waterfront nightclub down on the pier. Patience had half-expected Jace to say he was going back to his room to study, as he always had in college.

But he came along, and when they got to the club, he'd ended up sitting on the opposite end of the table, between Anne's cousin and Beth.

Patience nursed another bourbon and water and kept an eye on Jace while fielding questions from Ira and his wife Lauren, who were sitting next to her. They were both genuinely interested in her job at the magazine. Patience politely kept up her end of the conversation, but she couldn't help wishing they would go dance or something so that she could be left alone to watch Jace in peace.

Finally, Ira and Lauren got up when the band slid into a slow number.

So did Jace and Beth.

Patience straightened in her chair, watching them head toward the dance floor.

Patience was consumed by irrational jealousy as Jace led Beth around the tiny, crowded space in front of the band. And she didn't miss the semismug smile Beth tossed in her direction when they danced by.

Oh, well. She wasn't about to admit, even to herself, that it bothered her. She'd just dance with someone else. She cast a vicious glance around the table, skipping over Bryan, of course. He was busy doing shots of tequila with Anne's old boarding school friend Buffy, whose pearls and pageboy were askew. Patience noticed that the other available men at the table—Jack, John, and Henry—practically cringed when they felt her looking at them. As if she'd ever ask *them* to dance!

Well, she couldn't just sit here alone scowling. She picked up her drink and went down to the other end of the table, where Marnie the teacher was wistfully watching the dancers and sipping a frothy blender drink decked out in umbrellas and colored plastic animal stirrers.

"Hi, Marnie, having fun?" Patience shouted over the music, sliding into the chair Beth had vacated.

"Oh, yes," Marnie said, obviously thrilled to have company. "I usually don't go out on Friday nights. And I've never been to this club."

Patience felt sorry for her. She began asking Marnie about her students, her pets, her apartment—and all the while, she watched the way Jace's strong arms were holding Beth . . . and she seethed.

Jace hadn't wanted to dance with Beth—he hated dancing. It always made him feel uncomfortable and self-conscious. Besides, he hadn't wanted to leave poor Marnie alone at their end of the table, knowing Henry and Bryan and the other guys wouldn't talk to her.

But Beth had asked, and Jace had known it would be rude to say no.

Once they were out on the dance floor, he'd caught sight of Patience sitting with Marnie. She was watching him and Beth, though, and Jace had felt himself becoming stiff and clumsy under her piercing gaze.

Damn it! Why did she have the power to do this to him?

He maneuvered Beth through the crowd so that he couldn't see Patience and she couldn't see them.

Finally, the music faded, and Jace was about to release his hold on Beth.

But she was clinging to his neck. "Oh, I love this song," she exclaimed as the band slid into the next number.

Before Jace could reply, someone was tapping on his shoulder.

He turned to see Patience standing there. "Mind if I cut in?"

"Uh . . . no," he'd said, surprised. He'd looked questioningly at Beth, who shrugged.

"Thanks," Patience said, and slipped into Jace's arms, circling her own around his shoulders.

Jace's stomach did a curious little cartwheel when he tentatively rested his hands on the small of her back. She was so tall that she could rest her chin on his shoulder, and after a few seconds, she did.

*Relax,* Jace told himself. Every nerve in his body was on alert, and he fought the impulse to freeze up. *Just pretend she's Beth, or anyone else. Just listen to the music and forget about Patience.*

Jace had always loved this old song—"Unchained Melody" by the Righteous Brothers. He concentrated on the lyrics, on the tenor's melodic voice, on the gentle rhythm of the band.

Then he noticed that Patience was leading.

"Hey, cut it out," he muttered in her ear. "You're supposed to be following me."

"Oops, sorry," she murmured. Her breath was soft against the sensitive skin of his neck.

Her curls tickled his jaw, and he could smell her clean shampoo scent. It was fresh, herbal, outdoorsy— better than the spicy perfume Beth had been wearing.

Once Patience had stopped trying to lead, Jace actually found himself relaxing. As the song built to its romantic crescendo, he found himself wishing it wouldn't end. He wanted to keep holding Patience Magee close so that he could feel her heart beating against his own. He tightened his arms around her and twirled her around and breathed her scent and tried to ignore the sensations that were washing over him.

And then the song was over and another was starting—an old Commodores ballad, "Still." Neither of them made a move to stop dancing; they just slipped into the slower new rhythm.

As if of their own volition, Jace's hands moved, lightly rubbing her lower back. She reacted instantly, moving even closer until their bodies were locked in a tight embrace.

They weren't looking at each other or speaking, but so much was happening between them that Jace felt breathless and his mind was whirling. All he could think of was wanting to be alone with Patience. He longed to pull her out the door at the edge of the dance floor and kiss her senseless in the moonlight.

Patience had asked Jace to dance on impulse, jealous of Beth. It may have been nervy, but then, she'd never been a shrinking violet.

Still, her cheeks felt hot even now, hours later, when she remembered what she'd done when that second song was over.

She'd moved one hand down from around Jace's neck, and she'd clutched his fingers with it. When he'd glanced down at her in surprise, she'd gestured at the door with a toss of her head and said, "Want to go outside and get some air?"

She'd known what she was really asking, and so, she was sure, had Jace.

She'd wanted to go outside so he would kiss her. She was desperate, suddenly, to know what that would be like. She wanted to feel Jace's lips on hers more than she'd ever wanted anything in her life.

The way he'd looked at her had told her he wanted it, too, and that had filled her with an exhilarating anticipation.

She'd pulled him through the crowd toward the

door behind the bandstand, and they'd slipped out onto the quiet pier behind the club.

It was deserted and dark even in the light of the three-quarter September moon.

The air was chilly, and Patience shivered as soon as the breeze off the water hit her.

"I'll warm you up." Jace had pulled her into his arms. She'd leaned her cheek against his chest and listened to his heart racing before she tentatively pulled back and looked up at him.

He was watching her, his eyes so black and opaque that she couldn't read their expression. She held her breath, watching him, wondering how he could look so composed when her whole body was electrified with wanting him.

After a long moment, he finally leaned down toward her and she released a sigh, closing her eyes in the instant before she felt him gently cupping her face. He held her like that, his hands warm on her cheeks, while his lips came down over hers in a kiss that was at first gently searching, almost tentative.

But within moments, she was leaning back against the splintered wooden railing of the pier and he was leaning over her, brushing her lips repeatedly with his fervent, probing mouth . . . stroking her face, her hair, her neck with his hands.

Never before had Patience been kissed this way—thoroughly, passionately, and yet still with a tenderness, almost a *reverence*.

Jace made her breathless, carried away.

He was the one who finally pulled back.

He released her suddenly and took a few steps away.

When Patience opened her eyes, feeling dazed, she saw him beside her, leaning his elbows on the railing.

They'd stared at each other, both breathing hard.

Before either one of them could speak, the door of

the club burst open and they heard a voice. *"There you are! We've been looking all over for you two."*

It was Beth, and Bryan and Henry and the others were right behind her.

Patience had run a hand through her windblown curls, too rattled to speak.

"You guys look pretty cozy out here," Lauren commented, tossing a meaningful grin their way. "What's going on?"

Patience found her voice. "I, uh, started to feel really faint when we were dancing. So Jace helped me out here so I could get some fresh air."

"Oh, yeah?" Bryan and Henry nudged each other like the frat boys they had once been; but before they could make a big deal out of it, Ira said, "Listen, this place is getting too crowded, so we're going to leave and go to a different club."

"Okay, great," Jace said, pushing himself away from the railing. He looked as serene as he always did.

A moment ago, Patience would have sworn that he'd been as affected by their kiss as she had, but she must have been wrong. He seemed to have taken it lightly, judging by the way he kept a casual distance from her for the rest of the evening.

Well, she'd take it lightly, too. She'd vowed not to let one little kiss from Jace Hoffman get to her.

Unfortunately, that one little kiss had kept her awake all night.

And the last thing she realized before she finally drifted off to sleep was that the alarm was set to go off in ten minutes.


"Ladies and gentlemen," Father Bianco boomed, "may I present to you the new Mr. and Mrs. Ned Boylston!"

A round of applause echoed through the church as the newly married Ned and Anne turned, beaming, to face the congregation.

Organ music swelled in a recessional march, and Anne accepted her bouquet from her sister before she and Ned headed back up the aisle.

Jace couldn't help smiling as he watched them go. It had been a nice ceremony, even though he was so exhausted from not sleeping the night before that his legs felt wobbly and his eyelids burned.

He followed the other ushers, who were edging across the front of the church to meet their bridesmaids one by one.

Instinctively, Jace braced himself for Patience. After what had happened between them last night, he didn't know what to expect.

When he'd glimpsed her standing at the beginning of the aisle before the ceremony, he'd been stunned by how gorgeous she looked. The bridesmaid dress was an above-the-knee-length sheath, and it was cut so that it showed off Patience's tanned shoulders and delicate collarbone. The pale pink fabric made her skin glow, and she wore a big matching bow that caught her curls back from her face. She'd seemed almost demure as she'd stood poised to begin the procession, carrying an armful of long-stemmed wildflowers tied with a deeper pink bow.

Jace hadn't been able to take his eyes off her. Then the music had swelled and she'd started down the aisle, and it was apparent that with every measured step she took, she was fighting the impulse to break into a sprint.

When she arrived at the front of the church, she'd glanced in Jace's direction just before she'd angled off to the left. Her eyes had been flashing emeralds, full of spirit and fire despite her docile attire and semiladylike steps.

Jace had found himself flinching, as always, beneath her candid gaze. During the ceremony, he'd studiously avoided looking in her direction.

Now, as she walked toward him and he stretched out a hand to take her arm, he saw that same fiery expression in her eyes. It was as if she were daring him to touch her, as if she could tell what touching her did to him. What kissing her had done to him last night.

Jace reached out and clasped her arm, and she immediately started down the aisle. He tugged her backward and whispered, without looking at her, "We're supposed to wait until Father Bianco signals, remember?"

"He *did* signal," she responded in a low voice through a clenched jaw that was frozen in a big, fake, bridesmaid smile.

"He did not. He was adjusting his toupee."

Her melodic laughter spilled over softly.

Jace was hardly touching her, but he could feel the barely contained energy zinging through her. She was restless and excited and eager to get moving. She'd probably never stood still or kept quiet for as long as she had just now during the ceremony.

Finally, Father Bianco signaled and they stepped forward. Again, Jace found himself trying to keep Patience from rushing back up the aisle. He had to keep a firm grasp on her arm to do it, or he had the feeling she'd break free and leave him in the dust.

Once they were outside in the warm September sunshine, he abruptly let go of her arm.

Instead of pulling away, she turned and looked at him, a flicker of amusement lighting her green eyes. "What's the matter? Can't wait to get rid of me, Hoffman?"

"Huh?"

"Never mind." She shrugged and stepped into the receiving line, tossing over her shoulder, "See you in the limo."

Jace watched her meeting and greeting the wedding guests, laughing that tinkling laugh and making easy conversation. He saw her flirting with the single guys who went through the line, and he noticed, with an annoying flicker of rivalry, how they reacted.

How could they help it? She was so damned beautiful in that dress, flashing that dazzling smile and tossing her head with those glossy black curls glinting in the bright September sun.

Jace was staring, but he didn't care. It wasn't as if she were aware of it—she hadn't looked in his direction once.

He noticed that one of her curls had sprung free of the bow's constraints and was *boing*ing around her face. It was so like her not to notice and tuck it back in. He shook his head, irritated, yet strangely mesmerized.

For some reason, that one errant curl began to drive him crazy. The longer Jace watched, the harder he fought the inexplicable urge to walk over to Patience and brush it back from her face.

He remembered how surprisingly silky her hair had been when he'd run his fingers through it last night. How incredibly soft her lips had been.

She'd blown him away, given him a taste of blissful abandon before he'd struggled to get hold of himself. God only knew how he'd summoned enough willpower and presence of mind to collect his scattered emotions and quell the fierce physical craving that had threatened to blot out every ounce of his better judgment.

He'd been in a zombielike state by the time they were interrupted by Beth and Bryan and the others, so rattled he couldn't think straight for the rest of the night.

Never before had he been so profoundly stirred by kissing someone, and it had scared the hell out of him.

Jace had always liked to stay in control of his emotions. He'd never felt comfortable in situations where he wasn't completely in charge, where he couldn't think rationally and maintain a steady, even keel.

Patience Magee had always had a knack for throwing him completely off balance, even before this—*thing*—had started between them. Now he knew, beyond a doubt, that he had to stay as far away from her as possible.

No way was Jace going to get involved with a woman like Patience. He knew her—and himself—only too well. Not only did his unreasonable attraction to her threaten his sense of self-control, but she'd surely drive him crazy. She was utterly unpredictable, impulsive, stubborn . . . just plain *loony*.

In fact, at the moment, he couldn't think of one redeeming quality Patience Magee possessed.

Of course, when it came to *physical* qualities, she rated just about perfect.

But this wasn't about physical attraction. It was about sanity—and Jace's determination to keep his.

That meant he couldn't go near Patience any more than he was required to.

Which was probably why he couldn't seem to think of anything but how much he wanted to grab her and crush those pouty, pink-frosted lips with his own.

He told himself that it was just human nature to want her, since he couldn't have her. If he gave himself permission to kiss her, he probably wouldn't want to.

*Yeah, right.*

Jace sighed and dragged his eyes from Patience, determined to get her out of his mind.

Of course, it was next to impossible to forget about

her when she was right there in front of him in all her impetuous glory.

But after today, it would be a cinch, because Jace would never see her again.

# Three

Patience poked her head into the corner office and saw her boss, Camisha Thompson, sitting at her desk reading a manuscript.

"Are you busy?" she asked, rapping on the door frame to get the executive editor's attention.

Camisha didn't look up from the article. "I'm always busy," she murmured intently, still scanning the page. "What do you need?"

Patience walked into the office and flopped down into one of the cushy guest chairs. "I've run into a hitch with an article," she said, running a self-conscious hand through her curls as she noted her boss's smoothly coiffed hair.

Camisha, a lithe, beautiful African-American woman with high cheekbones and cat-shaped eyes, always looked as if she'd stepped out of the pages of the magazine she edited.

"Which article?" Camisha finally set down the red pencil she'd been using to mark the manuscript and looked up at Patience.

"The 'Six Sexy Studs' article."

At Camisha's blank look, Patience reminded her, "Remember? This is the piece where I'm going to videotape real live bachelors talking with each other about relationships and sex and turn it into an article. It used to be called 'Eight Excellent Eligibles,' then 'Seven Sensational Singles.' That was before Bachelors Number Eight and Seven lost their nerve and dropped out."

Camisha smiled. "Oh, yes, that's right. That article is going to be our lead feature in the April issue, not to mention the fact that it's due the third week in October . . . which happens to end tomorrow," she noted, glancing at her desk calendar. "What kind of hitch did you run into, Patience?"

"A fiancée hitch, to be specific."

"Come again?"

Patience sighed and shook her head. "One of the ground rules is that the guys in the article have to be unattached. They have to be genuine bachelors, you know? Anyway, the interview session is scheduled for tonight, and just now, one of the guys called and told me that he's engaged."

*"Engaged?"*

"Yup. In the six weeks since he agreed to do the article, he met someone, and he's flying to Vegas with her this weekend to get married."

Camisha raised her perfectly arched dark eyebrows. "So much for the commitment-shy man of the millennium."

"No kidding."

"Can't you just do the article without him?"

"And call it what? 'Five Fabulous Fellas'?" Patience wrinkled her nose. "I don't know what's with these guys—they're dropping like flies. And both of the guys who dropped out were our token cute businessmen. Now all we have left are the starving artist, the cop, the construction worker, the teacher, and the farmer.

"A farmer? Where'd you find a farmer in New York City?"

"He lives way out east on Long Island, but he's taking the train in for the interview tonight."

"Well, I guess you do need to balance the group with a businessman. You'll just have to go out and find one."

Patience smiled ruefully at her boss. *"You* are so very *married,* Camisha. You've obviously forgotten what it's like out there. I can't just go out into the streets of Manhattan and pluck a handsome, heterosexual, unattached, articulate, *employed* businessman out of the crowd. I'd have better luck convincing a total stranger to lend me a thousand bucks."

"I see what you mean. Did you check with the other editors in the office to see if they have any prospects?"

"If any of them knew any single and straight and available businessmen, do you think they'd have formed that floating Saturday night poker game?"

Camisha laughed, and Patience protested, "I'm completely serious, Camisha. You wouldn't happen to know anyone who fits the bill, would you?"

"If I did, you can bet I'd have been talked into fixing you or one of those man-hungry cardsharks up with him long before now." Camisha leaned back in her chair and stretched. "Come on, Patience, think hard. There must be someone who can pinch-hit for our eloping businessman.

Patience searched her brain. There was only one vague possibility, a name that had been nagging at her consciousness. She'd refused to acknowledge it because she couldn't imagine him agreeing to speak candidly with a bunch of other men about relationships and sex for an article in a national women's magazine.

"Patience? Something tells me you have an idea but you're reluctant to spill it."

She grinned at her boss. "There's no hiding anything from you, is there?"

"Nope. So, who is he?"

"Jace Hoffman. I went to college with him, and I bumped into him at a wedding last month. He works on Wall Street; he's single; he's straight; he's articulate . . . and he's also an extremely annoying individual."

"I see."

"You want me to call him, don't you?" Patience said, noting the look on her boss's face.

"I can't imagine why you think you have a choice."

"I can't imagine him saying yes to this."

"You never know."

"You do with Jace Hoffman." She shook her head. "If he's anything, it's predictable. I'm positive he's not going to do it. But I'll call and ask him if you insist."

"Good. And if he says no . . ."

"We'll call off the article?"

Camisha laughed. "No way, girlfriend. If he says no, just ask him again. And again. Bug him till he says yes."

Great.

Patience stood and glumly walked back out to her cubicle. She didn't have Jace's number, but she remembered the name of the firm he'd said he worked at. Lynde and Slater. It would be simple enough to look him up.

Actually, she already had—the day she got back to New York after the wedding. She'd found herself casually flipping through the Manhattan White Pages, running her finger down the column of Hoffmans in search of his name. There was no Jace Hoffman, but there were several J. Hoffmans, many of them on the Upper East Side. And since she didn't know which street he lived on, she had no idea which J. Hoffman was him, if any were.

Instead, she'd flipped through the business listings until she came across Lynde and Slater. She'd be able to reach him there . . . not that she was about to call him. Why would she want to do that? She had no intention of ever seeing him again.

Especially after the way he'd acted at the wedding reception. During dinner, he'd dutifully sat next to her, but he'd spent the whole time chatting with Marnie, who was on his other side.

And when it came time for the traditional bridal party dance—an incredibly romantic old Cole Porter tune—he'd acted as if he'd rather run barefoot through ground glass than come near her. Once they were out on the dance floor he'd barely touched her, and he was so rigid that she couldn't believe he was the same person she'd danced with just the night before.

Considering the way he was treating her, Patience hadn't been about to let him lead, and she'd managed to land the two-inch heels of her dyed satin bridesmaid pumps on his feet a few times, too. Sure, it was a rotten thing to do, but she was in a cranky mood from the lack of sleep, which happened to be Jace's fault, too.

Halfway through the song, she was about to tell him she'd had enough dancing with him, but the photographer suddenly appeared to snap a photo of them. Patience forced a smile through gritted teeth, and as soon as the flash had gone off, she'd said, "Okay, Jace, that's enough. You don't have to keep dancing with me."

"The song isn't over yet," he'd protested mildly.

"That's all right. I don't think anyone will mind if we drop off the dance floor."

He'd shrugged, and she'd slipped out of his stiff embrace and made a beeline for the bar. That was the last time she saw him that night, and she'd whispered "good riddance" as she'd hurried away.

After all, who did Jace Hoffman think he was, kissing her passionately one minute and ignoring her the next? Patience told herself he wasn't worth a second thought and she'd be lucky if she never saw him again.

But somehow, she hadn't been able to shake the thought of him, even though it had been over a month

# ASK ME AGAIN 55

since the wedding. Time had dulled the memory of how standoffish he'd been, but it somehow hadn't done the same to her memory of his passionate kiss.

Now, as she dialed the number of Lynde and Slater, she couldn't help feeling a tiny trace of apprehension. He might be a maddening individual, but there was no denying that something about him piqued her interest. She couldn't help it.

And even though she had no intention of getting involved with him and she knew there was no way he'd agree to do the article, she had to admit that she'd be mighty interested to hear what Jace Hoffman had to say about relationships and sex.

Jace was scanning a copy of *Kiplinger's Personal Finance* magazine and downing a pastrami on rye from the deli across the street when his personal line rang.

He reached for the phone. "Jace Hoffman," he said, still chewing and reading an article on junk bonds.

"Hi, Jace. It's Patience Magee. Listen, I need a favor."

He gulped, nearly choking on his sandwich.

Leave it to her to crash back into his life out of the blue, acting as though it were the most natural thing in the world that she'd be calling him at work. And she had the nerve to ask him for a favor on top of it?

"Patience," he said weakly when he'd managed to swallow and locate his voice. "How've you been?"

"Fine," she said tersely. "What are you doing tonight?"

He'd had a dinner date with a lawyer he'd met at a party up in Rye last weekend, but she'd canceled this morning because of a complication in a case she was trying.

"Nothing," he said cagily, "why?"

"Great. I need your help with an article I'm working on."

"You need *my* help? Why?" She'd caught him so off guard that he could barely keep up with her. He was still reeling from the shock of hearing her voice after more than a month of trying to get her out of his mind.

"I need someone to interview, and you're the only Wall Street guy I know."

"Oh yeah? What about what's his name, the guy you almost married? Crunchy?"

"Crispin," she said on a laugh. "Crunchy . . . very amusing, Jace. Anyway, I hear he's engaged. But you're not . . . are you?"

"No," he admitted.

"Good," she said, sounding pleased.

So, she was interested in him? Or just making conversation? Why did it matter to her that he wasn't engaged?

He had to remind himself that her motive for calling him was obviously purely professional. She'd said it was, hadn't she?

But still, the way she had asked whether he was engaged to anyone—and the way she had reacted to the news that he wasn't—well, it made him feel sort of—

"Grab a pen," she said briskly in his ear, "and I'll give you the address of my office. I need you here at seven."

"Whoa, wait a minute. Who said I was willing to be interviewed?" He reached for his bottle of seltzer and took a sip.

"You *have* to do this, Jace," she said pleadingly. "I'm really in a bind. This is a major article for me, and you can't let me down."

"Look, Patience, you act as if you can just call me up and bark commands at me, as if—"

"Listen, my other line is ringing and I've got to run. Do you have that pen?"

He automatically reached for one, along with a pad of paper.

She was already reciting the address, and he scrambled to get it down. "So, I'll see you tonight, right?" she asked breathlessly.

"Patience, I can't just—"

"Sure you can. Gotta run. 'Bye."

Jace stared at the receiver, listening to the dial tone that had followed her abrupt hang-up.

Patience Magee.

How like her to come barreling back into his life now, just when the memory of what had happened between them the night before Anne and Ned's wedding was beginning to fade at last. Not that he couldn't still summon the recollection of how she had looked in the moonlight, of what it had felt like to kiss her . . .

Damn!

Jace didn't want to remember. He'd spent the last month trying to forget. But she'd left an indelible mark on him, like a splotch of red wine on a white dinner jacket. Even though he hadn't seen her since the wedding, he'd felt her presence lurking in his life.

Every single day, as he rode the bus down the East Side to work, he found himself scanning the other passengers and the people out walking on the city sidewalks, half-hoping for and half-dreading a glimpse of those glossy back curls, of that bouncy, impatient walk.

It was ridiculous, he knew. There were eight million people in New York, and he'd never run into her yet in the five years he'd lived here. What were the chances that he would now?

Besides, he knew she lived in the Village, where he seldom ventured, and she worked in midtown. He knew that because he'd casually checked the address of the

*She* editorial offices in an issue his old girlfriend Sue had left in his apartment. He'd even flipped to the masthead and located Patience's name opposite Associate Editor, and he'd pretended not to notice the little thrill that shot through him at seeing it there in black and white.

In the past, he'd marveled over how just being in the same room with her could get to him. Now, being in the same city, even when he wasn't even in touch with her, was enough to keep him constantly on edge.

Knowing she was out there somewhere, that she could, ostensibly, pop up in front of him at any moment, left Jace with a constant sense of guarded anticipation, even though he'd assured himself that he'd never see her again.

And now look what had happened. Here she was, crashing into his peaceful lunch break, giving him orders that he . . . for some reason . . . had obeyed.

What was the *matter* with him?

Jace shoved the half-eaten sandwich aside.

There was no way he was going to meet her tonight.

Absolutely not.

No way.


"Jace! You showed!" Patience hurried across the reception area as soon as he stepped out of the elevator.

"You mean I had a choice?"

"Not really." She stopped a few feet from him and looked him over. He was wearing a charcoal-colored Brooks Brothers suit with a crisp white button-down shirt and a maroon-and-navy-striped tie. He carried a briefcase, and a black overcoat was slung over his arm.

He was every inch the young urban executive—and every inch of him was impossibly appealing, Patience noted. The other bachelors, who were already gathered in the conference room, paled by comparison.

Jace looked around the deserted reception area. "Where is everyone?"

"Most of the staff has left for the night," she explained, leading him down a long hallway. She reached up and smoothed her curls, conscious of his gaze on her back.

"What's this all about, anyway, Patience?" he asked, reaching out and halting her with a steady grip on her elbow.

She turned to look at him. "I told you. I needed to interview someone from Wall Street."

"Why? Are you writing some kind of financial feature?"

She avoided his gaze. "Sort of."

"What do you mean, 'sort of'?" he asked suspiciously.

"I mean, the article is kind of about . . . bachelors."

*"Bachelors?"*

"And . . . sex." She snuck a peek at his expression.

"Sex?"

Patience didn't realize that she'd been hoping to rouse him into some sort of reaction until she saw that there was none. Leave it to Jace not to raise his voice, let alone an eyebrow. Leave it to him to simply nod, as if he'd been expecting it all along. "I see.

"You do?"

He spun on his heel and headed in the opposite direction.

"Jace, wait! Where are you going?" Patience caught up to him and grabbed his sleeve.

"Where do you think I'm going? Home."

"Jace, you can't leave. Please don't leave, please-please-please. You've *got* to let me interview you for this piece. It's the lead story of the April issue, and if I do a good job, it could mean a promotion to full editor."

He stood watching her silently.

"Please, Jace?" Patience donned her most beseeching expression.

"Why me?" he finally asked.

She couldn't tell if it were a genuine question or merely an exasperated outburst. She decided to treat it as a question.

"Because you're the token businessman," she explained. "We have a teacher, a farmer, a construction worker, an artist, and a cop.

"So I'm not the only bachelor you're interviewing tonight? It's a group thing?"

She looked at him carefully, trying to see if he meant that in a positive way. Naturally, she couldn't tell. She never could, with him.

"We have five other eligible bachelors," she said carefully. "The other guys have been great, Jace—really cooperative. They're all waiting for you in the conference room. Jace, look, I'm going to be completely honest about this. If you don't help me out here, I'm going to have to call the whole thing off. These guys are going to be disappointed; my boss will be furious, and the entire production schedule is going to be thrown out of whack because we'll have an enormous hole in April. So you see, you've *got* to do this."

He sighed. "Patience—"

"Jace, please? I mean, you showed up. You can't back out now."

"I showed up because you practically hung up on me today, and I had no way of getting hold of you to tell you I wasn't coming.

*Oh yeah? You could have called information and asked for the main number at* She *magazine—there must be a reason you didn't,* she thought smugly, but she didn't dare say it.

"Look, I showed up because I'm a decent guy," he said, as though he'd read her mind.

"And you'll do the interview because you're a decent guy, too, right?" She tugged on his arm, pulling him toward the conference room again.

"I don't know, Patience."

"It's going to be fun," she assured him, tossing a glance over her shoulder. "And don't worry, you look exactly right for the picture.

*"Picture?"*

"Just a teensy weensy one, I promise. Okay, Jace?"

His only reply was a loud groan.

She took that to mean yes.

Jace should have known better than to have shown up tonight, and he definitely should have known better than to stay once he'd found out what this "interview" was all about.

But somehow, he found himself following Patience down the hall and into a conference room; and instead of thinking about how much he wished he hadn't gotten involved in this crazy scheme of hers, he was thinking about how great she looked.

She was wearing a narrow black skirt that nearly came down to her ankles, a cropped black-and-white-checked jacket, and black lace-up boots. She had some sort of filmy red scarf tied like a headband around her curls, and she wore dangling gold earrings that hung almost to her shoulders and jangled when she walked.

"Okay, here we are," she said, stopping in front of a door marked Conference Room. She threw it open and Jace followed her inside, thinking that in that getup, she looked like a cross between a Gypsy and somebody's maiden aunt. Okay, an impossibly *sexy* maiden aunt.

Uncomfortable with the thought, he shifted his attention to what was going on inside the room. Five men were seated around a long table, and two others, long-haired techie types, were over on the side, fiddling with some sort of video equipment.

"All right, guys, this is Jace," she announced, motioning him to take an empty seat before she went to stand at one end of the table.

Jace noticed how every eye in the room was fixated on her, and he felt himself bristling. These guys were all too aware of the charming Ms. Magee. Leering, almost. He could just imagine what thoughts were running through their heads as they watched her.

*So, what is this? Are you jealous?*

Irritated with himself again, Jace followed the direction of their collective gaze.

Look at her, confidently tossing her curls over her shoulder and talking with those broad gestures, probably describing what they were going to be doing here tonight. He wasn't listening to her words; he was merely watching her talk, feasting his eyes on her after a month that he had to admit had dragged by.

Okay, so he'd missed her. And he'd had to come tonight, just because he had to see her. Just one more time.

And maybe he didn't like the idea of being interviewed for an article in a women's magazine . . . all right, he *hated* the idea. But he'd found it impossible to walk out that door and leave her in a bind. And he'd been reluctant, too, to leave her alone with five eligible bachelors. For good reason, judging by the way they were all staring at her as if the *Sports Illustrated* swimsuit issue had suddenly come to life.

Patience didn't even seem to notice. She just kept talking and smiling and laughing and answering their questions, and Jace felt unreasonable jealousy boiling up inside of him.

"Okay, so are there any more questions?"

The room was silent. Jace couldn't very well ask her to repeat everything she'd just said, so he decided he'd have to wing it.

"Fine. You guys can go ahead and grab a beer or whatever—" She gestured at a beverage cart in the corner—"and we'll be ready to go in a few minutes."

Jace wandered over with the other guys and reached for a Rolling Rock. It was going to kill his ulcer, but what the hell.

When they were all seated again, Patience motioned to the two jean-clad guys who were working the video equipment, and one of them said, "Okay, rolling."

"Great," Patience said, and flashed a reassuring smile at the collection of eligible bachelors. "Listen, guys, just relax. I want this to be as casual as possible, okay? Forget about the cameras for the next hour."

"Yeah, right," someone muttered, and there was uneasy laughter.

"Okay, have any of you ever been married?"

Two of the men raised their hands tentatively. Patience smiled. "You're divorced now?" They nodded.

"What about the rest of you? You're all in your mid-to-late twenties. None of you has a significant other. Why not?"

"Why not? Who wants to settle for just one babe when you can have as many as you want?" one of the guys asked, and everyone laughed.

Everyone except Jace, who decided that it was going to be one long hour.

"Jace . . . wait a minute," Patience said, spotting him hurrying toward the conference room door. The taping was over, the bachelors beating a hasty retreat down the hall toward the elevator.

It had taken longer than she had expected, once the session got rolling. Get a few beers into these guys, and they were willing to spill all.

Well, except for Jace. He hadn't been silent, but he hadn't talked much compared to the others. She still didn't know what made him tick when it came to his love life.

"Jace!" she called again.

This time he heard her. He stopped and turned to look at her. "Yeah?"

She strode toward him. "I really appreciate your helping me out like this. You were terrific."

He shrugged, and she was surprised to see a small smile touch his lips. "Yeah, well, it wasn't as bad as I thought it was going to be."

"It was male bonding at its finest, if you ask me," Patience said, stretching up on her tiptoes, rubbing the aching small of her back, and giving a satisfied sigh. She checked her watch. "I'm starving. Want to go get something to eat with me?"

The words had just spilled out of her mouth, taking Patience as much by surprise as Jace obviously was. She braced herself for his flat-out no.

But he shrugged and said in his mild way, "Why not? I'm hungry too."

"Great. There's a coffee shop around the corner. Let me just talk to the video production guys for a second, and then I have to go back to my cubicle and grab my coat and bag.

"I'll wait for you by the elevator."

He walked out of the conference room, and Patience turned back to Mike and Ray, who were putting away the camera equipment. The whole time she was talking to them, her mind was focused on Jace, just as it had been during the taping session.

She made a quick trip to the ladies' room on her way back to her desk, inspecting her hair and makeup in the mirror. She freshened her lipstick and tried to tame her curls, all the while telling herself she wasn't trying to impress Jace. After all, it wasn't as if this were going to be a date.

One thing he had made clear in the session: She was about as far from the type of woman he was seeking as anyone could get. When it had been his turn to describe his ideal mate, he'd used words like "level-headed," "sensible," and "patient."

Had it been her imagination or had he been looking deliberately at her the whole time he was speaking, as if to prove a point?

And when he'd described the ideal first date, he'd said it would be a quiet dinner followed by a movie.

Patience couldn't think of anything duller and unimaginative. She personally hated going to the movies on a first date. It was such a cop-out—you couldn't get to know each other when you were sitting in the dark staring silently at a screen.

The other bachelors' answers had been far more appealing to her. When they'd described the perfect woman, most of them had used words like "creative," "fun-loving," "daring," and "free-spirited."

And their first date agendas had ranged from renting a limo and pulling an all-nighter in Atlantic City to bungee jumping, which Patience had tried several times and found exhilarating.

A quiet dinner and a movie.

Hah.

Well, it wasn't as if she hadn't already known she and Jace had nothing in common. She didn't know why she'd even bothered to ask him to go to the coffee shop with her.

But when she returned to the reception area and saw him leaning against the wall between the two elevators, she understood why she'd done it.

There was something about Jace Hoffman that undeniably attracted her. Call it chemistry, call it lust—whatever.

Patience knew it was a purely physical attraction, because every time Jace opened his mouth and made one of those perfectly reasonable, well-thought-out observations of his, she found him as infuriating as ever.

It wasn't fair that she should be this attracted to someone who was so obviously all wrong for her.

"Are you ready?" he asked, buttoning his overcoat and turning up the collar neatly.

"All set." Patience pressed the Down button.

She saw the way he was eyeing her black leather bomber jacket, which was silver studded and had fringe along the sleeves. She knew what he was thinking—that his ideal woman would be wearing a Burberry trench coat.

Well, her ideal man would have on ripped, faded jeans and his ear would be pierced. Maybe his tongue, too.

"Come *on*," she muttered to the missing elevator, punching the Down button again.

"That won't help," Jace observed, belting his overcoat.

Patience shot him a dark look, then hit the button again to punctuate it. A moment later, the elevator doors slid open.

She shot Jace a triumphant smile and stepped inside.

# Four

"I'll have a bowl of the split pea soup," Jace told the weary-looking middle-aged waitress who was standing over their booth with her pen poised over a pad. "No croutons, please."

"That's all you're having?" Patience asked.

He looked across the table at her. "It's late."

"So? Aren't you starved? I haven't eaten since lunch."

"Neither have I, but I can't eat a heavy meal at this hour. I'll never get to sleep."

Patience shook her head, looking amused.

"Anything to drink?" the waitress asked in a thick Hispanic accent, tossing her head so that her brunette ponytail swung behind her. "Coffee? Oh, wait, not at this hour, right? You'll never get to sleep."

Jace scowled at her. Just what he needed. "I'll have a seltzer, please."

"You got it. What about you, honey? Gonna go for the split pea, too?"

Patience made a face. "No *thanks*. I'll have a bowl of chili, a double bacon cheeseburger deluxe; and instead of fries on the side can I have onion rings?"

"No problem. You want a seltzer, too? You're gonna need it after you eat all that," said the waitress.

"I'll have coffee," Patience said, handing over her

laminated menu and adding pointedly, "Regular, not decaf."

"Coming right up."

Now they were officially alone together, Jace thought as the waitress walked away. This all-night coffee shop wasn't exactly deserted—no place in New York ever seemed to be deserted—but they were in a quiet corner at the back of the place, with the wall on one side of their booth and another couple in the booth on the other.

Jace was facing the wall, but there was a mirror and he had a full view of the lovebirds in the next booth. They were seated on the same side, their backs to the mirror; and from what he could tell, they were in the midst of heavy foreplay.

Great.

There was nowhere else to focus his gaze but on Patience.

He looked at her and found her studying his face intently. Probing, actually.

"What's wrong?" he asked.

"You have trouble sleeping when you eat before bed? I thought food was supposed to have the opposite effect."

"That makes no sense."

"Sure, it does. Like on Thanksgiving Day, people make gluttons of themselves and then fall asleep watching bowl games on television."

"I've never done that in my life," Jace lied, feeling ornery. He hated himself for sounding like a science professor as he went on, "You're not supposed to eat a heavy meal late at night because your body has to expend energy to digest it and that can keep you awake."

"That never happens to me. And I *always* eat before bed."

"What do you eat?"

She shrugged. "Whatever I feel like having. Ice cream. Pizza. Anything. No matter what I have, I always sleep like a baby."

*It figures.*

"It figures . . ."

He frowned. His own thought had come out of her mouth. How had that happened?

"Huh?" was all he could say.

"That you would have insomnia, I mean. You just seem like the type. You've never handled stress very well. I remember Bryan used to say you would get all nervous the night before an exam in college."

"I'm not nervous," he retorted, wishing the waitress would show up with their drinks.

"I didn't mean you're nervous *now*—"

*But I am,* he thought. He was definitely nervous sitting here alone with her, at such close range that he could smell the cinnamon gum on her breath. He didn't have to wonder what she would taste like if he kissed her; he knew. And he wanted to kiss her anyway, damn it.

"—I just meant that, in general, you're the nervous type," she went on, oblivious to the direction his errant thoughts had taken. "You probably have a lot of stress at work, huh?"

"Some," he admitted. "How about you? You're an editor. You have deadlines. You have to be under pressure."

"Pressure doesn't bother me," she said with a wave of her hand. "I get a lot done when I'm under pressure. And you know what?"

"What?" he asked reluctantly.

"No matter how stressed I am, I always, always fall asleep the second I get into bed."

"Always?"

"Well . . ." A faraway look drifted into her seafoam eyes. "Almost always. Once or twice, I guess, I've had sleepless nights."

And he was overcome with jealousy, because he just knew what she was talking about. He could tell by her sultry expression that she had lost sleep over a man.

"But hardly ever," she concluded abruptly, and he was glad she didn't look at him because the last thing he needed was for her to somehow sense the wistfulness that had overtaken him.

Maybe it was the image of her in bed . . .

Or the knowledge that she had been crazy about someone else . . .

The waitress materialized, effectively breaking the mood as she set a seltzer, a straw, and a cup of coffee on the table.

*Stay,* Jace silently begged her. *Don't leave me here alone with Patience Magee.*

But the woman was already briskly walking away again.

*Some help you are,* Jace thought, glowering at her retreating back in the mirror. He reached for the straw and busied himself unwrapping it.

Patience grabbed a handful of packets from the sugar dispenser.

Jace watched over the rim of his glass, fascinated, as she methodically ripped them open, one after another, and dumped them into her cup.

"How many sugars do you take?"

"As many as I'm in the mood for. And right now, I want something sweet." She stirred her coffee.

"Why don't you just have . . . I don't know, a doughnut or something?"

"Because I haven't eaten dinner yet. Maybe I'll have a doughnut later."

"You're just doing this to bug me, aren't you?" he asked, as she lifted her cup to her lips and took a sip.

"Doing what to bug you?"

"Just . . . I don't know. Never mind." He drank some seltzer.

"How can you drink that?"

He almost sputtered in his drink. "How can *I* drink *this*? You're sitting there with so much sugar in your cup that it must have soaked up all the liquid by now, and you want to know how I can drink something with no taste, no color, no smell?"

"Exactly." She wrinkled her nose. "I mean, how blah is that? It's just carbonated water. Why don't you at least get a soda or something? You know, some kind of flavor?"

"Soda is too sweet."

"It figures." She grinned and raised an eyebrow at him.

And God help him, he couldn't help grinning back.

He was all set to scowl and make some kind of retort, but instead he was sitting here with a dopey smile on his face. He knew it was dopey because he glimpsed himself in the mirror and saw that, the way he was looking at her, he appeared positively smitten with Patience Magee.

Which was unfair, because he absolutely *wasn't*.

"How are your parents?" she asked then, out of the blue, and he blinked.

"My parents?"

"Yeah. Saul and Myrna, right?"

"How'd you know that?"

"I met them that time they came up for Parents Weekend senior year."

"Oh." Now there was a scary thought. Siccing Patience Magee on dear old Mom and Dad. Why would he have done that? He searched his memory. "I don't remember introducing you."

"You didn't. I ran into your mom in the ladies' room at the dining hall and we started chatting. I told her not to eat the sloppy joes because everyone said they were made out of horse meat. She thanked me."

"I'll bet she did."

He didn't know whether to be horrified or amused at the image of his mother, the persnickety-yet-lovable Myrna Hoffman, coming face-to-face with someone like Patience.

"What else did she say?" he asked Patience.

"She introduced me to your father when we walked out of the ladies' room. He was waiting for her there. I don't know where you were. Probably in class or something."

"Probably. So, what did my father say?"

"He asked me if I knew you. I said I did."

"And?"

"He asked if we were friends."

"Oh." Jace looked at his straw, bending the tip back and forth. After a minute, when it became obvious she wasn't going to elaborate, he asked, "What did you say?"

"I said we weren't."

He looked up. His gaze crashed into hers. "You said we weren't friends?"

"Of course. I mean, I couldn't lie. And we weren't friends. You couldn't stand me."

"That's not true," Jace protested. "You're the one who couldn't stand me."

"Actually, I think it was pretty much mutal. Face it. We loathed each other."

"Did you tell my mother that?"

"Of course not! I just told her we didn't know each other very well."

He nodded, protesting mentally that he'd always thought he knew her through and through, knew exactly what she was about . . . but maybe she was right. Maybe they hadn't known each other at all.

"So, are your parents still living in the city?" she asked.

He nodded, sipping his seltzer.

"Queens, right?"

"Brooklyn." He smiled. "Good memory, though. You were close. Right city, wrong borough."

"How could I not know you were from New York with that accent?"

"Accent? I don't have an accent!"

"Oh, please, Jace. What am I drinking?"

"What are you drinking?" he echoed, confused. Once again, his head was spinning, trying to keep up with the pace of her end of the conversation.

She gestured impatiently at her cup. "Just tell me what's in this cup."

He smirked. "Sugar."

"Aren't we witty" She smirked. "I mean the beverage."

"Coffee."

"See?" She poked his arm triumphantly and echoed an exaggerated, " 'Co-awfee.' "

"I don't sound like that!"

"You do so."

He scowled. Maybe he did. "Well, you have an accent, too. Half the time I can hardly understand what you're saying."

But even as he said it, he was admitting to himself that she didn't have an accent, really. She just spoke in such a rapid-fire manner that he often had to pause and decipher her words before he could respond. It drove him crazy.

She looked intrigued, tilting her chin up. "Oh, yeah? What kind of accent?"

He hesitated.

She grinned. "You can't remember where I'm from, can you?"

"Actually . . . I have no idea," he admitted.

The waitress arrived then with a pot of coffee, saying, "Here you go."

"Pardon?" Patience asked.

"Didn't you want a refill? I thought I heard you calling for it."

"Oh, no, I was just making fun of his accent," Patience said easily as if that explained everything. "But as long as you're here, I'll take a refill."

"So, where *are* you from?" Jace asked again when the waitress had walked away.

"New Hampshire."

*"You're* from New Hampshire?" Somehow, he couldn't reconcile her black-leather, crazy-curled urban image with the serene New England farm scene that had just materialized in his head.

"Born and raised just outside of Laconia."

"Laconia? Where's—"

"You won't know," she dismissed him with a flip of her wrist and went on, "My family's old Yankee stock. Our line goes back to the Puritans."

"You're a Puritan." He stared at her, trying and failing to imagine her in a high-collared drab dress with one of those little white bonnets on her head.

"Don't laugh. Well, okay, you can laugh," she said, as he cracked up. "It is funny. My parents named me after an ancestor—some old spinster Patience who lived three hundred years ago. Same thing with my sisters."

"Yeah? What are their names? Mercy and Charity?"

"Hey, pretty close. Hope and Faith."

"You're kidding, right?"

"Unfortunately, I'm not."

"Wow."

"What?" She stirred another two packets of sugar into her steaming coffee.

"I just didn't picture you as coming from this old-fashioned New England-type family."

"Well, start picturing it, baby," she said breezily. "I'm the real thing. I grew up in a big old farmhouse with a front porch. My dad milks the cows at dawn. My mom makes her own butter."

"No way." He couldn't tell if she were pulling his leg or not. For all he knew, she'd been born and raised in Jersey. It would be just like her to come up with this crazy tale of life on the farm.

"I swear to God," she said. "My mother's been outdoing Martha Stewart since Martha baked her first batch of rugelach. She makes a huge home-cooked meal every single night of her life, and she does quilting and embroidering . . ."

"Embroidering?" A sudden memory popped into Jace's head. Patience, back in that dorm room the night she'd burst in looking for Bryan—she had been crying, and she had reached into her pocket to pull out an embroidered handkerchief. At the time, he had been flabbergasted.

He still was, unable to believe that she came from someplace like New Hampshire, from a regular family. Okay, maybe not regular, with a butter-churning mother and sisters named Faith and Hope, but still . . .

"Split pea soup . . ." the waitress announced, plunking a bowl in front of Jace.

"Thanks," he muttered, and found himself salivating as he caught a whiff of the rest of the food on her tray. It smelled much more appetizing than split pea soup.

"Chili, burger, rings, and I brought you some ketchup for the burger."

Patience's order took up most of the table.

"Could I please have some mustard?" she asked the waitress. "Oh, and some sour cream?"

The woman nodded briskly and reappeared with the items before Jace could pick up his soupspoon.

"Sorry . . . I hate to send you back again, but could we please have a few more napkins? This is going to be messy," Patience said.

"No problem," the waitress said, and cheerfully came back with a stack of them. "Can I get you anything else?"

"No, we're set," Jace said quickly, lest Patience send her on another mission.

The woman looked at Patience to be sure.

"All set," she said, squirting a huge dollop of mustard at the edge of the onion ring platter. Then she poured a glob of ketchup on top of that.

Jace knew it was rude to stare, but he couldn't help it. "What are you doing?"

"Did you ever try an onion ring dipped in ketchup and mustard?"

"Come to think of it . . . no," he said flatly.

"You have to try it, Jace."

"No thanks." He made a face and spooned some of the thick olive-colored liquid onto his spoon. "I'll just stick with my soup."

He watched her dredge a grease-slicked onion ring through the pool of condiments, half-expecting her to lift it to his lips and insist on feeding him a bite.

Instead, she popped it into her own mouth and said, chewing, "You don't know what you're missing."

*No, but I can imagine,* he thought, gulping a mouthful of soup as he tried to block out the intimate image of her popping morsels of food into his mouth. That was something lovers did.

And not even real-life lovers like that smoochy pair in the next booth. Lovers only fed each other in those romantic-comedy movies, the kind that had fifty-year-old Gershwin songs on their soundtracks.

"How's your soup?" She dumped the white paper cupful of sour cream onto her chili.

"It's great," he said.

"Can I taste?" She was already reaching across the table with her own spoon, dipping it into his bowl.

He was too surprised to protest. He watched as she brought the spoon up to those full lips of hers, sipping the hot broth.

"It is good," she agreed. "But it would be better with croutons. Did you ever have it that way?"

"Sure, but I'd rather have it plain."

"You wouldn't say that if you'd ever had soup with croutons here."

"I don't like it that way."

"Well, you would if you'd tried it in this coffee shop, because they make homemade croutons out of day-old challah bread, and they're all thick and crunchy and crusty, and you never had anything that good. Trust me."

He just stared at her. She didn't see him. She was dumping ketchup on her impossibly huge burger, then replacing the top bun and lifting it to her mouth. He didn't think she could possibly take a bite, because it was so thick, but she managed.

She had ketchup on the side of her mouth when she put it down again.

He wanted to lift a napkin from the pile the waitress had dropped on the table, and he wanted to put one hand under her chin and tilt her face up and wipe the ketchup off, gently. Then he wanted to kiss the spot where it had been, so he could taste the ketchup, taste *her* . . .

Just do it, a voice said, and he actually reached for a napkin, fixated on her mouth, ready to obey.

She snatched a napkin out from under him and smacked it against her mouth. "See? I knew this would be messy," she said glibly, wiping the ketchup away.

And it was over, his insane lapse in judgment, and the moment had passed without her being any the wiser, thank God.

Unless she was mistaken, Jace had been about to wipe a huge smear of ketchup off her mouth. Patience crumpled her napkin, tossed it aside, and focused on her chili.

Why would he do something like that?

The way he had been watching her—

His expression had been almost . . . well, tender was the only possible word she could think of to describe the look on his face.

*You must have been imagining it,* she told herself as she swallowed a heaping spoonful of spicy, chunky chili.

"Hey, how about those Yankees?" she asked brightly, not exactly to change the subject, because there *was* no subject, but she had to come up with one because the silence had grown uncomfortable.

Or maybe it was just her. Maybe he was totally relaxed. He certainly looked it, the way he sat there matter-of-factly spooning his bland soup into his mouth.

"I'm a Mets fan," he said.

"You're kidding."

"Nope." He unwrapped the small packet of saltines that had come with his soup. "Big, big Mets fan. Why?"

"How can you possibly like the Mets?"

"What do you mean, how can I like them? I'm from New York, and—"

"Yeah, but the Yankees are the true New York team. The Mets are practically on Long Island, out there at Shea Stadium."

"And Yankee Stadium is in the Bronx, practically in Westchester County," he said mockingly.

"I just can't believe anyone who considers himself a New Yorker can root for the Mets over the Yankees when the Yankee tradition goes back to—"

"Let me guess. You're a Yankee fan," he interrupted dryly.

"Absolutely. Always have been."

"I didn't know they made Yankee fans way up there in New Hampshire."

She grinned and asked him what he thought about the prospects of a subway series this year. As they discussed the latest round of major league playoffs, she found herself relaxing.

Until the bill came and he grabbed it before she had a chance to reach for it.

"I've got it," he said, reaching into his pocket and pulling out a black Coach billfold.

"You're kidding, right?"

"Why would I be kidding?"

"Because you only had a bowl of soup and I had a feast, Jace." She tried to grab the bill out of his hand from across the table but he held it above her reach.

"Patience, come on, it's no big deal," he said with maddening calm.

"Yes, it is." She reached into the pocket of her coat and fished several rumpled bills from amidst the crumpled tissues and gum wrappers. About to hand him a twenty, she looked up and saw him watching her with an incredulous expression.

"Don't you have a wallet?" he asked.

"I don't carry one."

"Why not?"

"Because this is New York and if it ever got stolen I would lose everything—credit cards, license, cash, everything. I prefer to be on the safe side," she said haughtily, resenting his expression.

"The safe side?" He eyed the wrinkled twenty in her hand and the litter of contents from her pockets, which she had spread on the table in front of her. "So you carry your money like that? And where do you keep the rest of your stuff? In your socks?"

"What stuff?"

He looked exasperated. "The stuff you would keep in a wallet."

"You mean credit cards?"

He nodded. "For one, yes."

"I don't carry them anymore."

"Why not?"

She hedged, not wanting to go into the whole got-myself-into-credit-card-debt-over-my-head-and-had-to-take-out-a-bank-loan-to-pay-them-off story. Somehow, she didn't think he would understand.

She had been right out of college then, on her own in New York, with an entry-level publishing job that paid peanuts and an apartment she shared with Beth, who never seemed to mind when Patience needed to borrow her half of the rent money . . . at first.

"I'd rather pay cash," was all she told Jace.

"Well, what about your driver's license?"

"Like I said, this is New York. Only cabbies and crazy people drive in the city."

"Yes, but shouldn't you carry your license with you? I mean, don't you need it as ID?"

She shrugged. "For what? I mean, it's not like I get carded when I go out, because I know all the bartenders at the places I go to, and even if—"

"That's not what I mean," he said, and she got the impression that he was fast losing patience with her for some reason.

"What do you mean?" She was losing patience with him, too, for that matter. Why all the questions?

"Look, what if you step out the door and God forbid you get hit by the Lexington Avenue bus? How are they going to know who you are when you're unconscious at the hospital?"

After the crack he'd made about her socks, she wasn't about to tell him she kept an ID card in her boot whenever she left the apartment. She wasn't *completely* irresponsible, although the way he was treating her, you'd think he had just found out she was living in a cardboard box by the East River.

"Look, Jace." She tossed the money on the table in front of him, "I don't have time to hang around here arguing. I've got to get home and feed my cat. So take this twenty and—"

He flinched, lifting both hands above his shoulders as if she'd thrown an explosive in front of him. "No," he said. "I told you, this is my treat. Okay?"

"No," she said stubbornly.

"Mind if I ask why not?"

"Because if you pay then it's either that you think I can't afford to pay for myself or that you think I ordered all that food because I thought you were going to pay, or worse yet, it's as if we're on a date . . ."

And that was certainly a horrifying thought.

"Because I want to pay my share," she said simply.

"Well, I'm not taking your money." He stood and pulled on his overcoat.

"Then I'll leave it there and our waitress will get a huge tip."

"Fine with me," he said.

"Great." She put on her leather jacket. "She was really nice about bringing me extra napkins."

"Twenty extra dollars worth of nice?"

"Whatever."

"Patience, you can't afford to go around throwing away money like this, can you?"

She bristled. "What's that supposed to mean? Just because you're a rich investment guy and I'm working in publishing doesn't mean—"

"I'm just trying to be nice, for God's sake!" he said, raising his voice. "I'm just trying to buy you dinner because . . . because . . ."

"Why?" she demanded. "Why is it so important to you that you buy me dinner?"

He faltered. "Actually, I have no idea."

"Because you want to have your way, right? You want to be in control, right?" A little voice inside of her head told her to shut up, that she was out of line, but she went right on blabbing away anyway. "You want me to know that you can afford to do stuff like this and you think I can't, right?"

"Wrong," he said quietly, and she felt sick inside. She hated the way he was looking at her. As if she was being totally childish.

"I'm sorry," she said abruptly, needing desperately to make that expression go away. "I don't know what's wrong with me, Jace. You were just trying to do the gentlemanly thing, and I'm acting like a little brat."

"No argument there."

He picked up the twenty from the table and tucked it back into her coat pocket.

She let him, and when he leaned toward her to do it, it was all she could do not to close her eyes and inhale his scent. How could he still smell so clean, like soap and aftershave, at this hour of the night? She wanted to ask him, but then she realized that he would know she had noticed something like that and he might think she was attracted to him or something . . .

And okay, to be totally honest here, even if she were attracted to him physically, a relationship with Jace could never work. He would drive her crazy. There was just no way around it. In the grand scheme of things, he was split pea soup—minus the croutons— and she was chili, and when you put the two together, all you got was an upset stomach.

"Ready?" he asked, putting the tip on the table, tucking it underneath the napkin holder.

"Ready," she agreed, yawning.

"Tired?" he asked.

"Must be that huge meal. See? I told you food makes me sleepy," she said.

For a moment she thought he was going to argue again, but he merely smiled.

They walked toward the register, past the booth with the lovey-dovey couple, who were now feeding each other French fries.

Patience rolled her eyes and said to Jace in a low voice, "I didn't know people did that in real life. I thought it was only in sappy movies."

He looked startled for some reason, but he smiled faintly and said, "Yeah, that's what I thought."

He paid the bill. She helped herself to one of those chalky pastel mints from the bowl on top of the cash register.

She saw him glance sharply at her, looking as though he wanted to say something but had thought better of it.

"What?" she asked, replacing the spoon in the bowl and chewing on her mint.

"Nothing." He held the door open for her.

"You were going to say something to me." They stepped out into the chilly October night.

"No, I wasn't."

"Sure you were. Spill it, Hoffman," she said good-naturedly as they headed down the nearly deserted cross street toward the avenue.

"I was just going to point out that it probably isn't a good idea to eat candy from a bowl that's out there for anyone to stick their fingers into."

"I used the spoon," she said, rolling her eyes for the second time in five minutes.

"Yeah, but most people probably don't. I mean, that's like opening your mouth and licking the germs off thousands of strangers' fingers."

"Ptooey," she said, spitting her mint into the gutter. "Thanks a lot, Jace. You really know how to ruin a perfectly good mint. Now I'm stuck with chili breath."

"I don't mind," he said, grinning at her.

"Oh, really? Then why are you walking way over there?" she teased, and poked him in the arm.

"No, really, it's not your breath," he said, and pretended to cringe away, flattening himself against a gated store window, and she cracked up. So did he.

It felt good to laugh with Jace.

She realized she had never done it before, which was startling when you really thought about it, because they had known each other all those years in college.

"How come we were never friends?" she asked him as they started walking again.

"You mean in college?" he asked, so promptly that she knew his thoughts must have wandered in the same direction.

"Yeah. Why did we hate each other?"

"I didn't hate you, really," he said. "I just thought you were a fool for going out with someone like Bryan."

"But I didn't go out with Bryan the whole four years," she pointed out. "And you never liked me before that, either."

"Well, you didn't seem too crazy about me, either."

"You were just so boring and uptight," she said without thinking, then slapped a hand over her mouth and snuck a peek at his face. "Oops, sorry . . . too much honesty?"

"No, it's okay. I thought you were too slapdash and immature," he said.

"Touché." She smiled up at him. "You still think that, don't you?"

"No," he said as they reached the avenue and stopped for the orange Don't Walk sign.

"So, you don't hate me anymore, Jace?"

"Nope," he said, looking down at her.

She shoved her hands deeper into the pocket of her coat. "Brrr," she said, her teeth chattering. But the sudden chill had nothing to do with the autumn night air. It was the expression she had glimpsed in his eyes—one that had nothing to do with hate.

"Patience," he said, and hesitated.

She couldn't seem to tear her eyes away from his. "Hmm?"

And then he was bending his head closer, putting one hand beneath her chin and tilting her face toward his. His lips came down over hers in a sweet, tender kiss.

She gasped when he broke away.

"What's wrong?"

"I don't know," she said, still shivering. "I guess it's just . . . shock."

He smiled. "Why are you shocked?"

"You kissed me."

"I know. Chili breath and all."

"But, Jace . . . Why did you kiss me?"

"I wanted to," he said.

"The Walk light is on," she announced, looking away from him because she absolutely had to.

They crossed the avenue. On the other side, she pointed downtown and said, "I go that way."

"So do I. We can grab cabs at the taxi stand in front of Grand Central."

"Oh, I don't need a cab," she said.

"Why not?"

"I'm taking the subway."

"At this hour?" He frowned.

She checked her watch and laughed. "Jace, it's not even midnight."

"So? It's not rush hour, either. The subway is too dangerous at any other time."

"Oh, please," She picked up her pace, her heels clicking along the concrete. Gone was the aura of intimacy, the feeling that you could just stroll along, laughing. The avenue was more crowded than the cross street had been. And anyway, the mood had been broken. Once again, he was looking and sounding completely irritated with her.

"Riding the subway alone at night is just asking for trouble, Patience."

"I do it all the time, and nothing has ever happened. It's perfectly safe. I get off on Bleecker Street. There are always a million other people around, even in the middle of the night . . . which it *isn't,*" she added pointedly.

"You're tempting fate. I'm putting you in a cab."

She stopped walking and folded her arms across her chest, glaring at him. "You're putting me in a cab?" she echoed. "You have no right to put me anywhere!"

"I didn't mean it like—"

"I'm sick of you talking to me like you're the oh-

# ASK ME AGAIN

so-wise parent and I'm the silly little child who doesn't know anything."

"I didn't mean to—"

"Why does every man who comes along think he has to take care of me and tell me how I should be living my life?"

"I'm not trying to—"

"Look, you don't know anything about me, okay? I can take care of myself. I've been doing it for years, and I like it. I don't want anybody telling me what to do. Got it?"

He had stopped trying to butt in and was just watching her mutely.

"Got it?" she repeated.

He shrugged. "Do whatever you have to do," he said, throwing up his hands. "You're right. I'll just keep my mouth shut."

"Good. Thank you."

"No problem."

They started walking again. Silently this time.

Patience busied herself looking in at the spotlit store-window displays they passed, pretending she was strolling alone. She might as well be. She got the impression that Jace couldn't wait to be rid of her now.

Soon enough, they were at Grand Central. "I'm going in here," she said, pointing to the Lexington Avenue side entrance. "I can get the subway right downstairs."

"I'm going around to the taxi stand on "Forty-Second Street," Jace said. "So, I guess I'll see you."

"I guess so."

There seemed to be nothing else to say. Patience turned and walked through the propped-open doors.

She turned around to remind Jace that she'd give him a call so that he could see the magazine article when it was written, but he'd already been swallowed up by the crowd on the sidewalk.

Just as well.

Maybe she wouldn't call him after all.

*So, it's good-bye, Jace Hoffman,* she thought. *Again.*

Clutching a mugful of warm milk, Jace padded from the kitchen back to the living room. He set the mug on a coaster on the glass coffee table and checked the clock. Still five more minutes until "The Odd Couple" started on cable.

He adjusted the wooden blinds, shutting out a view of the East River and the lights of Roosevelt Island, then straightened the oil painting on the wall beside the entertainment center. He had bought it at a gallery opening he'd gone to with Sue last April, right before they broke up. She had loved the painting—a monochromatic cityscape that wasn't really his taste. He'd bought it to please Sue, in a sense, and because he considered art a worthwhile investment.

He plopped down on the couch and picked up the remote control, flipping channels on his forty-inch television set. He had already watched the financial news report and had caught tonight's Mets playoff score on ESPN. He had checked the Weather Channel to see if he needed to bring an umbrella to the office tomorrow—he didn't—and sat through the opening monologue on a late-night talk show to see if any of tonight's guests sounded interesting—they didn't.

He looked around the living room, restless. The plants were watered, the magazines perfectly fanned on the coffee table, and the bills were all paid and waiting in a neat stack in the "Out" box on his desk in the corner.

The cleaning service had been here today, so the

place was in perfect order. Not that it wasn't on an ordinary day, anyway. Jace liked to keep things neat and organized. But he felt that he needed something to do, and it would have been helpful if he'd spotted a big pile of crumbs that needed to be swept up.

He picked up his mug, leaned back against the leather couch cushion, and sipped his milk. Cocoa would be better, but chocolate contained caffeine. A few years back, when he'd mentioned his chronic insomnia to his physician at his annual checkup, Dr. Katzenbaum had recommended warm milk before bed. It contained some kind of chemical that was supposed to make you drowsy.

It never worked on Jace, but he figured tonight was going to be one of those nights when he needed all the help he could get.

It was Patience Magee.

He never should have agreed to do that interview.

Okay, so he'd done it as a favor to her, on a strictly professional basis, but . . .

Why had he gone to the coffee shop with her?

And why, for Pete's sake, had he kissed her? In the street, no less, like some passionate fool.

Meanwhile, here he was, unable to relax because he knew that she was out in the dark Manhattan night on that damned subway.

Actually, he realized, she must be home by now. She'd said she lived someplace near Bleecker Street.

It figured. That neighborhood, in the heart of Greenwich Village, was as eclectic as Patience herself. Jace rarely ventured below Twenty-Third Street unless he was passing through on the way to his office in the financial district in lower Manhattan.

Unable to stand it a moment longer, Jace pressed the "mute" button and tossed the remote on the table. He stood and walked purposefully toward his desk, uncertain of his mission until he found himself pulling the enormous Manhattan phone book out of a drawer.

He muttered to himself as he flipped through the *Ms,* wondering why he assumed she would even be listed. For all he knew, she had a roommate and the phone could be under her—or *his,* knowing liberal Patience—name. And even if she were listed, she was a woman, and women never listed themselves under their full names, which would be an open invitation to obscene callers.

So, how many *P. Magees* would there be in the Manhattan phone book?

He didn't have to wonder, because she wasn't listed with a bunch of other *P. Magees.*

She was listed as *Magee, Patience.*

At least, he assumed it was she.

Okay, there could only be one Patience Magee in Manhattan . . . in the world, he corrected himself. A name like that was definitely one of a kind.

Besides, what other woman would brazenly list her full name in the phone book, like a neon beacon to any wacko with a phone?

He dialed the number, telling himself he only wanted to make sure she had made it home all right. When she answered, he would hang up. Then he would have peace of mind.

Right, he told himself. If you can live with yourself after a junior high stunt like this.

He hadn't called a female and hung up when she answered since he and Howie Nussman were in sixth grade and both had a crush on Lindsey Meyer. Of course, that was in the days before Caller ID, he thought, as his gaze fell on his own Caller ID box.

Realizing that if Patience had one, too—and these

days, who didn't?—his hang-up call wouldn't be anonymous, Jace stopped dialing and replaced the receiver.

Then, because he knew he would never be able to watch *The Odd Couple* in peace if he didn't know she had made it home safely, he went to the closet by the door and took his cell phone out of his briefcase. Cell phone numbers might pop up on Caller ID, but they weren't accompanied by a name. She would never know it was him calling.

Feeling foolish, yet unable to stop himself, he flipped open the phone and dialed her number again. This time he let it ring . . . and ring . . . and ring . . .

Then there was a click and an answering machine picked up.

She wasn't home.

"Hey, it's Patience. You know the drill."

She wasn't home?

He forgot all about staying anonymous as concern overtook him. Had something happened to her?

There was a beep.

"Hello, Patience, it's Jace Hoffman," he heard himself say. "You're not home, and I'm worried, because I left you an hour ago and—"

There was another click in his ear, and then Patience's voice said, "Checking up on me, Hoffman?"

"I was worried," he said lamely, wondering how he could have ever thought this was a good idea. Why hadn't he just hung up, the way he had planned?

Because he was too rattled at the thought that something might have happened to her.

He should have known better. If anyone tried to mug Patience or follow her off the subway, she'd probably strike a karate pose and send him yelping home.

"Why were you worried?" she asked, and to his surprise, she didn't sound antagonistic, for a change. She sounded almost . . . touched. Okay, and maybe a bit amused, too.

He felt his face grow hot. "Because you refused to listen to reason and insisted on taking the subway home alone," he said testily.

"Like I said, Jace, I do it all the time. I got home safe and sound forty-five minutes ago."

"Well, when you didn't answer the phone I thought—"

"I never answer my phone. I screen calls."

"All of them."

"Yup, every single one."

"Why?"

"Because I got sick of heavy breathers and sickos, okay?"

He opened his mouth to tell her that if she hadn't listed her first name in the phone book, she wouldn't be getting obscene phone calls. But he thought better of it. He'd had enough arguments with Patience Magee for one day.

Besides, it was just about midnight. Might as well get the new day off to a more peaceful start.

"Well, as long as you're all right . . ." he said, and paused. In the background, on her end, he could hear familiar music.

"Hey, that song—is that the beginning of 'The Odd Couple'?" he asked, turning to look at his own television.

He had pressed "Mute," but sure enough, there were the opening shots of Jack Klugman and Tony Randall.

She was watching it, too.

"I love 'The Odd Couple,' " she said. "I used to stay up and watch it with my dad when I was really little. Now I watch the reruns on cable every night. I know every episode by heart."

"So do I," Jace said, incredulous.

"I also know the whole opening by heart," Patience said. "You know, 'On November thirtieth, Felix Unger was asked to remove himself from his place of residence . . .' "

" 'That request came from his wife,' " Jace picked up quoting the familiar voice-over where she left off. She joined in, chuckling, and they recited it together, word for word.

Then, as if on cue, they launched into a simultaneous version of the instrumental theme song, singing, "Da-da-da-da-da-daaah . . . da-da-dah, da-da-dah, dah . . ."

"Hey, we actually have something in common," he said after they had erupted in laughter.

"Yeah . . . that we both like this really old television show about two New Yorkers who have nothing in common," she said dryly. "There's some kind of poetic justice there, don't you think?"

"I guess," He grinned and looked over at the TV. "Hey, isn't this the episode where Oscar goes to that dating service and ends up getting matched up with Felix's ex-wife Gloria?"

"The one where he uses the name Andre la Plume!" Patience exclaimed. "Oh, I love this episode."

"Okay, so . . . I'll let you go watch," Jace said, shifting his weight.

"Okay, you, too," Patience said. "Hey, thanks for calling."

"Yeah," he said, then added, impulsively, "Maybe I'll do it again sometime."

"Maybe you should," she said, and her voice was smiling.

So was he, as he hung up.

# Five

"How about you, Jace," Patience watched herself ask on the conference room television monitor. "How do you feel about sex on a first date?"

"I think it's a bad idea," the televised Jace said in his characteristically unflappable way. "I mean, it's great when you're in the moment, but I wouldn't want to get involved, long term, with the kind of woman who would hop into bed with someone she barely knows."

Patience leaned back in her chair, propped her feet on the table, and aimed the remote control at the VCR across the room, freezing the tape on a close-up of Jace's face.

She narrowed her gaze at his slightly out-of-focus image, studying the expression in his dark eyes, which were clearly aimed right at her—meaning, the televised Patience. There was a challenge in the way he was looking at her, she realized now. As though he assumed she might be the kind of woman who would sleep with someone on the first date.

She never had. Not that she had completely ruled it out, because anything could happen, in theory. But she had never been so swept away by a guy that she fell into bed on the first date—or the second, or even the third, for that matter. Relationships just weren't that simple—at least, not for her.

*Guess I'm just an old-fashioned Puritan gal after all,* she told herself, grinning. *Take that, Jace Hoffman.*

She aimed the remote at his frozen face on the screen, about to zap it into action again, when her friend Kaia, a petite, perpetually cheerful Asian woman who worked as one of the magazine's beauty editors, stuck her head in the conference room door.

"What'cha doin'?" she asked cheerfully, clutching a small bag of chips from the break room vending machine. Her tiny figure was chicly clad in a black velvet catsuit and provided absolutely no evidence of her penchant for junk food.

"I'm just going over the videotape from last night's interview," Patience told her.

"What interview?" Kaia plopped down in the chair next to her and peered at the screen.

"You know . . . for the 'Six Sexy Studs' article."

"'Six Sexy Studs'?" Kaia munched a potato chip and held the bag in front of Patience. "Wasn't it supposed to be 'Eight Excellent Eligibles'?"

"Where have you been?" Patience took a chip and crunched it loudly. "My bachelors were dropping like flies."

"You mean, backing out?"

"I mean, deciding to get married. The way things were going, I almost had to call it 'Five Fantastic Fiancés'."

"So, what's up with him?" Kaia asked, motioning at Jace's slightly blurred close-up.

"He's . . . I don't know what he is."

"Engaged?"

"No, he's single. I managed to find six single guys."

"And did they all look like him?" Kaia asked. "Because if I knew there were single, straight, available men in Manhattan who looked like that . . ."

"Actually, he's not your type," Patience said, pressing Play again and helping herself to another chip before settling back in her chair to watch the tape.

"How do you know?"

"Trust me. He's an uptight Wall Street guy. He likes to control people. He's incredibly anal-retentive. He thinks the Village is for freaks and drag queens. He doesn't like cats. And he's a Mets fan."

"You got all of that out of a one-hour interview with five other guys participating?"

"Nah, I've known him forever."

"You've known him forever?" Kaia sat up straighter in her chair. "How?"

"Well, not *forever*, but . . . we went to college together."

"Fix me up with him, Patience. He's cute."

"Can't," Patience said firmly, her eyes glued to the television, where the farmer and the teacher were comparing notes on pickup lines.

"Why not?"

*Yeah, why not?* Patience asked herself.

After all, Kaia was intelligent and fun-loving, and adorable—and one of her best friends. Plus, she was just dying to become somebody's wife. She'd been saying that if she didn't meet a decent man soon, she was going to resort to the personal ads.

So, why not fix her up with Jace? Maybe they would hit it off.

*Because . . .*

*You know why not,* Patience told herself, trying not to squirm visibly. *It's because you want Jace for yourself. Which is ridiculous because that's never in a million years going to happen.*

"If it's because you think he's not my type, get over it," Kaia said. "These days, my type is 'single.' Period."

"Kaia, believe me, you don't want to get tangled up with a man like Jace Hoffmann," Patience said, lifting her remote, taking aim, and fast-forwarding through a long-winded breakup sob story from the starving artist. When Jace's face popped up again, she pressed Play.

"Oh, I get it," Kaia said, looking from the television to Patience.

"You get what?" Patience frowned, pretending to be intent on what Jace was saying. As if she hadn't already watched this tape twice, pretty much memorizing his responses.

"You want the Mr. Cute Control Freak all for yourself. And I don't blame you."

"That's a laugh," Patience said, trying to muster one for effect. It came out a reedy warble. "I don't want Jace Hoffman. God, he's the last man I'd ever want to date."

Kaia crumpled the empty potato chip bag and brushed the crumbs off her lap before standing up. "I know you, Patience Magee," she said, grinning. "You're into him, whether or not he's your type. Anyway, didn't you ever hear the old saying that opposites attract?"

"It's a lie," Patience informed her. "My parents couldn't be more alike, and they're blissfully happy."

"Yeah? Well, so are mine. They still hold hands when they walk down the street. My mother's a right brain neat-freak lawyer, and my father's—well, you know."

Of course Patience knew. Johnny Chen, a longhaired music teacher at Manhattan's high school for the performing arts, was as offbeat as they came. He moonlighted as a stand-up comedian. She'd gone with Kaia to see him perform at Catch a Rising Star, and they'd sat with Kaia's mother, who seemed very prim in her well-tailored suit.

"Just because two people who seem to have nothing in common can occasionally wind up happily married doesn't mean I secretly want to date someone like Jace Hoffman," Patience said resolutely. "Your parents are a rare exception to the rule."

Kaia shrugged. "All right, I'll shut up for now. Just let me know when I can say 'I told you so,' okay?"

"It'll never happen. The day I say yes to Jace Hoffman will be the day . . . the day . . ."

"Pigs fly?" Kaia offered helpfully.

"I was looking for something a little more original, but that'll do in a pinch," Patience told her with a grin.


"I'll have two hot dogs with mustard and a bottle of water," Jace told the old man standing under an umbrella beside his hot dog cart.

"You want onions?"

"No onions," Jace said, "but I'll take an extra napkin, please," which automatically brought Patience to mind.

Everything he had done so far today seemed to inexplicably cause a vision of Patience Magee to pop into his head. Brushing his teeth, pressing the button for the elevator, buying a subway token—no matter what he did, he thought of her.

And he didn't want to think of her, because what was the use? Nothing was going to come of this . . . this *connection* they'd established. He had his life; she had hers . . .

*And never the twain shall meet,* he thought, reaching into his overcoat for his wallet, paying the vendor, and taking the napkin-wrapped hot dogs and bottle of water.

He crossed Broadway, glancing up at the overcast sky. It was sprinkling lightly, but not enough to put up his umbrella . . . or to go back to the office. For some reason, he was too restless to sit at his desk and eat today. That was what he usually did—read the papers and gobbled a quick sandwich.

He found himself wondering what Patience was doing right now. She didn't seem like the type to eat at her desk. She probably socialized during her lunch hours—probably met friends at restaurants that served frozen margaritas, chips, and salsa. He could just imagine her squeezing in a cocktail and some gossip before hurrying back to the office.

Needing to disapprove of her further, Jace told himself that she probably didn't take her publishing job seriously. But he couldn't help recalling how earnest she had been last night running that interview session. She had seemed to know exactly what she wanted to accomplish, keeping a tight rein on her subjects when they strayed toward rowdiness. He had been impressed. He couldn't help it.

Well, so what? That didn't mean he had to . . .

*What?*

Date her?

*Yeah, that's a joke,* he told himself, trying to find it funny. But he didn't. There was nothing humorous about the idea of seeing Patience Magee again, in a romantic setting. In fact . . .

*Nah.*

He found an unoccupied spot on a low concrete wall in front of an office building and sat down. As he munched his first hot dog, he gazed idly at the others seated on the wall—construction workers and secretaries and business people like himself. They all seemed to be in groups of two and three.

Suddenly, he felt conspicuous. Even . . . lonely.

Finishing the first hot dog, he wiped his mouth and drank some water. Then he started the second. As he chewed, a ridiculous thought popped into his head.

What if he called her at work, right now? Just to say hello, just so he wouldn't feel so damned lonely sitting here eating his lunch.

There was no reason not to. After all, he had his cell phone in the pocket of his suit jacket, and he could call 411 to get the main number for *She* magazine.

He finished the second hot dog in two enormous bites, wiped his hands carefully, and took out his phone. He called information. Then, before he changed his mind, he called her.

Moments later, he had been connected to her direct line. As it rang, he wondered what he would say to her if she answered . . . and what message he would leave on her voice mail if she didn't.

He had no idea.

Which was why, when she picked up breathlessly, he froze.

"Patience Magee," her voice said.

What was he supposed to say?

He fumbled silently and settled on, "Hi."

"Who is this?" she asked impatiently, and he could just see her scowling.

"It's Jace Hoffman."

"Jace!"

She was happy to hear from him? Surprised, he hesitated, uncertain what to say next.

"Where are you?" she asked. "It sounds like you're on a cell phone."

"I am. I'm on the street."

"Outside my building?"

"No. No, I'm actually on lower Broadway. Why?"

"Oh, no reason, I just thought . . ." She paused. "I don't know, for some reason I thought maybe you were going to say you were in the neighborhood and wanted to stop up to say hello."

"Really?" Taken aback, he switched the phone to his other ear and leaned against the stone pillar behind his shoulders. "Well, maybe I'll do that sometime."

"Yeah, that would be good." She cleared her throat.

"So, listen, I know you're probably busy . . ."

"Kind of," she said after a moment. "I mean, I'm trying to put together that article . . ."

"How's it coming?"

"Great. Really great. You were . . ."

"Great?" he supplied when she seemed to be searching for the right word.

She laughed. "Yes, you were great. Thanks again for helping me out, Jace."

"It was actually fun."

"You sound surprised."

"I am surprised. Well, I'd better let you get back to work. I've got to get back to the office myself."

"Okay," she said, but there was something searching in her tone. As though she wondered why he had called.

He wondered himself.

Then, because he impulsively decided that he really shouldn't be calling her for no reason, he said, "Listen, what are you doing later?"

"Later?"

"I mean, tonight. After work. Do you have plans?"

"Actually . . ."

"Because I thought maybe we could get together," he heard himself say. "If you're not busy."

"You mean . . ."

"I mean, go out," he said, unable to bring himself to say the word *date*.

"Go out?" she echoed. "Like . . . just the two of us?"

"That was what I was thinking."

"Wow, that would be . . . nice."

He was stunned that she'd said yes.

Even more stunned at what he'd done. He'd just made a date with Patience Magee, a woman he couldn't . . .

Well, okay, he could *stand* her . . .

And obviously, since he had kissed her last night, he was attracted to her.

But what made him think the two of them could possibly declare a truce and spend an entire evening together? What would they do? What would they talk about?

"What did you have in mind?" Patience asked. "Wait, let me guess . . . dinner and a movie?"

He knew she was referring to his comment during the interview about the ideal first date, and he resented the hint of sarcasm in her voice. This was a really bad idea.

But how was he going to get out of it now?

He couldn't.

So, reminding himself that he was a gentleman, he said, "Is there something you'd rather do instead of dinner and a movie?"

He figured she would have been a lady about it and say of course there wasn't—that whatever he wanted to do was fine with her.

He obviously forgot with whom he was dealing.

"Absolutely," Patience Magee said decisively. "I would rather go to see the Wired Lamps."

"The . . . what?"

"They're a band," she explained. "My favorite band, actually. And they're playing tonight down at The Dump."

"The Dump?"

"This club in Tribeca."

"Sounds charming," he muttered, wondering what

he had gotten himself into and how he could possibly get himself out without being rude.

"So, if you're interested . . ."

"I guess we could go. Would we have time to have a quick dinner beforehand, or—"

"Oh, God, yes," she said. "They don't go on until twelve."

"Twelve . . . midnight?"

"Uh-huh."

"The concert *starts* at midnight?"

"Is that a problem?"

"Well, it's just . . . I mean, it's a weeknight and . . ." He sounded like a real wimp, didn't he? But what was he supposed to do? Act as if it were no big deal to go out until all hours when he had to get up at five-thirty tomorrow morning and head downtown to a demanding job?

"If it's too late—"

"No, it's fine," he said quickly, feeling as if he were back in middle school and desperately wanting the cool kids to think he was one of them.

"Because I remembered that you said that you never go to bed until late because you can't sleep, so I figured you might as well go out and spare yourself some tossing and turning."

"Well, gee, that was very kind of you," he said, unable to keep a note of sarcasm from his voice. It was a defensive move, partly because he had the sudden feeling that she somehow knew he had lain awake pretty much all night last night . . .

Thinking about her.

"You know me," she said breezily. "Always concerned for your well-being."

He smiled in spite of his paranoia. "Okay, where should we meet? Do you want me to come to your office?"

"Nah, then you'd just have to go back downtown. Do you know any good restaurants in Tribeca? Because I know this place—"

"I'll just come to your office," he said quickly. "I don't mind coming up to midtown. I'll make a dinner reservation someplace."

"Okay, that's fine," she said unexpectedly. He had been expecting an argument. It just didn't seem that anything with her could be easy, but maybe he was wrong.

"What time should I be there?" he asked.

"Seven-thirty?" she suggested.

"Fine."

"Do you remember where my building is?"

He told her that he did and that he'd see her there tonight.

"Great. And Jace?"

"Yeah?"

"Thanks for calling. I'm really looking forward to it."

"Me, too," he said, unable to keep from smiling.

He hung up, tucked his phone back into his pocket . . . and realized the sky had suddenly opened up. It was raining in earnest. People were scattering in search of shelter.

Funny. He hadn't even noticed.

He put up his umbrella and splashed across Broadway, quelling a bizarre urge to make like Gene Kelly and dance his way through the downpour back to the office.

"Are you sure I'm dressed okay for this place?" Patience asked Jace across the small vase of roses in the center of the table after the waiter had taken their order.

"I told you, you look great," he said.

And though she wasn't a hundred percent certain that he meant it, she felt a prickle of pleasure just hearing Jace say anything complimentary about her appearance. Until now, she had gotten the impression that he wasn't exactly crazy about her style. Not that she minded. She didn't dress to please anyone but herself.

Still, she was grateful that she had dashed out this afternoon to buy a new outfit. Nothing outrageously expensive, but Bloomingdale's was having a sale and she had found this body-skimming mocha-colored shift that just happened to match her shoes and lipstick. She had been tempted to ask Kaia to help her put her hair up for the occasion, but couldn't stand the thought of hearing her say "I told you so," especially so soon.

After all, this was just a date. She and Jace were hardly poised to join the ranks of happily married polar opposites.

So she had done her own hair, piling it on top of her head and pinning it the best she could. She couldn't keep some wisps from tumbling down, but she had to admit that she liked the effect. It was kind of . . . sexy. And right now, that was exactly what she wanted to be for Jace Hoffman. She couldn't help herself. She wanted him to be attracted to her, damn it, because that was how she felt about him.

Look at him sitting there across from her in his black Paul Stuart suit and tie and perfectly starched white spread-collar shirt. He was Tall, Dark, and Handsome personified, and she couldn't deny any longer, even to herself, that she was drawn to him. Even if it were purely on a physical basis, which she was no longer even sure of . . . not that she was ready to consider any other kind of feelings for him.

So here she sat across from him at a round candlelit table in this small French restaurant in the east Fifties, one of those small, exclusive places frequented by society people and celebrities, not poverty-stricken magazine editors who lived in the Village.

It wasn't her kind of restaurant and she wasn't crazy about French food, though she'd acted enthusiastic when he'd told her she had to try the duck l'orange and to save room for crème brûlée. Mexican was more her style—the kind of place where you could munch tortilla chips and salsa and down a frozen margarita or two while you waited for your order.

She would give anything for a basket of chips now. Not so much because she was hungry, but because she was nervous and needed something to do.

She couldn't help it. She didn't know if it was because she felt out of her element in this place or because she was with Jace again, but her heart was beating a little too fast and she couldn't keep from tapping her foot under cover of the white linen tablecloth. Her hands wanted something to do, so she reached for her glass.

She sipped her wine and asked brightly, "So, how was your day?"

"Not bad," he said, and started to tell her about it. He went into detail about what had happened with one of the blue chip stocks, and it should have bored her out of her skull, but she found herself hanging on his every word. He made it interesting somehow.

"Why are you looking at me like that?" he broke off to ask.

"Like what?"

"Like . . . I don't know. I guess like you're really interested in what I'm saying."

"Because I am," she said, "and I shouldn't be."

"Gee, thanks," he said, but he looked amused.

"Oh, come on, Jace, stock? What a snore. I mean, that's what I'd have thought. Except that you make it seem so fascinating somehow. You're really passionate about what you do, aren't you, Jace?"

He nodded. "I love it. Why is that so surprising?"

"I guess I just assumed you were in it to make money."

He shrugged. "That's a part of it. I'm not going to pretend that I'm not well paid for what I do, but . . . I wouldn't do it if greed were the only thing motivating me. It's just like any other career. Why do you do what you do?"

"Honestly? Because I need to pay the rent," she said without hesitation. "No, I mean, I really enjoy my job. But I can't stand the confinement of working in an office. I'm just not cut out for the nine-to-five grind, and I absolutely live for weekends and days off. In fact, I've unfortunately already used up all my vacation time and all my sick days for this year, and it's only October."

"You've been sick that often?"

"Oh, I never really get sick," she said. "I take echinacea."

"You take what?"

"Echinecea. It's an herbal supplement." He looked disapproving. Surprise, surprise. "It boosts the immune system."

"So you're never sick, but you've used all your sick time? Why?"

"I consider those days necessary for my mental health."

"You mean, you call in sick when you're healthy just so you don't have to go to work?"

"You bet," she said, noticing the disapproval in his eyes.

*Don't let him start in on you,* a warning voice said.

*Don't ruin what was shaping up to be a nice evening with an argument.*

"How does your boss feel about that?" Jace asked, although she could tell he wanted to say more.

"Camisha? Who knows? She hasn't said anything to me about it. I never blow a deadline, and the company gives you ten sick days, anyway. I guess they figure you're going to use them."

"But what if you get the flu between now and Christmas?" Jace asked.

"I won't. I get a flu shot every year down at the drugstore. They have this free clinic—"

"Well, there are other things you can get besides the flu. Strep throat, bronchitis . . ."

"I told you, I never get sick," she reminded him.

"But how do you know you won't?" He sounded exasperated. "Everyone gets sick sooner or later. What if you do?"

"If I do, I'd have to worry about it then." She sipped her wine and looked him in the eye. "Come on, Jace. Why stress about *what ifs?*"

"I'm just trying to see where you're coming from," he said, and she could tell it took great restraint for him to maintain good humor about this. Obviously, what he really wanted to do was lash into her for being so irresponsible. "Don't you feel guilty?"

"For playing hooky from work?" She searched her soul, wanting to be completely honest here. And she was when she told him, after a moment, "No, I honestly don't feel guilty."

"But what do you do when you stay home?"

"Anything I want," she said, smiling at the very thought of such delicious freedom. "I stay in bed until noon; I watch bad made-for-TV movies on cable; I eat cookies for lunch. You should try it sometime."

"Eating cookies for lunch?" He wrinkled his nose.

"Calling in sick. Giving yourself a break. It might make you a new man, Jace," she said teasingly.

He shook his head. "I couldn't do it."

"You're right," she said. "You probably couldn't."

For a moment, they were silent, sipping their wine.

"Don't you ever worry about tomorrow, Patience?" Jace asked her, toying with the stem of his goblet. "Do you always just assume that problems will take care of themselves—that things will automatically work out somehow?"

"They always have," she answered promptly. "At least, for me. And seriously, Jace, haven't things always worked out for you?"

"What kind of things?"

"Anything. Everything. A job. A place to live. Friendships. Relationships."

"Most of the time, I guess . . ."

"You sound hesitant. You're thinking of your ex-girlfriend."

"Sue?" Looking surprised, he shook his head. "She's the farthest thing from my mind, actually."

And maybe she had been. But Patience had been trying to think of a way to bring up the subject, and now was as good a time as any. She was bursting with curiosity about the woman who had almost snagged Jace Hoffman's heart.

"What was she like?" she asked him. "I'm being completely nosy, but I'm assuming you don't mind."

"No, I don't mind. She was . . ." He shrugged.

"Wait, let me guess. She was the complete opposite of me."

He seemed to be considering that, then said, "Pretty much."

"Did she work on Wall Street, too?"

He shook his head.

"Well, I'm guessing she's not an actress. Or a stripper."

He grinned. "She was a corporate accountant."

*Figures.* "How did you meet?"

"At a party."

"Is she beautiful?"

"Sue?" He seemed to be considering it.

Gee, Patience thought, if he has to actually think about it, then—

"She was definitely beautiful."

"Oh." She felt deflated. She had almost expected him to say that his ex was nothing special. Well, maybe not expected. Hoped was a better word. "What did she look like?"

"Like a cross between Sela Ward and Courtney Cox."

"She must be stunning."

He nodded—unenthusiastically, she noted, feeling a bit smug.

"Was she Jewish?" she asked. "Because I was just thinking that if she were so gorgeous and successful, there must be some reason why you didn't marry her. I thought maybe it was the religion thing."

"She was Jewish," he said. "It wasn't that."

*Is that important to you, Jace?* she wanted to ask. *Do you only date Jewish women?*

Well, she wasn't Jewish, and this was a date, wasn't it? But it wasn't the kind of date that could go anywhere, she reminded herself. It was just two old acquaintances getting together . . . for French food and wine at a romantic candlelit restaurant.

"So, what was it?" she asked Jace, forcing her attention back to his ex-girlfriend. "Was she a horrible person or something?"

"You really are nosy, aren't you?" he asked, but it

sounded like a mere observation, not as though he were irked by her questions.

"Incredibly nosy. So spill the dirt. What went wrong?"

"I thought I told you this once before. In Newport. Didn't we have this conversation?"

"You told me that what went wrong between you and Sue was that she wanted to get married. So, why didn't you want to marry her?"

"I just wasn't ready. Or maybe it was more that she wasn't the right person."

"So, you're a subscriber to the 'one right person' theory?" Patience asked. "Like, everybody in the world has only one soul mate—one perfect person they're supposed to be with?"

"I take it that's not what you believe?"

"We're not talking about me."

"Yet," he said with a grin.

"So, you just haven't found her yet, is that it? Your special someone?"

When he didn't nod—when he didn't react at all—she suddenly found herself feeling flustered. *Had* he found Ms. Right? Was he hopelessly, secretly in love?

*Please, God, don't let that be true.*

She wanted him to be still searching, still available . . .

*But why? Not so that you can have him, because you've already concluded that'll never happen in a million, trillion years.*

"I always thought that when I found the right person," he said slowly, twirling his glass so that the wine that was left swirled in the bottom, "I would know it in an instant. Like you just get struck by a thunderbolt when you look into her eyes or take her hand . . ."

"Like Meg Ryan and Tom Hanks at the end of *Sleepless in Seattle*?" she asked.

He looked surprised, and amused. "Exactly."

"And it wasn't like that with Sue?"

"No. I mean, I was attracted to her right away, but . . ."

"No sparks?"

"Oh, there were sparks," he said, and Patience was so consumed with hating Sue for a moment that she almost missed his saying, "At first."

"So, the sparks died?"

"Pretty much. And I realized that she was everything I should be looking for in a wife—smart and beautiful and successful and a good person—and that if I married her, we would probably live a very nice life. But not a life that was . . ." He paused, searching for the right word.

"Scintillating?" she provided.

He burst out laughing. "Exactly. Perfect word. 'Scintillating' is what I want."

She raised her glass to him. "Here's to your finding your Ms. Right, then, Jace. Because everyone should have a scintillating marriage."

He clinked her glass. They drank some wine.

He said, "How about you? What was wrong with Crispin? No sparks?" he added—a bit hopefully, she couldn't help noticing with satisfaction.

"Oh, there were sparks," she said, hoping there was a sufficient gleam in her eye. She might not have a future with Jace, but it couldn't hurt to make him a little jealous.

"There were?"

"*Major* sparks." Okay, a lot jealous.

"But he wasn't Mr. Right?"

"I don't believe in that," Patience said. "I figure there are a lot of people who could be right for you. You just have to click with one of them when the time is right."

"So, the time wasn't right with Crispin?"

"Oh, that wasn't all that wasn't right with Crispin. I was just talking in general terms."

"What was wrong with him?"

"He was just . . . dull. Once I got past his looks—and the English accent—"

"You like accents?"

"Not necessarily," she said quickly, remembering that she had told him just last night that he had one. "But I've always thought British men are sexy. At least, rock musicians are."

"And Crispin wasn't a rock musician?"

"God, no. He had some boring financial job."

"Like mine."

She shrugged. "Only yours doesn't seem so boring, for some reason. His did. And he kept talking about how we were going to get married and buy a house in the suburbs and have children. I felt smothered."

"So, you don't want to get married or buy a house or have children."

"No, that's not it. I do want those things—I mean, I *might* want those things. But not now."

"Or maybe just not with him."

"I think it was both," Patience said resolutely, though she wasn't entirely sure anymore.

Being married . . . well, maybe there was something kind of appealing about it. Maybe it wasn't something that would happen to her years from now, when she was in her midthirties, as she had once assumed. Maybe it could happen sooner.

"I think that if you met the right person tomorrow, you would give up everything for him," Jace said.

"Give up everything?" she echoed. "What do you mean by that?"

"I mean that if you fell head over heels in love with

Mr. Right and he wanted you to move to Jersey and get pregnant on your honeymoon, you would."

"No way."

"I think you're wrong."

"Who says falling in love means you have to give up everything?"

"It doesn't. But the point is, you would."

"I would not!"

"I can see right through you, Patience Magee," he said smugly. "I can definitely see you getting swept away, becoming a wife and mother overnight, moving to the suburbs . . ."

"Not in this lifetime."

*And not with you,* she added silently, seething that he thought he knew her so well. He knew nothing about her. Nothing!

"We'll see," Jace said with maddening calm. There was something almost glib about him.

"We'll see?" she repeated. "What's that supposed to mean? If you think you're going to convert me into a Suzy Homemaker with—"

"Me?" He looked horrified. He plunked his glass down on the table. "I didn't mean you should marry *me.* I was talking hypothetically."

"I know *that!*" she retorted, though for a moment there, she hadn't been sure. "Can you see *us* married?"

He laughed. Hard. Maybe too hard.

For a moment, she was insulted—and a bit hurt. But then her own glass of wine kicked in and she saw the humor in it. She giggled as she said, "You're the farthest thing from my Mr. Right . . . assuming there *is* such a thing. Which I don't believe in."

"Well, I do. And you're the exact opposite of my vision of Ms. Right," Jace pointed out good-naturedly as the waiter appeared with their soup course.

"Well, now that we have that settled . . . I'm starved," Patience said, and added, "I suppose your Ms. Right eats like a bird?"

"Actually, I like a woman who has an appetite. I'm Jewish, remember? Food plays a huge role in family get-togethers."

"So, Sue liked to eat?"

"Sue was the most finicky eater I've ever seen. When I brought her home to meet my parents, she wouldn't touch the noodle pudding—it's my grandmother's specialty—or put cream cheese on her bagel or eat a rugelach. She was always worried about her weight."

"I've never had noodle pudding; but for the record, I love rugelach, and I always put lots of cream cheese on my bagel," Patience said lightly. "Too bad I'm not your type, Jace."

"Too bad you're not." He grinned and leaned back as the waiter set his consommé in front of him. "But maybe you can come home to Brooklyn with me sometime anyway, since you've already met my parents. You'd love Bubbe's brisket."

"Who's Bubbe?"

"My grandmother. She lives with my parents. She'd be thrilled if she saw the way you can put food away. She loves to feed people."

"I'd like to meet her." She raised an eyebrow at him across her bowl of vichyssoise. "Does this mean we're going to be friends?"

He picked up his spoon and held it poised over his bowl. "Do you want to?"

She shrugged. "Why not?"

"See you later, Patience!" bellowed Tommy, the doorman, over the throbbing live music.

"Later, Tommy!" She ran back and gave him a quick squeeze. "Say hi to Andre for me!"

"Who's Andre?" Jace asked as they walked past the crowd lined up along the velvet ropes on the sidewalk.

"His lover. He's a performance artist. He used to be a woman—Andrea," Patience said matter-of-factly. "But then she went to Europe and had an operation and now she's Andre."

"Oh." And here Jace had thought nothing else could shock him tonight.

"Did you have fun?" Patience asked, zipping her leather coat.

"It was—"

"Interesting?" she asked, her green eyes twinkling up at him.

"Definitely." He glanced back over his shoulder at the eloquently named The Dump. Aside from the doorman, velvet ropes, and crowd, you would never know the place was a nightclub. It looked like a warehouse, and there was no sign. The otherwise deserted block was lined with run-down buildings and strewn with garbage, and it was easy to imagine a mugger lurking in the shadows of a nearby alley.

Yet the club seemed to be one of those happening New York nightspots, judging from the hip clientele. He had recognized a couple of well-known actors and actresses in the throng, and Patience had pointed out several other notables—mostly musicians he had never heard of.

He had to admit, he was impressed by the way the waiting crowd had parted when she'd arrived, as though sensing she belonged here. Jace had felt their eyes on him as he passed and knew they were wondering what he was doing here, with her. He had almost expected to be turned away at the door, but the doorman had greeted Patience by name and waved them right inside. She had known everyone—the bartenders, the crowd, even the band members who took the stage and blasted something that Jace didn't exactly consider music.

"So you didn't have fun, Jace?" Patience asked, looking disappointed.

"No, I did," he said truthfully, realizing he had had fun . . . because of her. She was fun to talk to; she made him laugh. "You must do this a lot, huh? I mean, they all knew you in there."

"Pretty often," she said, nodding. Then, around a sudden yawn, she added, "Maybe not as much now as I used to. I mean, there was a time when I was out every night, but . . ."

"You're slowing down with old age?" he asked, amused.

"That, and I was in a relationship for a while, which meant I didn't do this sort of thing as much."

Oh. "Did you ever bring Crispin here?"

She nodded.

Disappointed, he asked, "What did he think?"

It wasn't that he wanted The Dump to be "their" place, or that he ever intended to set foot inside the club again. It was just . . .

Okay, he didn't like picturing her here with another guy. He couldn't help it.

"Crispin hated it," she said, smiling—though not fondly—at the memory. "He called it a bloody nightmare, and he insulted Andre. I was furious with him."

Jace wanted to tell her that he might not meet transsexual performance artists every day, but *he* would never insult Andre. And he didn't think The Dump was a nightmare, exactly. Just . . . different. Really different. From every place he had ever been—or imagined being—in his life.

Jace spotted a cab turning the corner from Canal

Street and hailed it. When they were settled inside, he snuck a peek at his watch and gasped.

"What's wrong?" Patience asked over the twanging sitar coming from the front speakers.

"It's after three."

"Wow, it's that late?" she asked blandly.

"I have to be up for work in about two hours."

"Why do you get up so early?"

"I have stuff to do."

"At that hour? Like—?"

"I go to the gym—"

"Where the heck is it? In Connecticut?" she asked dryly.

"No, there's one in my building."

"I'm not surprised. I pegged you for living in one of those luxury East Side towers, right?"

"Pretty much," he admitted. "And then I make coffee and have breakfast and check the financial news, and then I head to the office."

"Wow," she said. "You're nuts."

"Nuts?" You'd think he would be used to her by now, but he still found himself raising an eyebrow. "Why? What time do you get up?"

"Eight-thirty."

"Eight-thirty? What time do you have to be at work?"

"Nine, officially, but nobody shows up until at least nine-thirty," she said. "And how long does it take me to jump into the shower and throw on some clothes?"

"How long?" he asked, trying to banish the sudden image of her in the shower, soaping her naked body.

"Like, ten minutes tops."

"Don't you have breakfast?"

"I usually grab a doughnut and a can of Pepsi on the way to the subway . . . and don't give me that look. I need the sugar and caffeine to get me going in the morning."

About to lecture her about the benefits of a morning workout and healthy breakfast, he bit his tongue. It was no use. She wasn't going to change. Besides, why should it matter to him what she ate for breakfast? It wasn't as though he had any say over what she did. She was just his friend. Nothing more.

To prove it, he said, "We should get together again."

"Sure we will. Isn't that what friends do?" She smiled at him.

Her face was only inches from his in the dark cab.

He fought the inexplicable, familiar urge to haul her into his arms and kiss her. They had already decided a romance wouldn't work. And friends didn't kiss each other. Not the way he wanted to kiss her.

"What do you want to do?" he asked. "I mean, the next time we get together."

"I don't know . . . I'll leave it up to you. Come up with something fun."

"I'll try."

Great. Talk about a challenge. What would she consider fun? He had the feeling a movie wouldn't cut it.

The cab sped around a corner, jostling them so that she landed against him, the whole right side of her body running the length of the left side of his. They were both fully dressed, wearing coats, yet he felt a jolt at the unexpected contact—as if it were far more intimate.

He sprang away, steadying himself against the door.

"I'm busy the next few nights, though," she said unexpectedly.

Busy? With what? He wanted to ask her, but he

didn't dare. It was none of his business if she had several dates lined up, or with whom.

Still, he was irked. "So am I," he lied. "I was thinking more like next weekend."

"You mean, what? Like, ten days from now?"

He nodded, noting that she seemed disappointed. Well, so was he. But *he* wasn't the one who was too busy to get together this weekend. In fact, all he had planned was a visit to Brooklyn on Friday night for the weekly Sabbath meal with his family.

"Okay," she said, and shrugged. "That's fine. You can call me next week."

He nodded. That wasn't what he wanted. Why couldn't he just say it? Why couldn't he admit he didn't really want to wait almost two whole weeks until they got together again?

Because they were just friends, that was why. You weren't supposed to be that eager to see your friends. Friendship was casual. It didn't make your heart beat faster when you looked at the other person . . .

Which was exactly what his heart was doing as his eyes met Patience's.

Much as he tried, he couldn't tear his gaze away. There was something in the depths of her expression that fascinated him. Something that begged him to say what he was thinking. To tell her that even though they had established that they were all wrong for each other and that all they could ever be was friends, he had this crazy urge to kiss her again, to see where it would lead if they forgot, for a moment, who and what they were supposed to be.

"Patience," he blurted, "I—"

The cab screeched to a sudden stop, effectively interrupting whatever was happening between them. He swallowed the rest of the words just as quickly as they had sprung to his tongue, realizing how utterly inappropriate they were.

"I live there," she said, pointing out the window at a narrow six-story building that housed a deli on the first floor.

He realized, with a mixture of disappointment and relief, that they hadn't stopped at a light, as he'd assumed. They were at their destination—rather, she was at her destination.

"I'll walk you inside," he said, and tapped on the glass between the seats, instructing the cab driver to wait.

"You don't have to walk me inside," she told him. "I'm fine."

He didn't bother to argue, just climbed out of the cab after her.

At least the quiet, tree-dotted Village side street was well lit, and it wasn't deserted even at this hour. There were a few pedestrians, mostly clusters of NYU students and bohemian types heading toward or coming from a bar across the street. She inserted her key into an almost hidden door set back to the right of the deli entrance. "Okay," she said, pushing it open, "I'm in. Thank—"

"I'm walking you to your apartment, Patience."

She seemed about to argue, then shrugged as if to say *suit yourself*.

He followed her up a flight of steps, and then another. He looked up and saw several more flights rising above them.

"What floor are you on?" he asked, and then, before she could reply, he answered it himself. "The top."

"How'd you know?"

"Just a lucky guess," he said, continuing to climb. He was winded despite his regular workouts.

She wasn't even out of breath when they reached

the top. She stopped in front of a door marked 6D and unlocked two locks.

He was relieved to note that there was a dead bolt . . . and a peep hole. But for the first time he realized just how vulnerable a woman living alone in New York really was. An unexpected protective instinct washed over him. He suddenly didn't want to leave her here alone. But he had no choice. The cab was waiting downstairs, and he had to be up for work in two hours, and besides, they were just friends.

She stepped inside and flipped on a light. Curious, he peered over her shoulder.

"Want to come in?" she asked, catching him.

"No, I can't. The cab . . . and I was just being—"

"Nosy?"

He smiled. "No, that's you, remember? I was just being cautious. Making sure everything was all right. You live alone?"

"If I say yes, Rufus will be offended."

"Rufus?" Who was that? Another British boyfriend? He asked, as casually as possible, "Who's Rufus?"

"I'll show you," she said, and motioned him over the threshold, whispering, "Shh . . . he's sound asleep."

The apartment consisted of one room, with high-beamed ceilings and two walls of exposed brick. There were two tall windows, and hardwood floors, except for a few squares of tile in one corner that marked the kitchen area—little more than a sink, fridge, and stove. Still, the place was homey. There was one of those huge basket chairs with a floral print cushion, and the windows were framed by puffy white curtain valances. A bunch of flowers were stuck in a drinking glass on a trunk that apparently served as a coffee table, positioned as it was in front of the futon—which must double as a bed, because there wasn't one. On the walls were eclectic framed posters—one from

Cirque du Soleil, another from a concert featuring bands he didn't recognize, another a Picasso print.

There was clutter everywhere, he noticed—and he wasn't surprised. The apartment was definitely lived in, from the piles of newspapers on the floor by a chair to the stacks of paper on the computer desk. Rumpled clothes were strewn over the furniture, a hardcover novel was opened facedown on the futon, and there were dishes in the sink.

"Rufus is in here," Patience said, pushing open a door that was ajar.

He peered into the tiny bathroom and saw an enormous black cat asleep in the tub. It was snoring loudly.

"Rufus is a cat," he announced, relieved.

"Yeah, I know." She grinned. "Were you expecting a human?"

"I forgot you said you had a cat."

She pulled the door closed with a quiet click and said, "You don't like cats."

"What makes you think that?" he asked, though of course it was true. He hadn't liked cats ever since his Aunt Goldie's Siamese had leapt on him and scratched his face when he was a kid.

"You mentioned it during the interview last night."

"Was that only last night?" he asked.

"Tuesday," she said. "Technically, it was two nights ago, since it's pretty much Thursday morning now."

He yawned. "I've got to go get some sleep, and so do you."

"Okay," she said. "Thanks for a fun evening. I really had a good time."

"So did I."

"You look surprised."

"I am, in a way."

"I know what you mean." She smiled.

He smiled back.

And then—he would later try, and fail, to recall exactly how it had happened—she was in his arms and they were kissing. Her mouth opened beneath his, and she moaned softly as he threaded his fingers through her hair, knocking out the few pins that held it up, letting it spill over her shoulders in a glorious tumble.

She tasted of wine and crème brûleé; he buried his face in her neck and inhaled herbal shampoo and crisp October evening air. He nuzzled his mouth into the hollow beneath her ear and she threw her head back, pulling him against her tightly.

This was it. The point of no return. He knew it, fuzzily, as he kissed her deeply, knowing that if he didn't stop now, he wouldn't. He would make love to her right here, right now, with the apartment door standing wide open and the cab waiting downstairs and the fat cat with the crazy name snoring in the tub.

"Jace," she said, dragging her lips from his, and he looked down at her.

"I know," he murmured, and he pulled himself away. "I've got to go."

"It's late, and we're tired," she said quickly, as if to explain what had just happened. "And we were drinking."

No, he thought, even as he nodded. He was wide awake, and he hadn't had a drink since the beer he'd ordered when they first got to the club. There was no excuse for kissing her, except that he was wild about her.

But he couldn't tell her. He wouldn't tell her. Even if he were willing to admit to himself that he secretly longed for something more than friendship with Patience Magee, she had made it absolutely clear that he wasn't her kind of man. She wanted him as a friend, and nothing more.

"I've got to go," he said again, striding to the door. "I'll call you."

"Or I'll call you," she said. He looked back at her.

She grinned. "I know you, Jace. You'll start thinking about what just happened, and you'll let it ruin everything. You won't call, because you'll be afraid that it'll happen again."

"Won't it?" he asked, allowing himself a flicker of hope.

"Not if we don't let it. So don't worry."

"Good," he said, feigning relief.

"We'll go out next weekend, and we'll do strictly friend stuff," she told him.

"Definitely." He cleared his throat and hesitated only a moment longer in the doorway before telling her good night.

Then he took the cab home to his uptown apartment.

He made a pot of coffee before taking a long, cold shower. Then he drank two cups of it and dressed for the gym, afraid that if he allowed himself to sleep, he might dream of her . . . and wake up wanting—*needing*—what he could never have.

# Six

"I'll have the western omelet with extra cheese—that comes with hash browns, right?—and a side of bacon. Oh, and could you please bring ketchup and Tabasco sauce?" Patience closed her menu, handed it to the waiter, and looked at Beth.

"I'll have the fruit cup," she said, and shook her head. "I don't know how you can put away food the way you do and never gain weight. You don't even work out."

"Good genes, I guess."

"And all that nervous energy that has you bouncing off walls most of the time," Beth said, turning her head to watch the waiter walk away. "He's cute."

"Very cute."

"Too bad he's a waiter."

"You're such a snob, Beth," Patience said, leaning back in her chair and glancing out the plate glass window at Fifth Avenue, which was teeming with Sunday afternoon pedestrians despite a steady drizzle.

"I can't help it," Beth said, shivering as the restaurant door opened and people came in off the street. She pulled her pink cashmere sweater closer around her. "I want a guy with money. What's so wrong about that?"

"Absolutely nothing, except that it's pretty shallow,"

Patience said, thinking about Jace. It had been days since she'd heard from him. They hadn't spoken since he'd left her apartment that night—er, morning.

Well, what did she expect? She had told him she'd be busy all weekend, and she had been. But when she'd checked her answering machine each time she got home, she had found herself hoping for a message from him—and bitterly disappointed when there wasn't.

"So I'm shallow," Beth told her with a shrug, and reached for her cup of herbal tea. "I just want someone who can support me in the style to which I'm accustomed."

"You have a trust fund. Why do you need a rich guy? Your grandfather's money can support both of you," Patience said with a snort, dumping several packets of sugar into her coffee and giving it a stir.

"Because the kind of man who would live off my grandfather's trust fund isn't the kind of man I want. How lazy is that? I want someone who has worked hard and become successful on his own."

"The way you have?" Patience asked, raising a wry eyebrow. They both knew that Beth was just biding time at her public relations job for the Metropolitan Museum of Art. The minute she met Mr. Right and got engaged, she planned to quit.

"Exactly." Beth smiled good-naturedly. "So—I've already told you about my boring Saturday playing golf in Connecticut with my parents. What did you do all weekend?"

"What else? I worked," Patience said, rubbing her shoulders that still ached from hunching over a desk for hours on end. "The magazine just went to print."

"That time of the month, hmm?" Beth asked, familiar with Patience's editorial deadlines. "So all you've done since brunch last week is slave away, and you don't have anything juicy to tell me?"

"Well . . ." Patience shifted her weight and watched a couple kissing under an umbrella at a bus stop down the block.

"Tell me. Did you meet someone?"

"No."

"I could have sworn I saw an 'I'm in lust' gleam in your eye."

"You did. But it wasn't because I met someone new."

"You and Crispin got back together?"

"Oh, please." Patience waved her hand as if to shoo away an annoying fly. "He's history, thank God. No, it was somebody else. Somebody I used to know—somebody you knew, too."

"Jace Hoffman!" Beth said triumphantly. "You finally hooked up with Jace Hoffman."

"What are you talking about?" She tried to hide her shock. How had Beth guessed on the first try?

"Come on, Patience. It was obvious at Anne's wedding last month that you two had something going, even though you kept talking about how you couldn't stand him."

"I didn't *keep* talking about him," Patience protested. "In fact, *you* were the one who was interested in Jace, remember?"

"Yes, but it was obvious he wasn't interested in me, or, for that matter, in anyone but you."

"He ignored me during the entire reception!" Patience pointed out.

"You had him rattled. You think a guy like Jace Hoffman is comfortable being attracted to someone like you? He probably wanted to run away as fast as he could. No offense."

"Gee, none taken," Patience said dryly.

"You know what I mean."

"I know. You're more his type, Beth. He even said so."

"He said he was interested in me?" A flicker of intrigue lit Beth's blue eyes.

"No," Patience said, adding with a smirk, "no offense."

Beth grinned. "None taken."

"What he said was that I wasn't his type. That his type is exactly the opposite. Which means you."

"That doesn't explain why or how you and Jace happened to get together since I saw you last Sunday."

"We didn't exactly get together," Patience admitted. "At least, it wasn't intentional."

She told Beth what had happened between them. By the time she was finished, their meals had arrived, been eaten, and cleared away.

"So, what do you think?" Patience asked, sipping the last of her coffee, which had grown cold.

"All you've done is give me a blow-by-blow description of the time you and Jace spent together. You haven't said anything about how you feel about him."

"That's because I have no idea," Patience admitted, toying with her saucer.

"Sure you do."

She looked up at Beth, who was nodding.

"It's obvious. You're falling for him, Patience."

"But I can't be."

"Why not?"

"Because we both know it would never work out. And why get involved in a relationship that has no future?"

"How can you know it has no future?"

Patience tilted her head and gave Beth a look. "Can you see me settling down with someone like Jace?"

"No, but—"

"Can you see us being together for the rest of our lives without driving each other completely insane?"

"No, but—"

"There's just no way, and we both know it. That's why I have no idea what to do with this thing that's happening between us. Or I should say *happened*. Because whatever it is, it's over."

"I don't agree."

"With what? You just agreed with everything I said."

Beth shrugged. "I can't necessarily see you two together long term, but I don't think that whatever is going on is over . . . or that it has to be. Why can't you and Jace spend time together without dwelling on how the relationship is doomed from the start?"

"How can we ignore something like that? You, of all people, should know that you only date people you can imagine marrying. Anything else is a waste of time."

"And you, of all people, have never subscribed to that theory. You've gone out with plenty of people you would never imagine as a future husband, Patience."

Patience considered that. "Maybe, but . . ."

"But what? You aren't even sure you want to *get* married. You're making excuses, here. Your personal philosophy is never to worry about tomorrow. Why does it have to be different with Jace?"

"I don't know," Patience said slowly, tracing the edge of her placemat with her spoon. "It just *is* different with him."

"I think you should go for it with him."

"Come on, Beth. Go for *what*?"

"Whatever happens."

"Nothing is going to happen. Because as I said, it's over. He hasn't called me."

"You told him you were busy. Besides, you told him you'd call him."

"I know, but I don't think I meant it. I was just so rattled from that kiss, and I knew he was, too, and I had to say something to show him that it was no big deal."

"Even though it was a big deal."

Patience nodded. "I can't handle stuff like this. I don't like to sit around obsessing about a man. It's not my style. It's too . . . draining."

"So, do something about it."

"What?"

"Call him," Beth said. "For God's sake, if you don't, I will. He's cute; he's single, and he's rich. Plus, I'm his type."

"Then call him," Patience said, as though she could care less.

"Nah. He may think that he wants someone like me, but you're the one he's crazy about."

Patience took her napkin off her lap and tossed it into the center of the table. "You're the one who's just plain crazy, Beth," she said, exasperated. "In fact, this is making me see just how ridiculous I'm being. I'm going to forget about Jace."

"We'll see about that," Beth muttered.

"I swear. I'm not going to think about, talk to, or see him. Why bother?"

"I'll bet when we meet next Sunday, you'll be singing a different tune," Beth said, looking so smugly certain Patience vowed to prove her wrong at any cost.

Jace waited until Wednesday night to call Patience, having thought that if he put it off, the desire to see her again might fade.

If anything, it had grown more intense. She was all he could think about, whether he was lying in bed trying to fall asleep or running on the treadmill at the gym or closing an investment deal. The first thing he did when he walked into his apartment Wednesday night was to go straight to the phone and dial her number.

He got her machine, of course. She'd said she screened all her calls.

"Hi, Patience, it's me, Jace. Are you there?"

There was no answering click and breathless hello.

"Patience?"

He waited.

Still, no reply.

"Give me a call when you get in," he said quickly, and hung up.

Had she been sitting by the machine, screening calls? Had she decided not to pick up for him? But why? They had agreed to be friends, and he'd said he would call her. She had even said she'd call him—which she hadn't.

*Okay, don't get paranoid,* he warned himself. *Maybe she wasn't home.*

He busied himself in the kitchen, chopping vegetables for a stir fry. He was in the mood for takeout, but he didn't want to tie up his phone placing an order, just in case she called back. Which struck him as behavior more suited to a teen-aged girl than to a grown businessman, but he couldn't help it. He didn't have call-waiting—an invention that struck him as rude—and he wasn't certain she would call back again if she tried once and got a busy signal. Knowing her, she would immediately get distracted by something else and he would never hear from her again.

Not that he expected to, anyway.

So when the phone rang suddenly as he was standing by the stove, tilting the wok to heat the oil, he jumped—and splattered oil all over the front of his shirt. Luckily it wasn't yet hot enough to burn him, but the shirt was ruined. And that was the last thing on his mind as he snatched up the receiver.

Even as he said, "Hello?" he knew it wouldn't be her. No sense getting his hopes up.

So when it *was* her, he almost gasped.

"Jace, it's me, Patience," she said. "I must've been in the shower when you called."

Patience in the shower. Not an unfamiliar image. He forced it aside reluctantly, reminding himself that they were just friends as he said, "How have you been?"

"Fine. Busy. In fact, I just started a pottery class tonight. That's why I had to take a shower. I was covered with that slimy muddy stuff from head to toe."

Another dangerously off-limits vision popped into Jace's head. Again, he tried to ignore it, but his voice cracked a little as he said, "Sounds messy."

"But fun. You should try it sometime. It's a great way to get rid of stress."

"Who says I'm stressed?"

"Didn't we have this conversation already?" she asked, and he could hear the grin in her voice.

"You're right. Let's change the subject. I'm glad you called me back, because I remembered we had made plans for this weekend"—remembered? As if he had forgotten, even for a moment—"and I wanted to figure out what we were going to do."

"Do you have any ideas?"

He was going to suggest ice skating—an activity that seemed different enough to interest her, yet harmless and playful in a 'just friends' sense.

But before he could open his mouth, she said, "Because I'm dying to see that new musical that's getting rave reviews and I thought maybe we could go."

"A musical?" He was pleasantly surprised. He, too, had seen the reviews for the Rodgers and Hammerstein production that had just opened on Broadway, but a revival of a classic musical that had been popular almost forty years ago hadn't struck him as anything that would appeal to her.

A Broadway show was even more civilized than ice skating, and there was no chance that he'd make a fool out of himself by falling on his butt. "That sounds good."

"Great. I'll get the tickets. I can get them for free through work."

"Are you sure? Because Broadway tickets are expensive and if you can't—"

"It's not Broadway, actually. It's off-off-Broadway, and—"

"Which show are we talking about, Patience?" he cut in, with a sinking feeling.

*"Vampire Cheerleaders on Parade,"* she said, then, after a pause, added, "Aren't we?"

"Actually, I thought you meant something else," he said, thinking he should have known better.

*Vampire Cheerleaders on Parade?*

He held back a sigh, saying, "But that sounds . . ."

"Let me guess. 'Interesting'?" she said on a laugh.

"Exactly." He grinned. "Are you sure you can get the tickets?"

"Positive. Is Friday night all right with you?"

He hesitated. He always spent Friday nights in Brooklyn with his family. Mom and Bubbe cooked a big dinner, served it on fine china, and lit the Sabbath candles. It was a tradition.

For a moment, he considered inviting Patience to come with him. Just as quickly, he dismissed the thought. He wasn't ready for Patience to descend on his family just yet. In fact, despite the invitation he had offered when the topic had come up last week, he couldn't imagine ever bringing her home to meet his family. They would think . . . well, he wasn't quite sure what they would think. That was the problem.

Either they'd think she was out of her mind and wonder what he was doing spending time—even as friends—with someone like her . . .

Or they'd fall in love with her and ask him when he was going to marry her.

Either way, he'd be in trouble.

"Jace?" she prodded. "Is Friday a bad night for you? Because we can do it another time."

"No," he said hastily, "Friday's fine. Friday's great."

"Good. Look, I've gotta go—the Yankee play-off game is about to start."

After a quick—and good-natured—argument about the Yankees' chances of making yet another World Series and a discussion on where and when to meet Friday night, they hung up.

Jace smelled something burning.

He hurried over to the stove and turned off the burner. Hot oil smoked in the bottom of the wok. Great. Another few minutes on the phone with her and he'd have burned the place down. That should be a hint that Patience Magee was a distraction he didn't need in his life.

He chose to ignore it.

Picking up the phone again, he pressed the speed dial number that automatically connected him to his parents' Brooklyn brownstone.

"Hi, Dad," he said, when Saul Hoffman picked up the phone.

"Jace. What's the matter?"

"Nothing's the matter." His parents always assumed something was wrong when he called. They always, always picked up the phone and said "What's the matter?" when they heard his voice, as if it were the middle of the night and they were expecting the worst.

"Good," his father said. "Did you see the Mets game last night?"

"Of course. Two more wins, and we're in the World Series."

"The Yankees are playing right now. If I were a betting man, I'd have my money on a subway series, Jace. How about you?"

"You never know," he said briskly. "Listen, Dad, do me a favor and tell Mom I can't make it this Friday night."

"Tell her yourself. She's right here, wanting to talk to you."

Jace squeezed his eyes shut, frustrated, as his mother's voice came on the line. "Jace, how's that cold?"

"I'm fine, Mom." He had lied and told her he had a cold when he'd seen her last Friday night. Still exhausted after losing a night's sleep when he'd been out with Patience, he had been run-down, and his mother had noticed immediately.

"Did you finish the chicken soup Bubbe sent home with you?"

"It's all gone, Mom," he said. "And you were right, it did the trick, because I'm a hundred percent better."

"Hang on. What are you saying, Saul? I can't hear you and Jace at the same time."

Jace sighed. Why his parents didn't just get on separate extensions when he called, he'd never know. Instead, they just hovered next to each other, constantly interrupting whoever was on the phone to ask what was being said.

"Your father's asking me why you're not coming Friday night," his mother said after a brief consultation on the other end. "I should know? This is the first I've heard of it. Why aren't you coming, Jace."

"I made plans with a friend," he said.

"What kind of friend? A woman?"

"Not that it matters, because it's *just a friend,* Mom, but yes. A woman." He cursed himself for not lying and saying he had to work late.

"So it's a new girlfriend?"

"No. No, it's absolutely not a new girlfriend."

"Is she Jewish?"

"No. Not that it matters."

"I know it doesn't matter, Jace," his mother said. "You know we don't have our hearts set on a Jewish bride for you. It's a new world. Even Uncle Ira"—that would be his mother's youngest brother, the apple of Bubbe's eye—"married a Catholic girl, and you know how much we all love your aunt Sheila—"

"Mom, calm down. This has nothing to do with me getting married. She's just someone I knew a long time ago, in college. I bumped into her again, and we're getting together. Very simple. It's not a date."

"Call it what you want, Jace," his mother said, and he was irked at the implication. "Is it anyone I know?"

"No," he said, because it was easier than going into the whole story, and he was certain his mother couldn't possibly remember meeting Patience briefly in the ladies' room ten years ago.

"Well, why don't you bring her to dinner here? You know what Bubbe says. There's always plenty of food for one more."

"I can't bring her there, Mom. We have tickets to go see a show."

"Just a minute, Saul, I'm trying to ask him something," his mother said to his father, and then asked Jace, "What show?"

*"Vampire Cheerleaders on Parade,"* he said.

"What kind of show is that?" his father asked, apparently having wrestled the receiver back from his mother.

"I don't know, Dad. It's just a show."

"Does it have nudity?" his father asked, lowering his voice. "Is it one of those?"

"I have no idea, Dad," Jace said, feeling as if he were sixteen again. Which was pretty much how he felt every single time he spoke to his parents.

"Tell him to come on Saturday instead," his mother said in the background. "Lena's coming with the kids."

"Your mother says—"

"Tell her that's fine," Jace said. "I'll be there."

He loved his sister Lena, who was married and lived on Long Island. And he adored his young nephews, Ben, six, and Zach, three, who pretty much idolized him in return. They used to come to Brooklyn regularly for Sabbath dinner, but he hadn't seen much of them since Ben had started playing soccer on Friday nights when school started in September.

After a few more minutes chatting with each of his parents, he managed to extract himself from the conversation by mentioning that he hadn't eaten dinner yet.

"At this hour?" his mother said, stunned to think that a person could delay dinner until nine o'clock in the evening.

He *was* hungry, he realized as he hung up the phone. Really hungry. And no longer in the mood for stir-fried vegetables.

He tossed the wok into the sink, put the cut-up vegetables into a baggie in the fridge, and ordered take-out pizza.

"Is that it?" barked the kid on the other end of the line. "Just one small cheese pizza?"

"Make it extra cheese," Jace said impulsively.

It was something he'd always been tempted to do. Something Patience probably did without thinking.

Patience, again.

He was whistling as he headed into the bedroom to change his clothes.


Patience opened her fridge and put back the can of Pepsi she'd just taken out. She removed a bottle of Poland Spring water instead. As she padded back to the futon and flopped down on her stomach, she told herself choosing water over soda had nothing to do with Jace.

But it did, and she knew it. She hadn't slept well these past few nights. Instead of dropping off as soon as her head hit the pillow, she'd found herself lying awake, thinking of Jace.

Thinking of her vow not to see him again, wondering what she would do if he called her.

Well, now he had.

What she had done, when she'd heard his voice coming over the answering machine, was stand and stare at the phone, trying frantically to decide whether she should pick up or not. He had hung up just as she reached for the receiver.

She hadn't planned to call him back.

So why had she?

She had no idea. Maybe just to prove to herself that it was no big deal. That she and Jace were just friends, and that was what friends did—they returned each other's phone calls.

Friends didn't necessarily lie to each other about being in the shower when they had actually been screening calls, she reminded herself. But that had just popped out.

"Besides, it wasn't really a lie," she told Rufus, who

had heaved his enormous body onto the futon and settled at her side, purring.

He looked up at her with those unblinking cat eyes, and she was overcome with guilt.

"It wasn't a lie, Rufe," she said again. "Well, not exactly."

She *had* gone to a pottery class, and she *had* taken a shower. It just wasn't what she was doing while Jace was talking to her answering machine.

"Let's watch some TV, Rufus," she said. "That'll take your mind off your troubles."

She reached for the television remote control, flipping channels with one hand as she gulped some water.

*Bleh.* What a blah thing to drink.

What she really wanted was that Pepsi. She loved a sweet, fizzy can of it before bed.

But maybe it was the caffeine and sugar that had been keeping her awake lately. It had to be. She *wanted* it to be. That was something physical, something she could control.

She didn't want it to be something other than the Pepsi. Something emotional.

Emotions, she couldn't control.

She could tell herself that she wouldn't let her feelings rule her actions—that common sense alone decided what Patience Magee did. That she wasn't ruled by her heart or her libido.

But it seemed, alarmingly, that all she had to do was hear Jace's voice and she went all woozy. Now she had a date with him for Friday night. She really had been planning to go see *Vampire Cheerleaders on Parade*. In fact, she already had the tickets. Camisha had given them to her this afternoon because she'd done such a great job on the bachelors article. She had been planning to ask Kaia to go with her; but as long as Kaia didn't know that, there was no harm done.

She thought of Kaia, who so desperately wanted to meet the right guy and get married.

She thought of Beth, who wanted the same thing.

"If I were a real friend, I would introduce Jace to Kaia," she told Rufus. "Or I would suggest to him that he take Beth out on a date."

Yes, even Rufus seemed to agree, judging by the intent way in which he regarded her, that it was what she should do.

And it was what she *would* do . . .

If she weren't interested in Jace herself.

"Well, I can't help it," she argued with Rufus. "There's something really sexy about him. I know, I know, you're right. Maybe Beth is right, too."

Maybe she was making too big a deal out of this attraction. If something were going to happen between them, who was she to fight it? What was wrong with having a fling with a guy who clearly wasn't your type? A guy who stood for everything you loathed in the world?

Patience sighed and gulped more water.

"We'll see what happens Friday night, Rufus," she said as the cat hopped off the couch and walked toward the bathroom. "Are you going to bed? Me, too. Only I haven't been sleeping as soundly as you do, Rufe."

She got off the futon and pulled it out, flattening the mattress into a full-sized bed and pulling out the quilt she stowed in a low basket beneath the frame.

"One more restless night," she muttered aloud, "and I swear I'm going take a cue from Rufus and try the bathtub."

# Seven

"Well?" Patience asked as she and Jace stepped out onto the Bowery. "What did you think?"

"I thought it was pretty good," he said, buttoning his leather coat. It was brown, rich, and creamy as cocoa, a shade that exactly matched his eyes, and it had probably cost more than Patience made in a month. He also wore well-pressed khakis, loafers, and a brown cashmere sweater she was dying to touch—simply because it looked so soft, she reminded herself.

"You liked it?" She shoved the program into the pocket of her vintage black wool pea coat that had once belonged to her grandfather.

"Yeah, I did. *Vampire Cheerleaders on Parade,*" he said with a chuckle as they walked away from the theater. "I never would have expected to sit through something like that, let alone enjoy it."

"See, Jace? It's good to try new things. You never know when you'll surprise yourself."

"Yeah," he said, and his eyes met hers.

Her stomach turned over. He looked as if he wanted to kiss her.

"Should we call it a night?" she asked, suddenly feeling frantic. If he kissed her, she would just . . . crumble. She would lose every ounce of the self-restraint that had kept her from stroking his sweater, from letting her arm brush against his in the theater, from leaning against him when the crowd jostled them on the way out.

"Call it a night now?" He looked taken aback. He checked his watch. "But it's only eleven o'clock."

"I know you don't like late nights—"

"It's Friday. I don't mind when I don't have to get up at five-thirty in the morning."

"I thought we had already concluded that you don't have to do that anyway."

"That was your conclusion. And anyway, I thought we also concluded that you would be better off setting your alarm a little earlier so you can have something other than a doughnut for breakfast."

She grinned up at him. "Fine. Let's try it."

"What?"

"On Monday, I'll set my alarm for . . . eight."

"Seven-thirty."

"Seven-forty-five," she said grudgingly. "And you set yours for eight."

"Seven-thirty."

"Seven-forty-five," she said again. "You skip the gym, and I'll make myself some whole grain toast for breakfast."

"And a grapefruit," he said.

"But it takes forever to cut into all those little sections!"

"And it's worth it." He chuckled. "Think of how much energy you'll have if you eat a square meal before you start your day."

"More energy! What am I going to do with more energy?" she asked, and saw a glint in his eye.

"Oh, I'm sure you'll find something to do with it," was all he said.

But there was something flirtatious in his tone.

"So, if we're not going home, where are we going?" she asked, to change the subject.

"I don't know the neighborhood," he said with a trace of irony. "This is your territory."

"There's actually a great little bar around the corner. Want to go have a drink?"

"Sure," he said, and she could tell by the look on his face that he was expecting it to be some kind of grungy dive.

She had to smile at his surprised expression when they walked up three steps from the street and stepped into the small, crowded cabaret. A soloist was at the piano, singing a soulful rendition of an old blues tune.

"I've got to learn to expect the unexpected with you, Patience," Jace said when they had squeezed into a small table by the bar and ordered their drinks—bourbon and water for her, beer for him.

"You should always expect the unexpected, Jace. Period."

"Is that how you live your life?"

"I try."

"You just go wherever the wind takes you, don't you?"

"Funny you should mention it," she said, tapping her hand on the table in rhythm with the music. "I was talking to a friend of mine just the other day about that very thing."

"Really?"

"Yes. It was Beth, actually. You remember Beth."

"Beth Stenner? From college?"

"Right. She seems to think I should just keep on going with the flow."

"And you think . . . what? That you should change? *Now?*"

"Sometimes I wonder," Patience told him, not wanting to meet his gaze. If she did, he might sense somehow that she and Beth had been talking about her feelings toward him.

"For the record, I honestly don't think a person can change the way they live their life, Patience."

"You don't?"

"Not that drastically. I mean, it's one thing to say you're going to set your alarm earlier as an experiment, but to suddenly decide you're going to become a methodical, organized, practical person . . . I just don't think that could happen. It wouldn't be you."

"I guess not," she said, somehow disappointed, though she knew he meant it as a compliment.

Maybe she had wanted him to say that anyone could change. She wanted to believe that it was possible. Because then they just might have a chance together.

So she was back where she had started.

Hopelessly attracted to Jace, and helpless to do anything about it, aside from have a quick fling . . . if he even wanted to do that. And she wasn't sure she did.

Tantalizing as it was to imagine herself in Jace's arms, seeing where this passion led . . . well, she just didn't think that would be enough. Not with him. With him, she would want more. She wouldn't be able to stand knowing that he was going to leave her sooner or later and marry some perfect upscale wife type like Beth or Sue.

*But of course that's going to happen. What other option would there be? For him to marry you?*

She sighed.

She wasn't even aware that she had done it until Jace touched her hand and said, "What's wrong?"

She looked up and found him watching her intently. "Nothing," she said. "It's just the music. The blues always get to me."

"She's singing 'Happy Days Are Here Again,' Patience," Jace pointed out, nodding his head at the soloist, who had indeed launched into the upbeat number.

"Oh. Well, I'm just tired, I guess."

"You look distracted. And upset."

"Trust me. I'm fine."

Their drinks arrived.

The Jack Daniel's burned her throat as it slid down, leaving her infinitely more relaxed than she had been a few minutes ago.

Perhaps it was the bourbon that allowed her to look Jace in the eye and say, "You still consider us friends, Jace?"

He nodded, looking wary. "Why?"

"That's what I told Beth. That we're just friends. That we could never be anything more than friends, because we're just not suited to each other."

"What did she say?"

"She said . . . never mind," Patience said, waving her hand.

"No, tell me. What did she say?"

"She basically said we should sleep together and get it over with."

She expected him to fall back in his chair, or at least choke on his beer. But all he did was raise his eyebrows and say, "Why does she think that?"

"She says it's meant to happen. Because . . . you know."

He shook his head. He was going to make her say it.

"Because I find you attractive, Jace, and I'm pretty sure—judging by the way you kissed me the other night—that you find me attractive, too. And since it's not like we're destined to fall in love and get married or anything, we might as well just hop into bed."

"Beth said that?"

"Well . . . pretty much," Patience said. She was beginning to feel a bit fuzzy on the details. She took another sip of her drink.

"Do you want to sleep with me?" Jace asked. He looked . . . fascinated by the turn the conversation had taken.

"Do *you* want to sleep with *me?*"

They stared at each other across the tiny table. Then he leaned over and kissed her. There was nothing gentle or tentative about his kiss; it built quickly from passionate to insistent.

She forgot that they were in a public place, forgot that they were just friends, forgot that there was no future in any of this.

There was nothing but the here and now, nothing but Jace.

"Let's go," Jace whispered raggedly in her ear.

"Where?" Her hands were on his shoulders, at last stroking the velvety cashmere of his sweater—yet now the soft folds of fabric only seemed to be in the way.

"Your place. It's closer," he murmured, already standing and taking her hand.

He threw some money down on the table and led her through the bar to the exit.

On the street, amid the reality of chilly night air and honking taxis and bright lights, she half-expected him to change his mind.

"You still want to go to my place?" she asked.

In reply, he pulled her into his arms and crushed her against his chest, kissing her until she felt limp.

"Guess that answers my question," she said weakly, and saw that he was already raising his arm to hail a cab. "It's only a few blocks from here, Jace. We can walk."

He shook his head as a yellow taxi slowed at the curb.

They climbed into the back seat, and he kissed her

again as the cab pulled into traffic. She leaned against the seat, her senses whirling. His hands were on her cheeks, cupping her face as his lips moved over hers.

"You are an amazing kisser," she murmured in his ear when his lips moved away from her mouth to brush against her ear.

Finally, they were at her building. He held her hand as they climbed the five flights of steps to the sixth floor, their arms linked and fingers laced warmly together. As soon as they were inside the apartment, he kicked the door closed and put his arms around her again. Lips searching, clinging, roaming, clinging again, they undressed each other quickly, letting their clothing fall in a heap at their feet.

Then she pulled him backward several steps and they fell on her unmade, still folded-out futon. He pressed kisses down her neck and over her bare breast. She arched her back as she felt her nipple pucker against his suckling tongue. His body was warm and masculine and insistent against hers, and she writhed beneath him, urgently needing him inside of her.

"Please, Jace," she moaned, and he lifted his head.

"Please . . . now," she whispered.

He smiled. "Impatient Patience," he said softly. "This is one time you're going to have to slow down."

She sighed as he moved his tongue to her other breast. She stroked his hair, quivering at the exquisite sensation building in her core.

When finally he lifted his head, locked his gaze on hers, and entered her, she exploded around his single thrust. Gasping at the intensity, she clung to his shoulders until the ripples had subsided.

"You okay?" he asked softly, poised, motionless inside her.

She could only nod as, incredibly, the heat began to build again within her.

They began to move together, silently, staring into each other's eyes until the building rhythm shattered in a blinding crescendo. He buried his face against her breastbone, shuddering as she gasped his name.

For a long time they stayed like that, entwined in each other's arms. Then he propped himself on his elbows and looked down at her.

"You okay?"

She nodded, smiling.

He rolled off her, and she pulled the quilt up around them before he pulled her against his chest, his arms snug around her. Her fingers lightly played upon his muscular chest.

"Jace?" she asked after a few minutes, when his panting had slowed to even breathing.

He didn't answer.

She lifted her head and saw that he was sound asleep.

Smiling to herself, she settled her ear against the steady throbbing of his heart, certain it would lull her to sleep.

Coming slowly awake, Jace stretched, rolled over . . . and caught himself before he rolled off the edge of the bed.

"Careful," a female voice said.

And he realized all at once, in the instant before he opened his eyes, that he wasn't in his bed, that he was on Patience's futon in Patience's apartment.

But Patience wasn't beside him.

He blinked rapidly, unused to the sunlight that streamed through the window, and he looked around for her.

There she was, curled up in that crazy round basket chair, looking like a content little bird in a nest. She wore an enormous gray sweatshirt and navy sweatpants, and her curls were darker than usual and damp.

"How'd you sleep?" she asked him.

"I slept incredibly well," he realized, rubbing his eyes.

"I thought you had insomnia."

"I do. Apparently, I've just discovered the cure," he added with a grin. "How'd you sleep?"

"I didn't." She lifted a mug she'd been clutching in her lap, and he smelled coffee wafting through the room. "I finally figured I might as well get up."

"I thought you always sleep like a rock."

"I do." She shrugged. "At least, I did until you came along."

"I kept you up? Was I snoring?"

She smiled. "I think it was that other thing you did. Right before you went to sleep. It was pretty . . . exhilarating."

"Exhausting, too," he said, sitting up. "What time is it?"

"Almost seven. I haven't seen seven in a long time. I've already taken a shower—and I even cleaned up the place in your honor."

He looked around. The heap of clothes they had strewn on the floor in their haste to undress were now draped over a standing lamp. The magazines, books, and newspapers that had littered the surface of the coffee table/trunk were now stacked haphazardly in a towering pile that appeared on the verge of toppling over. The papers on the computer desk had been formed into a heap with a round glass paperweight plopped in the center.

"I even washed the dishes in the sink," she said, watching him look around, apparently pleased with her efforts.

"That's . . . terrific," he managed. "Do you have a towel? I'll take a shower."

"In that closet," she said, pointing, then added, "Just kick Rufus out of the tub."

"Are you sure he won't mind?"

"Nah. I do it every day. Sometimes he doesn't wake up, though, and you have to lift him out. He's really old. Pretty heavy, too, so don't say I didn't warn you."

"Okay," he said uncertainly. He couldn't quite picture himself hauling that enormous, sleeping cat out of the tub. Then again, there were a lot of things he hadn't imagined himself doing until Patience Magee careened back into his life.

He got out of bed, naked, yet somehow unselfconscious though he knew she was watching him unabashedly. He was inexplicably comfortable with her in a way that he had never been comfortable with a woman before.

Opening the door she had indicated, he found a walk-in closet with a clothes rod on one side, shelves on the other. The rod was crammed with clothing-laden hangers, their weight bending the rod almost into a U-shape. The shelves were stuffed with everything imaginable—old dolls, hats, photo albums, office supplies.

"I'm sort of a pack rat," she called apologetically as he searched for a towel.

"I see that," he said weakly.

If he had ever, for a brief moment, entertained the notion that he and Patience could somehow make a go of it as a couple, this closet demolished it completely. Clearly, they were destined to be friends, and nothing more.

As for what had happened between them last night—well, he had no idea what to do with that. It had been pure lovemaking, charged with emotion as well as passion. Nothing had ever felt so utterly right in his life.

Maybe they *did* have a chance.

He spotted a couple of towels on a high shelf, beneath a stack of board game boxes. He reached up to pull one out—and got bopped in the head as Monopoly slipped off the shelf and fell to the floor. There was a clattering noise as the dice and the small metal board markers scattered around his feet.

"What was that?" Patience asked, appearing in the doorway.

"I just knocked your game off the shelf by accident." He bent and picked up a small silver iron, then a few pieces of paper money, the Kentucky Avenue card, and a miniature antique car.

"That's okay," she said with a wave of her hand. "Leave it. I'll get it later."

"No, I'll pick it up," he said, starting stacks of the paper money, laying out bills by denomination.

"Jace, don't worry about it. I usually just cram it all into the box anyway. It's no big deal."

"No, I don't mind," he said, snatching a Get Out of Jail Free card from the open toe of one of her sandals.

"Then I'll help. Here's some more money." She knelt beside him, scooping up several pink play money bills and, without straightening them, put them on the neat pile of yellow bills.

"Those go here," he said tersely, arranging them neatly so that the numbers all faced in the same direction and laying them on the pink pile.

"Gee, sorry," she retorted, standing. "Didn't mean to mess up your big plan."

"It's just that I like things to be in order." He checked through the group of board markers and determined that the silver shoe was still missing. Monopoly was one of his favorite games.

"No kidding. Well, maybe you'll want to come over sometime and help me organize my stuff, Jace."

"That would be great," he said, relieved. Maybe she was starting to realize that a person couldn't possibly go through life with chaotic closets. Maybe there was hope, after all.

"Oh, please," she said tartly. "I wasn't *serious*. I like things just as they are."

"But how can you stand living in a mess?" He retrieved the silver shoe and blew a dust bunny off the toe.

"Because I grew up in a household where everything had to be in its place all the time. When I was a kid, I had to keep my toys in neatly labeled bins and my books in alphabetical order by author. I vowed that when I had my own place, I wouldn't have rules like that."

"So you do know how to keep things organized?" he asked, surprised. He continued to pick up the money as they spoke, placing a rubber band around each finished stack and placing it back into the box.

"Of course I know how. I just don't like to live that way."

"I don't see why not."

"Because I have better things to do with my spare time these days, Jace. Like have fun."

He shrugged, snapping a rubber band around the stack of hundred dollar bills. Then he scanned through the real estate cards.

"Baltic Avenue is missing."

"Why am I not surprised you noticed that?" she asked, mostly to herself "It's been lost since I was twelve, Jace. This is my sister Hope's old game. That's why she gave it to me—she didn't want it after our dog ate Baltic Avenue."

"And you did want it."

Patience shrugged. "Sure. I just make sure that I never buy the purple properties. Whomever I'm playing with always snatches up Mediterranean Avenue—"

"But without knowing Baltic Avenue is missing."

"Right. Then he never gets to build houses or hotels on the property, and he loses."

"That's horrible," Jace said, so appalled that he stopped straightening the cards in his hand. "It's cheating."

Patience shrugged. "Well, I actually only did it to Crispin. And he deserved it. He thought he would win automatically because he was such an expert on finance."

"Oh." Maybe it wasn't so appalling after all, Jace decided, banding the real estate cards together, putting them into the box, and folding the board on top.

She handed him the cover, which was naturally torn at all the corners. He resisted the urge to ask her for some tape so he could repair it. Instead, he plopped it on the box and put the game back on the shelf on top of the towels and other board games.

"Take your shower," she said, "and then we can go get something to eat. There's a terrific Ukrainian diner a few blocks from here. You wouldn't believe their blintzes. Do you like blintzes?"

"Of course I like blintzes."

"Great. Hurry and take your shower. My mouth is watering already."

He hesitated. He had been planning to go home . . . but why? Why not spend more time with Patience? He didn't have to be at his parents' apartment until two o'clock.

"All I have to wear is my clothes from last night," he remembered.

"You can borrow a sweatshirt from me. It'll fit," she said, seeing his expression. "I always buy men's. Extra large. I like them big."

"I can see that," he said, noticing that the sleeves on the one she was wearing covered her fingers. There was something adorable about the way she looked in that oversized shirt, though. Something that made him suddenly want to kiss her.

He took her into his arms.

"What are you doing?" she murmured against his mouth as their lips met.

"Kissing you."

"I thought we were going out for blintzes," she protested, tearing herself away after a few moments.

"We are . . ." He slid his hands beneath the folds of her sweatshirt and stroked her warm skin. "In a few minutes."

"Mmm," was her response as she lazily raised her arms so that he could lift the shirt over her head. "The blintzes can wait a half hour."


Four hours later, Patience popped the last bite of her blintz into her mouth and closed her eyes briefly. "I'm stuffed."

"Gee, are you sure?" he asked wryly, eyeing the three empty plates in front of her.

They were at a booth in Kiev, a noisy Ukranian diner—as it turned out, Jace used to come here with his grandfather when he was still alive. He had told her that he still remembered taking the subway here from Brooklyn with a man he still referred to—charmingly, Patience thought—as Pop-pop.

"Hey, how about you?" Patience asked, nudging his

arm playfully across the table. "I see you're a member of the clean plate club, too, Mister Hoffman."

He grinned. "I haven't eaten this big a breakfast since I shared a roof with Bubbe. Which reminds me . . ."

"What?" She drank the last of her orange juice.

"I should probably get going."

"Oh." She wasn't prepared for the pang of disappointment that shot through her at those words.

"Yeah, I've got some stuff to do today."

"Oh."

Why couldn't she think of anything else to say?

After all, she had known he would probably go home after breakfast. What else was he supposed to do? Spend the day with her?

Well, she *had* thought of suggesting that they wander over to Broadway and browse for a while at the Strand, her favorite bookstore in the entire world, then go up to the open market at Union Square and get some of those tart, crunchy apples you could only find in New York State in October.

It was one of those crisp autumn days with just enough bite in the air to remind you that nice weather was waning, so you had better enjoy it while it lasted.

"I'd much rather spend the day with you," he said, reaching across the table as though he'd read her mind.

"But?"

"But I've got to be someplace by two."

"Oh." She tilted her head and smiled at him. "It's okay. I mean, I figured you must have plans. I usually do, too."

"Really? What do you do on Saturday afternoons?"

"Go to museums or shopping or to the movies. Roller blade or jog in the park. Just walk around the city. Hang out with my friends, drinking coffee. That's the great thing about New York. There's always something to do."

"Not so in New Hampshire?"

"There's stuff to do there, too," she said. "Especially at this time of year. You can go apple picking or hiking or to a craft festival. You can—"

"Somehow, Patience, I think you'd keep busy anywhere," Jace cut in, smiling.

"You're in such a good mood today," she said, smiling back. "A good night's sleep can do wonders."

"A good night's sleep . . . among other things."

"Jace, we haven't even discussed those . . . other things," Patience said reluctantly. "We should, shouldn't we?"

"You mean . . . what does it mean that we slept together?"

"That's exactly what I mean." She watched a shadow slip over his face and wondered why she'd had to bring it up.

"What do you think it means?" he asked—cautiously, she thought.

"I'm not sure. I mean, we're friends, right?" she asked, just as cautious.

"Absolutely." He nodded vigorously.

"And we're not each other's type, right? I mean, romantically."

She held her breath waiting for his response, thinking that he might tell her they'd been wrong, that they were suited to each other after all.

"I guess we're not," he said, though he seemed a bit unwilling to admit it. "We drive each other crazy."

"I know." She forced a smile. "So where does that leave us?"

"Friends," he said.

"And last night . . ."

"Was an experiment."

"Right," she said. Then, after a moment, she asked him, "What was it, exactly, that we were trying to find out with the experiment?"

"What it would be like if we . . ." He cleared his throat. "And now we know. Right?"

"Now we know," she agreed, thinking, *Now we know it would be fantastic.*

"So now that we have that out of the way, we can get on with being friends. Is that it?" she asked him.

"What do you think?"

"It would be fine with me if we keep hanging out," Patience said, trying to ignore a hollow feeling inside.

What she had wanted him to say was that despite their differences, they could find a way to work things out. That they shouldn't rule out a long-term relationship just because they couldn't didn't see eye-to-eye on how to put away a Monopoly game or what time a person should get up in the morning.

She told herself that those things didn't matter to her—that she could get past them if she and Jace were a couple. That they could make it work as long as they had passion and affection for each other.

But in her heart, she wasn't sure. Could she really be happy with someone who always seemed to be disapproving of her? Could she really live the rest of her life with someone who didn't agree with how she was living it?

"Listen," Jace said, reaching for his coat and pulling it on over the navy Barnbury College sweatshirt she'd loaned him. "I just had a brilliant idea."

"What is it?"

"Why don't you come with me today?" He almost looked startled as he said it, as though he were as shocked at his own impulsiveness as she was.

"Where is it that you're going?" she asked cautiously, lest she show too much enthusiasm and scare him off.

"Didn't I tell you? I'm going home to Brooklyn to visit my family."

He wanted to bring her home to his family after this whole conversation about just being friends? Granted, he had mentioned it once before; but for some reason, it seemed like the kind of thing you did with a girlfriend. If she ever brought Jace home to New Hampshire, her parents would assume they were dating, no matter what she tried to tell them.

Well, maybe his family was different.


"Jason! Who's your girlfriend?"

The moment he stepped through the door, he found himself squashed into Bubbe's viselike arms, as usual.

"This is Patience," he said, extracting himself from his grandmother, whose round, short body was clad, as usual, in an apron worn over a double knit pantsuit. Her chubby feet were stuffed into the terry cloth scuffies she always called her "carpet slippers."

"Patience!" His grandmother exclaimed, as if she were greeting a long-lost friend.

"She and I are old friends," Jace said mildly, glancing at Patience to make sure she wasn't taken aback. What was he thinking? He knew Patience took pretty much everything in stride; it was one of her more fascinating qualities.

"Old friends? What, old friends." His grandmother chucked him under the chin and shook her white head, newly styled from her standing Friday morning beauty parlor appointment.

"I didn't know your name was Jason," Patience said to him, looking amused, as his grandmother clasped her hand. She added, "Hi, Bubbe. I'm Patience. I've heard a lot about you."

"See? She even calls me *Bubbe*," his grandmother said, pleased.

"Isn't that your name?" Patience asked, looking confused.

"*Bubbe* means grandmother," Jace explained. "It's Yiddish."

"Oh. Sorry," Patience said, but she didn't look particularly embarrassed.

Jace was impressed. Sue would have been mortified if she'd made that kind of mistake. In fact, she had been extremely nervous the first time he'd brought her home to meet his family. Of course, maybe that was because, unbeknownst to Jace, she was assuming she was about to meet her future in-laws.

As for Patience, she couldn't look more relaxed. She wore jeans, a sweater, a barn coat, and hiking boots, looking for all the world as if she had popped out of an L.L. Bean catalog. Wholesome. The girl next door.

*Wife material*, he thought, inexplicably.

"So you're a *shiksa*?" Bubbe asked, sizing her up with a gleam in her eye. She was still clutching Patience's hand.

"I don't know." Patience looked at Jace. "Am I?"

"A *shiksa* means a girl who isn't Jewish."

"Yup, I'm a *shiksa*, all right," Patience said easily. "But don't worry, because as he said, we're only friends."

"Who's worried?" Bubbe hunched her shoulders to her ears. "My son Ira married a Catholic girl, and I love her like a daughter. We all do. Saul, tell her about Sheila."

"What about her?" asked Jace's father, who had just come in from the living room with a folded newspaper and his reading glasses in his hand. He wore the blue lambs wool cardigan sweater Jace had bought him last Hanukkah, corduroy slacks, and slippers.

"Dad, this is Patience Magee," Jace said. "We went to college together."

"She's just a friend," Bubbe said with a nudge and a wink, wink.

"We've met before, Mr. Hoffman," Patience said, shaking his hand. "I introduced myself to you and your wife when you were up at Parents Weekend at Barnbury."

"Patience!" Jace's mother came out of the kitchen, arms outstretched, just as his father said, "Oh, I remember you!"

Jace blinked. "You remember her?"

"I should forget someone who gave me such good advice? She told me not to eat the sloppy joes," his mother said. "She said they were made out of horse meat."

"Horse meat?" Bubbe made a disgusted sound and said something in Yiddish.

"Remember, Saul?"

"I remember. She told me about that shortcut back to the interstate. It was helpful when we went back for graduation," he said appreciatively. "Cut twenty minutes off the trip."

Patience gave Jace a smug look.

"You didn't tell me you were bringing anyone home with you, Jace," his mother said disapprovingly. "I would have cleaned up the house."

He grinned. "That's not necessary for Patience, Mom. She's not a neat freak like you."

"Anyway, the house looks spotless to me," Patience said, looking around.

Jace followed her gaze, trying to see the place through her eyes. It was one of those small brick rowhouses so typical of the outer boroughs, fronted by a wide, high stoop and a chain-link fence surrounding the yard. Inside, the walls were a mosaic of framed family pictures; the lampshades were still encased in plastic; the tables displayed well-dusted knickknacks. All the windows were hung with blinds and sheer drapery panels. The worn spots in the gold wall-to-wall carpeting were strategically covered by runners and area rugs. There was nothing elegant about the furniture that crammed the small living and dining rooms; it wasn't antique, but just plain old. Still, his mother cared for each piece as carefully as if it were a priceless heirloom.

Jace inhaled deeply through his nose.

"Do you have a cold?" his mother asked promptly.

"No," he said, just wanting to breathe that familiar home smell—a mixture of lemon furniture polish, Glade air freshener, freshly baked bread, and whatever happened to be bubbling on the stove. Jace realized that he was deeply comforted, as always, by the sight and the smell of the home where he had grown up. He found it oddly gratifying that he was sharing this with Patience.

"Oh, I love your ring, Bubbe," Patience said suddenly. She reached for Bubbe's hand and examined the platinum-and-diamond antique band on the fourth finger of her left hand.

"Thank you," Bubbe said, obviously flattered. "It's my engagement ring. It had been in my husband's family for three generations before he gave it to me. I wanted Lena to have it when she got engaged; but her husband, he's a jeweler. He had his own ideas. So I kept it."

"You never really wanted to give it up anyway, Ma," Jace's mother pointed out. "You love that ring."

"I loved your father," Bubbe said, her eyes clouding over. "The ring is nice, too, but it's him that I loved."

For a moment, they were all silent, aware of the old

woman lost in her bittersweet memories. Then Jace's mother—wearing full makeup, a nice blouse, dress pants, and shoes and stockings as she always did in the house—spoke up, telling Patience that she would show her around the house.

"That's okay, Mom," Jace said, wanting to spare her the tour. "She doesn't need to—"

"No, it's all right," Patience said. "I'd love to see everything."

His mother gave Jace an I-told-you-so look. She was proud of the house; she had grown up in a two-room apartment not far from here. Pop-pop had worked as a deli counterman and Bubbe had been a seamstress. When Jace was in middle school, Pop-pop had had his first heart attack and been forced to stop working. He and Bubbe had given up their apartment and moved into Jace's bedroom, and Jace had moved into the tiny guest room behind the kitchen. He hadn't minded. He loved having his grandparents under their roof. He still missed Pop-pop fiercely whenever he came home, and his grandfather had been gone since the summer after Jace graduated from high school.

Jace watched his mother and Patience walk up the stairs chatting easily.

He looked at his father. "I can't believe Mom remembers her."

"So do I. She's not easy to forget." His father put his reading glasses on again and held up the sports section. "So, Jace . . . no subway series this year."

"The Mets lost?" He hadn't even remembered there was a game last night, let alone thought to check the score. The realization threw him for a moment. Had he been that caught up in Patience Magee?

"And you say she isn't your girlfriend," Bubbe said, elbowing him. "I've never seen you lose track of a ball game score. Come into the kitchen, Jason. I've got some fresh challah I just took out of the oven."

"Where are Lena and the boys?" he asked as his father went back to his reading chair and he followed Bubbe into the kitchen.

"Out in the yard. She's letting the little ones run off some steam. They were hyper from being pent-up in the car for the trip in from Huntington. Such a long way. Such a shame they had to move all the way out to the island."

"It's only an hour, Bubbe."

"An hour." Bubbe threw up her hands and shook her head. "That's a trip, an hour. But look at you. You moved from the neighborhood, too—living the fancy life in the city."

"The city? This is the city, too." Jason took the piece of hot, yeasty bread Bubbe offered him. "It's all the same city, Bubbe. Just because I live in a different borough . . ."

She shook her head and said something dark in Yiddish, then went over to stir something on the stove.

Jace opened the back door, calling back to her, "Tell Patience where I am."

"Uncle Jace!"

Two miniature tornados were already hurtling toward him, nearly knocking him off his feet. He took turns lifting Ben and Zach, tossing them into the air and tickling them.

"You want to take over for a while?" his sister asked, breathless, giving him a hug. "We were playing hide-and-seek."

Tall and slender, Lena looked like a younger, darker version of their mother, who had been dying her hair blond for as long as Jace could remember. Lena was far more casual, though, wearing a ponytail, very little makeup, and jeans.

"Hey," Jace said, kissing on the cheek. "How's Paul?"

"Busy," Lena said. "As usual." Her husband owned a jewelry store in a Long Island mall and could never get away on weekends.

"Listen, I'll play with the boys if you go inside and rescue Patience from Mom."

"Rescue what?"

"She's a *who,* Patience. She's a friend of mine. Mom is giving her the tour."

"Oh, God." Lena rolled her eyes and started for the door, then called back over her shoulder in a big sisterly teasing tone, "Is this a 'special friend,' Jacey?"

"Just a friend, Lena." Jace caught Ben by the shoulders and flipped him upside down as he shrieked in delight.

"Will I like her?"

"You'll love her."

"Then why is she just a friend?"

Jace pretended to be busy with Ben and Zach so he wouldn't have to respond to that question . . . partly because he suddenly wasn't sure he knew the answer.

"You have an amazing family," Patience told Jace as they stepped onto the F train headed toward Manhattan. He had agreed to take the subway as it wasn't quite dusk. Besides, it wasn't easy to find a cab in his parents' residential neighborhood.

They made their way through the crowded car as the train lurched and moved ahead. There were no seats, so they stood on opposite sides of a pole, clutching it to keep their balance.

"Amazing?" Jace echoed. "I don't know about amazing. High maintenance, yes. Overwhelming, yes."

"Amazing. And I can't believe your parents remembered me."

"Why not? You remembered them."

"But I remember everything. I'm one of those people who never forgets details. Most people think it's strange to remember things that happened years ago."

"Not my parents. They're still talking about the time I fell backward in my chair at Joey Leibowitz's bar mitzvah. 'I told you not to rock like that or somebody would get hurt,' " he mocked, doing a perfect imitation of his father.

She smiled, opening the plastic baggie full of cookies Bubbe had made and insisted she take. Not that Patience had argued.

"Want one?" she asked Jace.

He groaned. "No thanks. I'm stuffed." He watched her bite into a small, jam-filled triangular cookie.

"What are these called again?"

*"Hamantashen,"* he said.

"They're fantastic. Your grandmother gave me the recipe."

"I know. You have to make them now. She's going to keep bugging me until I tell her that you tried it."

"I will make them." She popped the last bite into her mouth and brushed the crumbs from her hands. Then she reached into the bag again.

"You know how to bake?"

"Of course. Why else would I ask for the recipe?"

"I thought you were just trying to make Bubbe feel good."

"I think I made her feel good when I had a second helping of her noodle kugel. Also yummy, by the way."

"Bubbe loved you," Jace said. "My parents did, too."

"What about your sister?"

"Are you kidding? Lena's easy. She's crazy about anyone who pays attention to her kids . . . which you did."

She smiled. "I loved those little guys."

"You must have, considering that you let them use your jacket as a tent."

"We were playing camp-out. Every camp-out needs a tent."

"I thought it was sweet of you." He reached out and brushed a small dusty footprint off the sleeve of her barn coat.

Her heart skipped a beat at his touch, though it was brief and casual and not the least bit intimate. She couldn't help it. After today—after spending so much time with him—she wanted there to be more between them. No. Not just *more*. *Everything*.

Now that she had glimpsed Jace surrounded by his warm, loving family, had seen him playful and carefree with those two little boys who so obviously adored him . . .

Well, it was all too easy to envision him with a family of his own, with children and a wife to love, to bring home to those welcoming arms in Brooklyn.

And damn it, *she* wanted to be the woman who would join that family.

*She* wanted to be the bride Jace would marry under a *chuppah,* as the others in his family had been married. His mother had shown her all the wedding pictures—pointedly, Patience had thought, especially the one of Jace's Uncle Ira and Aunt Sheila, who was also a *shiksa.*

*She* wanted to be the mother of grandchildren whose pictures would someday hang beside Ben and Zach's.

*She* wanted to call his mother *Mom* instead of *Myrna,* and his father *Dad* instead of *Saul.*

And Bubbe—well, Bubbe had told her to call her *Bubbe* anyway, saying it felt right.

When Patience had hugged her good-bye, Bubbe had whispered in her ear, "If you live up to your name, you'll be back here as more than just his friend."

"What does *that* mean?" Patience had whispered back, after making sure Jace was busy arguing with his parents that his coat was warm enough for the weather.

"My grandson takes a long time to make up his mind about everything. When he was a boy, my husband asked him if he wanted a puppy for his birthday," Bubbe said in a low voice. "He said he had to think about it. His birthday came and went. He was still thinking about it. A year later, he told my husband he had decided he wanted a puppy. Reuben said, 'What kind of puppy?' and Jason said, 'I have to think about it.'"

"And?" Patience still didn't get why Bubbe was telling her the story. It wasn't until the end, when she saw the knowing gleam in Bubbe's eye, that she caught on.

"Jason walked down to the pet store every Saturday afternoon," Bubbe told her, "and he spent time with every dog there. He even went to the library and researched breeds. He wanted to pick the perfect dog. Two years later, out of the blue, he came home one day with a stray, mangy mutt that had latched onto him in the park. I've never seen Jace so happy. He kept that dog and he cleaned her up and he was devoted to her as long as she lived."

"What are you thinking?" Jace asked above the rattling train.

*What am I thinking? That Bubbe thought she was being so subtle with her little story, when actually she was comparing me to a stray, mangy mutt—a mutt, incidentally, that you happened to love unconditionally. I was thinking that Bubbe was telling me to live up to my name—to be patient—because she thinks you're going to realize that you want to bring me home and be devoted to me as long as I live. I was thinking that Bubbe is either a loony old lady or she makes more sense than anything else has lately.*

"Nothing," she said, hanging onto the pole as the train lurched again. Jace reached out to steady her. Again, his touch sent a jolt through her.

She focused her gaze on an outdated poster over his shoulder, pretending to be fascinated by the advertisement for a miniseries that had aired on television last spring during May Sweeps.

This was wrong.

The more she knew about Jace, the more she wanted him to be . . . well, not a just friend. She wanted him to be her boyfriend. Her lover. Her husband.

But she wasn't in love with him. She *couldn't* be in love with him, because there were things about him that still drove her crazy. A lot of things.

For instance, the way he refused to cross a street if the Don't Walk light had started blinking. She had tried explaining to him that it was more like a warning—that it didn't actually mean Don't Walk until it stopped blinking and stayed lit. He had said that didn't matter, that it wasn't a good idea to walk when it was lit, regardless of what the blinking meant. He had asked her if she wanted to get hit by a bus.

What kind of question was that?

It was the kind of question that drove her crazy, that was what kind of question it was.

Of course she didn't want to get hit by a bus. Nobody wanted to get hit by a bus.

She sighed, exasperated just thinking about it.

"What's wrong? You look irritated," Jace said to her.

"I'm fine." She flashed him a tight smile.

"You're not fine."

"I guess I'm just tired."

She faked a yawn and let go of the pole for a moment to rub her shoulders . . . which really were starting to ache, come to think of it.

"Oh." He looked disappointed.

"Why? What's wrong?"

"Nothing. It's just . . ."

"What?"

"I was going to ask if you wanted to see a movie or something."

"I think I'll just get off when we get to my stop," she told him, suddenly exhausted. "I didn't get any sleep last night and I've got to meet Beth for brunch in the morning and . . ."

*And I've got to get away from you, Jace Hoffman, before you either infuriate me again or make me fall in love with you.*

Either way, we'll both be in big trouble.

# Eight

Jace waited three days before calling Patience. It wasn't that he didn't want to talk to her, because he definitely wanted to. Very badly.

Desperately, even.

In fact, it seemed as though he thought about her every minute from the time they parted on the subway on Saturday night until the time he actually picked up the phone on Tuesday night.

The time apart had allowed him to analyze things. He was feeling unsettled about whatever it was that was happening between them.

It wasn't Just Friends. It was Sleeping Together.

And Sleeping Together was suspiciously similar to having a Relationship.

Which was the last thing Jace wanted with Patience Magee.

Yet how could he deny that he was crazy about her? She did something to him, something that made every shred of common sense fly right out of his head—hell, maybe it even made his *brain* fly out of his head, because when he was with her, he found that he didn't do as much thinking as he did feeling.

And what he was feeling, when he was with her, was . . .

Who knew?

It definitely wasn't Just Friendly.

But what were you supposed to do with a Relationship that had nowhere to go? If you couldn't imagine spending the rest of your life with someone, shouldn't you cut your losses early and move on?

Well, shouldn't you?

Somehow, Jace was no longer sure.

He only knew that he couldn't go any longer without talking to her, or seeing her.

So when he came home from the office on Tuesday night, the first thing he did—after changing into jeans and the sweatshirt she had loaned him, which he couldn't bear to wash because it still smelled like her—was to sit on the bed and dial her number.

She answered on the first ring.

Caught off guard, he stammered, then blurted, "I was expecting your answering machine."

There was a pause. "Jace?"

"Yeah."

"I actually . . . I just thought you were going to be someone else."

"Sorry to disappoint you," he said lightly, doing his best to hide the overwhelming doubt that suddenly overtook him.

Whose call was she expecting?

Was it another guy?

Was she disappointed that it was him instead?

He rose and paced into the living room, looking moodily out the window as she talked on in a halting way that wasn't at all her style.

"No, it's not that . . . it's just . . . Beth and I were just on the phone . . . but she had to go because her doorman buzzed her with a delivery, and . . . well, she said she'd call me right back, so I just assumed . . ."

"Oh, Beth," he said, relieved. He brushed a fleck of dust from the sill.

"I just thought you were her calling back . . ."

"Look," Jace said uneasily, toying with the cord that opened the blinds, "if you have to go . . . I mean, if she's going to be trying to get through . . ."

"No, it's just—I can talk for a minute," she said, and he could tell she was reluctant.

Why the hell was she reluctant to talk to him? After all, they were friends, weren't they? Just the way she and Beth were friends.

Friends called friends on the phone. That was what friends did, damn it.

"Look, I'll let you go," he said abruptly, striding away from the window, heading back to the bedroom.

"Wait, Jace—"

"What?" He paused in the doorway, the phone propped between his shoulder and his ear, his arms crossed in front of him.

"What's the matter? You sound angry."

"Why would I be angry?"

"I have no idea, but you are."

"No, I'm not."

"Yes, you are, Jace."

Irritated by the blatant certainty in her voice, he muttered, "It's just like you."

"What? I can't hear you."

"I said," he raised his voice, "It's just like you to tell *me* what *I* am."

"What's that supposed to mean?"

He exhaled heavily and crossed to the bed. He plopped down on the edge of the mattress. "Nothing, Patience. Just . . . go back to whatever you were doing. Waiting for Beth to call, or . . . whatever."

"But you called me. Why?"

*Because I'm a fool. Because I've spent the last three days imagining that there was something between us—something that obviously doesn't exist.*

"Why did you call, Jace?" she repeated.

"I just wanted to say hi," he told her, realizing he wasn't even sure whether or not it was a lie.

He obviously hadn't thought things through before calling her. He hadn't considered the objective. He'd just picked up the phone and dialed, never entertaining the possibility that she might not be happy to hear from him.

And yet . . . how could that have failed to enter his mind?

After all, he hadn't exactly heard from her these past three days.

Patience Magee was the kind of woman who would definitely call if she felt like it.

And if she didn't want to talk to you . . .

Well, she was the kind of woman who would let you know.

Which was what she seemed to be doing now.

"Look, Patience," Jace said, "I'll let you go. Beth is probably trying to get through to you, and I've got . . . stuff to do."

He waited for her to argue.

He wanted her to argue.

She didn't.

"Okay," she said simply. "See you."

And with a click, she hung up.

Patience stared at the phone in her hand, her thumb still firmly pressing the "talk" button. Why had she been so quick to sever the connection?

*Because Jake caught me completely off guard, that's why.*

For some reason, she hadn't been expecting him to call. She had assumed the ball was in her court.

When she'd left him on the subway on Saturday

night, she'd tossed a quick, "I'll give you a call next week" over her shoulder.

She hadn't meant it, though.

In fact, in the three days since she'd seen him, she had all but decided never to have any contact with him again.

She had actually been rehashing that very decision with Beth when Beth had to hang up. And Patience was so eager to continue the discussion that she had snatched up the phone the instant it rang, assuming it was Beth with more advice.

Beth's advice ran along the lines of, "So, if you don't want to see him, don't."

Not exactly what Patience wanted to hear, but maybe what she needed to hear.

*Don't see Jace.*
*Don't even think about Jace.*

The phone rang again.

Patience hesitated before pressing Talk.

What if it were Jace again?

Nah. He wouldn't call back.

Still, just to be sure, she screened the call.

"Patience, come on, must you screen every call?" Beth's voice came over the answering machine after the beep. "Pick up, it's me."

Patience pressed Talk. "I'm here."

"Why did you screen? You knew it was me."

"Because I just thought I knew it was you when it rang a minute ago, and it wasn't you."

"Who was it? Another obscene caller?"

"Jace."

"Really?" Beth was chewing something.

"Really." Patience remembered she hadn't eaten since lunch. She walked over to the kitchenette corner and opened a cupboard, looking absently at the contents.

"Did you tell him to get lost?"

"Not in so many words, but . . ."

"But he got the message?"

"I think so." She took out a can of SpaghettiOs.

"Good. Then he won't be bothering you again," Beth said around a mouthful.

"What are you eating?" Patience demanded, irritated with her friend's casual approach to this life-and-death conversation.

How could Beth eat at a time like this?

How could *she* think of eating at a time like this?

She put the SpaghettiOs back.

"Some out-of-this-world Belgian chocolates, if you must know," Beth was saying. "Mother expressed them to me. She's in Brussels."

"I thought you were on a diet. I thought you told me when I saw you on Sunday not to let you eat anything but steamed broccoli ever again.

"For breakfast today I had black coffee. For lunch I had a Certs. This is dinner. Okay?"

"Cranky, cranky," Patience said, feeling cranky herself "Listen, getting back to what we were saying . . ."

Beth sighed.

Patience ignored her. "Last week you were rooting for me to get together with Jace. Why are you telling me to tell him to get lost all of a sudden?"

"Because, as I said Sunday at brunch, you obviously can't handle an in-between relationship, Patience. With you, it has to be all or nothing. And since you can't have it all . . ."

"I get nothing?" Patience glowered, taking the SpaghettiOs out of the cupboard again.

"You have no choice, Patience. You said yourself that Jace isn't right for you. In fact, if I recall correctly, your exact words were, 'He drives me up a wall.' You did say that, didn't you?"

"Probably."

"You said it. More than once, actually. So, what else can you do? You have to cut him out of your life. You can't keep seeing someone who makes you miserable."

"I didn't say he makes me miserable. I said he drives me up a wall."

"There's a difference?"

"Of course there's a difference." Patience jammed the can opener on the edge of the can of SpaghettiOs and began turning the handle. "Just because someone drives me up a wall doesn't mean I have to cut him out of my life. My parents drive me up a wall sometimes, and I'm not estranged from them. You drive me up a wall sometimes, too, and you're still my friend."

Beth gave an exaggerated sigh. "Then be his friend, Patience, if that's what you want."

"I don't know if I can." She pried open the top of the can, then opened a drawer and hunted for a clean spoon. There wasn't one. She settled on a fork instead.

"If you can't be friends, but you can't have a relationship, but you can't not see him, then what else is there?"

"I have no idea," Patience said moodily, shoveling some cold SpaghettiOs into her mouth right out of the can. "Listen, I have to go. I'll call you later."

The phone rang.

Jace looked at it and frowned.

Probably his mother.

Or maybe Lena, who had said she'd call him this week to talk about what they were going to do for their parents' thirty-fifth wedding anniversary in November.

Or it could be Ned, who was supposed to meet Jace for a game of racquetball tomorrow. He set down the salad spinner and cutting board he'd just taken from the cupboard and picked up the phone.

"Jace?"

"Patience?"

"Sorry I hung up so quickly before."

"It's okay. I know you were waiting for Beth to call back."

"Yeah." She paused.

He waited, sensing something more was coming.

"That's not why I hung up," she said after a moment. "It was because I really didn't want to talk to you."

He bristled. "So you called me back just to make sure I understand that you don't want to talk to me?"

"No, I called you back to tell you why I don't want to talk to you."

"All right," he said, trying to be reasonable, trying not to be hurt by her words. It didn't work. He *was* hurt. Angry, too.

"The thing is—"

"Yes?"

"I thought I knew exactly where we stood. I thought we were going to be friends. And then . . . last weekend . . . well, that really messed things up. The fact that we . . ."

He clutched the phone tightly, making himself say the words when she didn't. "Slept together? Is that what you mean?"

"I mean all of it. Going to Brooklyn, meeting your family."

"Look, my family's a little crazy," he said, relieved that it wasn't about making love. "They're loud and they can be presumptuous and overbearing, but they mean well and—"

"No, it's not that. They're wonderful. It was just that everyone assumed I was your girlfriend."

"I told you, they're presumptuous."

"But it didn't bother me! That's the point, Jace. Can't you see what I'm trying to say?"

"I'm not sure."

"When we were together, I wanted to be your girlfriend. I wanted us to be in a relationship. And I know that we can't."

"Maybe we can," he heard himself say.

There was silence on the other end of the phone.

He didn't blame her.

He, too, was stunned by his words.

What was he thinking? How could he and Patience be in a relationship? It would never work.

Which was exactly what she said when she found her voice. "It would never work."

"Why not?"

"Because we're just . . ."

"Too different. I know," he said heavily.

"I keep thinking about the whole cliché about opposites attracting," Patience went on. "And I think it's true—that opposites do attract. Maybe I see in you qualities that I lack—qualities I might subconsciously admire."

"Subconsciously?"

"Well, it's not as if I go around consciously wishing I worked on Wall Street, or had all my CDs in order by record label."

"I don't have my CDs in alphabetical order by record label," he retorted. They were actually in alphabetical order by artist, but he wasn't about to admit it to her.

"Whatever, Jace, the point is that maybe I subconsciously wish I were more like you, and maybe you subconsciously wish you were more like me, and maybe that's what's drawn us together. Maybe opposites do attract. But did you ever notice that the cliché doesn't mention anything about opposites getting married and living happily ever after?"

He flinched. "No, but . . ."

"I just don't know what we're supposed to do with this," she said helplessly. "With *us.*"

"I don't, either," he admitted.

"But you just said maybe we can be in a relationship," she reminded him.

"Obviously, you don't agree, and you're probably right. It wouldn't work."

"Unless we give it a try," she said tentatively. "Like you said."

A thrill shot through him.

"Do you want to try, Patience?"

"I don't think we have any choice. If it doesn't work out, well, then . . . at least we'll *know.* And we can get past all this . . . *not* knowing."

"Right," he said, unable to keep a big grin from taking over his face.

"So what do we do now?" she asked, and he could hear the smile in her voice, too.

"I guess we . . . get together."

"Tonight?"

"No, we can just—"

"No, Jace, let's get together tonight," she said firmly. "I want to see you. Now that we've made this decision, I don't want to wait."

He realized he didn't, either. Why wait? They'd already made this completely impulsive decision.

They might as well act impulsively on it.

"I'll come over," Patience said.

"Or I can come there," he offered.

"You've already been here. I want to see your place."

"There's not much to see," he said, looking around

his tidy apartment. "Just a living room, kitchen, bathroom, and bedroom. It's not that big a deal."

"I want to see it," she insisted. "You know I'm nosy. So let me find a pen and I'll write down the address."

He heard her opening drawers, rattling things around.

He waited patiently.

"Find a pen yet?" he asked after a few moments.

"No, but . . . oh, there's an eyebrow pencil."

"Okay, it's two-seventy-two East—"

"Wait, I can't find anything to write on," she cut in, and he heard her rustling papers.

He waited.

Not quite as patiently, this time.

"Did you find some paper yet?" he asked.

"No. Well, never mind. I'll just write on my hand."

He forced himself not to find that absolutely ridiculous.

So she couldn't find a piece of paper anywhere in her apartment.

So he was the type of person who kept a clean scratch pad and a cupful of sharpened pencils by the phone.

So what?

It didn't mean their relationship wouldn't work . . .

Did it?


"Wow," Patience said, standing in the middle of Jace's living room floor and spinning slowly in a circle, gaping. "This place is so . . ."

So masculine.

So empty.

So clean.

"So *big*," she settled on, tactfully. "You could fit my entire studio in that entertainment center."

"I doubt that," he said, chuckling.

*He is incredibly good-looking,* she thought, glancing at him, finding it impossible to recall the scrawny, bespectacled image of the Jace she had once known. The very embodiment of tall, dark, and handsome. And dressed impeccably as always, she noted, in a cream-colored cable-knit sweater, beige corduroys, and Gucci loafers. She wanted to hurl herself into his arms and beg him to kiss her.

*Patience, Patience,* she commanded. *Good things come to those who wait, remember?*

She hooked her thumbs into the back pockets of her jeans and walked over to the entertainment center, conscious of his eyes on her. She checked the collection of disks on the shelf below the state-of-the-art DVD player.

*Bor-ing,* she thought, scanning the titles. A few black-and-white classics, a couple of recent blockbusters, and some financial titles that must be work-related.

She turned back to him and said brightly, "Interesting."

"Yeah, right." He grinned.

She grinned back. "Okay, but it's not as if I figured you'd have the latest indie films or foreign documentaries or porn stuff. This is pretty much what I expected."

"Somehow that doesn't sound like a compliment. Have you eaten?"

"Just cold SpaghettiOs from the can. I'm starving. How about you?"

"I was about to make a salad when you called. And I have some chicken breasts marinating in the fridge."

"You *do?*" She was impressed. "You're going to cook dinner for me?"

"Well, before I knew you were coming, I was going to cook dinner for me. Now I'm going to cook dinner for both of us. How about a glass of wine while I get busy?"

"Sounds good."

She wandered around the living room while he went into the kitchen. She checked the magazines that were perfectly fanned on the glass coffee table. *Newsweek, Sports Illustrated,* and *Kiplinger's Personal Finance.*

The couch was tan leather; the walls and carpeting, beige. The end tables held a couple of nondescript lamps, a stack of coasters, and a healthy philodendron. The wide window was covered by closed wooden blinds. Patience peeked through the slats and saw a breathtaking view of the river far below, with the twinkling lights of Roosevelt Island and Queens beyond.

She turned back to the living room and noticed the oil painting hanging on the wall near the entertainment center. It was a monochromatic cityscape, and she could tell by the frame that it was expensive. Why had Jace chosen such a blah image? If he were going to invest in art, you would think he would want something with a little pizzazz. Something to liven up the place.

*No, that's what* you *would do if* you *were going to invest in art,* she reminded herself. *Jace is different. And different isn't bad, remember? It's just . . . different.*

Still, she couldn't help feeling uncomfortable in his apartment. It wasn't just the minimalist decor or the fact that everything was neatly in its place.

The problem was, the apartment was an in-your-face reminder of just how opposite she and Jace really were. She could never live in a place that looked like this.

And, she had to admit, she couldn't see Jace living in her place, either.

But she wasn't supposed to be thinking about living together, was she?

*Of course you are. You're trying a relationship. A relation-*

*ship leads to commitment if it's successful. Commitment means living together. Getting married.*

Panic set in.

*Marriage means compromise. It means giving up your freedom. It means giving in even when you really want your way.*

Was she ready for that?

"Here's your wine," Jace said, reappearing with two goblets and handing her one. He clinked his glass against hers. "Here's to us."

Was she ready for *this*?

"Are you all right?" Jace asked, leaning toward her and looking into her face.

"I'm fine." She sipped her wine. "Let me help you make dinner, Jace. I'm stir-crazy."

"Patience, stir-crazy?" he asked dryly. "Gee, that's hard to imagine."

She swatted his arm and followed him into the spotless, sparkling kitchen. After setting her glass on the expensive marble countertop, she shoved the sleeves of her navy cardigan sweater past her elbows.

"What do you want me to do?" she asked, looking around at the gleaming stainless-steel appliances, the polished copper pots and pans hanging from a rack overhead, and the glass-front cupboards with their neatly arranged contents plainly visible.

"Why don't you make the salad while I cook the chicken?" He handed her a clear plastic produce container filled with organic mesclun greens.

"Sure," she said, glad to have something to do. She walked over to the empty wooden salad bowl on the counter, conscious of Jace watching her as she glanced at the label, then opened the container.

What, didn't he think she was capable of making a salad? Apparently not. She was about to dump the greens into the bowl when Jace grabbed her on the arm.

"Wait!"

"What?" She looked up at him, startled.

"You didn't wash it yet."

"I don't have to. It says right here that it's triple washed. See?" She pointed to the label.

"Yeah, but you should wash it again."

"Why?"

"Because, it's . . . because you just should," he said, and she could tell it was killing him not to just wrench the greens out of her hand and do it himself.

She frowned, deliberately stalling. "But if it's already been washed three times—"

"You don't *know* that."

"It's what the label says."

"But you should wash it. Just to be sure."

She shrugged and carried the container over to the sink. "Do you want me to use soap?"

"No!"

She was pleased to see that he looked horrified.

"Relax, Jace," she said, laughing at his expression. "I was only kidding."

"I knew that," he said mildly.

"No, you didn't."

"Okay, I didn't," he admitted, then said, "Here." He handed her a white plastic container with a funnel top and a strainer insert.

"What's this?" she asked, mystified.

"A salad spinner. It's for washing greens. Here, I'll show you."

Half amused, half annoyed, she watched as he put the greens into the strainer basket, replaced the top, ran water through the funnel, then turned a handle on the lid. Water dripped through the bottom of the container as the greens whirled inside.

"See? It gets all the water out so they won't be soggy," Jace said, opening the top and showing her.

"That's just . . . nifty," she said, flashing him a smile.

"I usually pat it with a few paper towels just to be sure," he said, gently doing just that.

She bit her tongue. All this fuss just to make a salad?

Well, okay. It was his kitchen. Determined to show him that she was willing to do things his way, she carried the salad spinner back to the bowl. She dumped the greens in, then turned to see him watching her intently.

"Don't you have chicken to make?" she asked irritably.

He nodded and opened the fridge.

She surveyed the vegetables lined up on the counter beside the cutting board and a paring knife. A cucumber, a tomato, and a couple of radishes.

"Do you have an avocado to jazz up the salad a bit?" she asked as she began peeling the cucumber. "Or some of those crunchy bacon thingies?"

"No avocado," he said, rummaging through the fridge. "No bacon *thingies,* either. I'm Jewish, remember?"

"Yeah, but it's not real bacon. It's not even meat. It's those fake little pieces that come in a jar. Never mind," she added quickly, seeing his expression.

"If you want to jazz up the salad, you can add some black olives," he offered, opening a cupboard and taking out a can of the ripe, pitted kind.

"Nothing like walking on the wild side," she quipped, taking the olives from him. "Next thing you know, you'll want to put in diced onion."

"No onion," he said, carrying a plastic container full of marinated raw chicken to the counter.

"No onion? Why not?"

"Because," he stood very close to her, "I plan on kissing you later."

"Oh . . . I have to wait till later?"

"Not necessarily." He put his hands firmly on her shoulders and bent toward her.

She closed her eyes as his mouth met hers. What she expected to be a light kiss quickly grew intense as his tongue slid past her willing lips. She leaned into him, pressing against the length of his body, feeling his arousal against her hip.

He broke the kiss to say raggedly, "If we keep this up, we're never going to eat."

The hoarseness in his voice sent a shiver through her. She was thrilled by the realization that she had the power to do this to him—to make unflappable Jace all flushed with pleasure.

"It's okay, Jace. I'm more hungry for this than for food," she said, standing on her tiptoes to kiss him again.

He groaned and swiftly lifted her onto the counter, standing between her spread legs as she wrapped her arms around his neck. His kiss grew hotter, more urgent, and his hands wandered beneath her sweater. She pulled back slightly and raised her arms, and he took her cue, lifting the sweater swiftly over her head.

"You're not wearing anything under it," he murmured, trailing his searing mouth along her collarbone, and then lower.

"I don't always wear a bra," she told him. "Sometimes it's just too—"

She was swept into silence by a wave of pleasure as his tongue swirled against her taut nipple. His hands found the buttons of her Levis. She lifted her hips when he had them open, allowing him to tug them past her thighs, hearing them drop to the floor at his feet. He slid his thumbs beneath the waistband of her black panties, and moments later they, too, hit the floor.

She arched her back and opened her legs at his coaxing as he bent before her, moaning his name when she felt his tongue graze her most intimate flesh. She moaned softly, holding his head, her fingers clenched in his hair as his mouth did incredible things to her.

"I want you inside of me, Jace," she whispered, squirming with hot, wet need.

He didn't stop, didn't speak, just kept doing what he was doing until, moments later, she careened into blissful oblivion, gasping as her body pulsed and quaked.

Only when she had quieted did he lift his face away from her.

"Patience?" He looked up into her eyes, searching. "You okay?"

"That was unbelievable," she said with a sated sigh, smiling, and he smiled, too.

He stood. She collapsed against his chest. He stroked her hair, traced her jaw. Then, finally, he brushed his lips tenderly against her cheek. "I'll finish making dinner," he said, and started to move away.

"Not so fast," she said, catching his hand and pulling him back. "You have to finish something else you started, first."

Their eyes met and held.

It was her turn to lift his sweater over his head, to fumble with the buttons on his fly, to undress him until he stood naked before her. Still seated on the counter, she pulled him into the apex of her legs, and he sank into her with a low groan. She wrapped her legs around his hips, moving with him, her hands splayed on his shoulders, feeling his muscles clench in the moments before his body shuddered violently.

Moments later she was there with him, trembling and whimpering and clinging to him.

"So good," he murmured, holding her close when it was over. "This is so good. How could we have thought this wouldn't work?"

"Oh, Jace, I don't know," she whispered, unwilling to venture consideration of anything prior to or past this moment. "I don't want to think about it."

All she wanted, all she needed, was the here and now.

And what they had right here, right now, was perfect.

"One boring salad, complete with quadruple-washed lettuce, coming right up," Patience quipped, taking the tongs and the bottle of gourmet salad dressing Jace handed her.

"I can't believe it's almost midnight and we still haven't eaten," he said, turning back to the chicken on his stovetop grill.

"It's no big deal." She poured some of the balsamic vinaigrette over the salad.

"But I promised you dinner hours ago," Jace said, turning a piece of chicken and reaching for his basting brush.

"So? I'm the one who suggested a tour of the rest of the apartment—starting with the bedroom."

He turned to see her grinning at him. She looked gorgeous, clad only in one of his starched custom-made shirts. He was just in time to see her spatter balsamic vinaigrette onto the collar as she tossed the salad.

"Oops," she said, wincing. "Sorry. I wasn't watching what I was doing."

He shrugged. "It's okay. I have a dozen shirts just like that one if it doesn't come out."

She raised an eyebrow. "What's this? A new, relaxed Jace Hoffman who isn't stressing over the sloppy ways of Patience Magee? It's amazing what a roll in the hay can do for a man's mood."

"A *few* rolls in the hay, if I remember correctly," he said, leaning over to kiss the tip of her nose. Then he kissed her mouth. He couldn't get enough of her.

She kissed him back, then pulled away and pointed to the clock on the microwave oven. "It's almost time for 'The Odd Couple,' Jace," she warned. "If you keep this up, we'll miss the show and the chicken will burn."

"So?" He kissed her again.

"So, the smoke alarms will sound and the neighbors will start evacuating and the building's sprinklers will go off, we'll be soaked, your furniture and carpet will be ruined, and—"

"So?" He grinned at her.

"Who are you, and what have you done with Jace?" she asked, pretending to cower.

He went back to basting his chicken, whistling 'The Odd Couple' theme as he slopped extra sauce on two pieces for her.

"I'll set the table. We'll eat in the living room so we can watch TV, right?" she asked.

He nodded, interrupting his whistling to say, "There are placemats in that drawer, and the plates are in that cupboard."

She busied herself scurrying back and forth between the kitchen and living room.

"The chicken's done," he called to her.

"Good. The show's starting," she called back.

He loaded the food onto a tray and carried it in. She was curled up on one end of the couch, looking for all the world as though she had sat there a million times. As though she belonged there.

He stopped short, realizing that this was what it would be like to be married to Patience.

"What's the matter?" she asked, seeing him standing there. "You're missing it."

"Nothing's the matter," he said. "I was just thinking . . ."

"What?"

"Nothing," he told her quickly, setting the tray on the table.

It was too soon to get carried away by wistful dreams of cozy domesticity. Much too soon. Just because they were good together in bed and had gone a few hours without an argument . . .

Well, that was hardly grounds for a proposal.

Still, if things kept up this way . . .

*Hey, you never know,* Jace told himself, feeling giddy.

"What did you say?" Patience asked, looking up sharply.

Oops. He must have spoken aloud.

"I said, what do you know, it's finally time to eat," he improvised.

"No, you didn't." She was watching him carefully.

He shifted his weight. "Doesn't *anything* ever slip past you?"

"Nothing," she said blithely, shaking her dark curls. "So you'd better watch your step, Mr. Hoffman."

"I fully intend to, Ms. Magee," he said, and settled contentedly next to her on the couch.

# Nine

Too good to be true.

That was the only way to describe what had been going on between Patience and Jace for a month now, ever since the night he'd cooked dinner for her at his apartment.

She almost dared to believe they had a future together.

*Ha!*

She should have known they couldn't last, these peaceful days of making love, traipsing around the city, lolling in each other's arms.

She should have realized that constant passion wasn't the only thing simmering beneath the surface whenever they were together.

She should have recognized that she was trying to be somebody she wasn't; that Jace was, too.

But she was deaf, dumb, and blind to any of it until it was too late. The beginning of the end happened innocently enough.

"Oh, by the way, there was a message on my machine from Anne," she said, looking up from the arts section of the *New York Times* one lazy Sunday afternoon in late November.

She had flown back from Thanksgiving in New Hampshire the night before, stopping in her apartment only long enough to deposit her luggage and check her machine before heading uptown to Jace's place. They hadn't been out of each other's sight ever since, except for the two hours when she'd dashed down to midtown to meet Beth for their weekly brunch date. She had hurried straight back and they had fallen back into bed for long hours of languid lovemaking. Pure bliss.

"Jace?" Patience prodded.

"Mmm?" he said absently, running his finger down a column of stock quotes in the financial section.

"She and Ned invited us over for dinner next Saturday night. Beth said that everyone's going. It's sort of a holiday get-together, and they want to show us their wedding and honeymoon pictures."

"Oh, right." Jace looked up, peeking around the newspaper that was still poised in front of his face. "She called here, too. I told her we couldn't make it."

"Why not?" Patience asked, surprised.

"Because." Jace made a face. "Do you really want to go over there and spend hours oohing and ahing over their wedding pictures?"

"Yes," Patience said, irritated. "Which is why I called her and told her we'd be there." He lowered his newspaper. "When did you do that?"

"Last night, when I got the message. I called her back right before I left home to come over here. *On the subway,*" she added pointedly, knowing it would rankle him to realize she hadn't taken a cab, even though it was after dark on a weekend night.

His mouth tightened, but to his credit, he didn't address the subway issue. All he said was, "Well, didn't she tell you that I'd already said no?"

"She didn't tell me anything, because she wasn't there. I left a message on their machine saying we would come."

Jace went back to his paper, saying, in a maddeningly detached tone, "Oh, well. You can call her back later and tell her we won't be there after all."

"No, I can't," Patience said flatly, tossing aside the arts section.

He looked up. "Why can't you?"

"Because I want to go. Everyone will be there. It'll be fun."

He groaned. "Patience, why do you want to see all those people?"

"Because they're my friends, Jace," she said in a *duh* voice. "They're your friends, too. Remember?"

"Ned is my friend," he conceded. "And Anne, because she's his wife. But those other guys—I hadn't seen them in years before we stood up in the wedding together, and I haven't seen them since the wedding, and I don't want to. We have nothing in common anymore except that we went to college together. Think about it, Patience. You don't really want to go either."

How dare he—

*Whoa, don't jump to conclusions,* she cautioned herself *Slow down. Get inside his head. Try to figure out what's motivating him, here.*

She contemplated the situation, gratified when she quickly realized what the problem must be. Nothing a little reassurance wouldn't cure.

*See? That wasn't so hard. Aren't you glad you didn't jump all over him?*

Now that she knew exactly what he was thinking, she could approach him calmly and rationally.

"Look," she said with uncharacteristic patience, "if it's because Bryan will be there, I can assure you there's nothing to worry about."

"Because *Bryan* will be there?" he echoed, looking stunned.

"I mean, if you're afraid that I still have feelings for him after all these years—"

He laughed. "Believe me, that never even entered my mind. The guy is a loser. He always has been. Anyone can see that."

She was seething, and she wasn't even sure why.

All she was certain of was that he was on the verge of ruining everything, and he didn't even seem aware of what he was doing.

"I want to go to Ned and Anne's," she said, glaring at him.

He didn't even notice. He wasn't looking at her. He was once again running his forefinger down a boring column of boring stock quotes as though it were the most fascinating thing he had ever seen.

"Okay, that's fine. Go to Ned and Anne's," he said blandly. "You can come back here afterward. I'll rent some movies and we can—"

"No!" She snatched the newspaper out of his hand.

"Hey!"

"Jace, you're barely even paying attention to what I'm saying. This is important."

He opened his mouth.

He closed it.

He opened it again, and said with utmost care, "Okay, I'm listening."

" 'I'm listening'? Who are you, Frasier Crane?"

"Who?"

"Never mind," she said, exasperated. Aside from "The Odd Couple," Jace didn't watch television sitcoms. Suddenly, that, too, bothered her. Why had she ever thought they had anything in common?

"Patience, come on," he said, touching her arm.

She pulled it away as if she'd been burned by his fingers. "Why did you think you could just make a decision like that for me?"

"You mean, that we wouldn't be going to Ned and Anne's?"

"Of course that's what I mean," she snapped. "That's what we're talking about—although I'm the one who's doing most of the talking while you read the paper."

"I'm not reading the paper now. Talk to me."

She took a deep breath, shaking.

She looked at him.

He seemed so . . . composed.

Didn't he realize how terrifying this was? Didn't he know they were on the brink of losing each other?

This wasn't an ordinary fight. Couldn't he see that? With some couples, it might be the kind of thing that would just blow over. But not with them.

This was the very problem she had been afraid would surface all along. She and Jace were just too *different*. They weren't meant to be together. This proved it.

"You didn't even check with me to see if I might want to go to Ned and Anne's," she said, and her voice quavered.

Oh, Lord. She was going to cry.

"Are you going to *cry?*" he asked, incredulous.

"Yes!" she bit out hotly as tears spilled from her eyes. "Of course I'm going to cry."

"Over a stupid dinner party? Look, if it means that much to you, I'll go. Okay?"

"I don't want you to go."

Exasperated, he said, "I thought that was what this was about."

"That's the problem! You have no idea what this is about."

"Then tell me," he said, and she noticed that his hands were clenched in his lap. He was doing everything he could not to lose it.

She resented him for that, too. She was sitting here

with tears streaming down her face, her nose running—damn, she needed a tissue—and he was completely unruffled.

That just proved he didn't care.

He was oblivious to her needs.

He was coldhearted.

He was everything she didn't want in a man, and she had almost made the mistake of believing they had a future.

She got off the couch, feeling shaky, and went to the closet.

"What are you doing?" Jace asked.

She ignored him.

She took her coat off the hanger and fumbled in the pocket for the neatly ironed handkerchief her mother had given her in the car on the way to the airport yesterday. Mom always did that because Patience always cried when she said good-bye to her family.

It wasn't that she was homesick—not most of the time. She loved her life in New York.

But good-byes in airports were hard, and there was always a moment, right before she boarded her plane, that she wondered deep down if she really wanted to go. If it wouldn't be easier, wiser, *better,* just to stay in New Hampshire with the people she loved; the people who loved her—her parents and her sisters. If it wouldn't be better to live life in a place that was comfortable and safe and predictable.

Yet that wasn't what she wanted. It had never been what she wanted.

Patience had always craved adventure. Unpredictability. Spontaneity.

That was why she lived in New York.

That was why she always got on the plane and soared back through the sky to New York, where she belonged.

Still, maybe there was a part of her that secretly longed for the security of home.

Maybe that was why she always shed a few tears in the airport.

The thing was . . .

And she didn't realize it until she had blown her nose noisily into Mom's neatly ironed handkerchief while standing in front of Jace's closet . . .

She hadn't cried last night in the airport.

For the first time ever, she had left New Hampshire and her family without a single tear, without a shred of regret.

Why?

*Maybe you're finally over that homesickness,* she told herself now, wiping her eyes. *Or maybe you were eager to get back to Jace, because Jace . . .*

Well, maybe he had become the safe, secure, comfortable thing she secretly craved.

"Patience?" he asked, behind her.

"What?"

"What are you doing?"

She sniffled. "Blowing my nose."

He appeared beside her, eyed the coat in her hand. "You're not planning on leaving, are you?"

She wavered.

Yes. She had been planning on leaving.

But now . . .

"Don't go," he said softly. "Please. Don't go."

She hesitated.

She didn't want to go.

She wanted to hurl herself into Jace's arms and hear him say he was sorry.

She wanted to hear him say . . .

*I love you.*

There. It was out there . . .

At least in her mind.

She wanted Jace to love her. Because if he loved her, then everything would be all right. None of this other stuff would matter. If he loved her, they would have a future, because love conquered everything. Everyone knew that.

*Do you love him?* a little voice asked in her head.

It was a voice that had been trying to intrude on her thoughts for a month; and now that it had gotten through, she was forced to consider the question.

*Did* she love Jace?

She was *afraid* to love Jace.

Because . . .

What if she loved Jace, and Jace didn't love her back?

"Patience," he said in a low voice, taking a step toward her.

They were face to face, inches apart. There was an expression on his face she had never seen before, tenderness mingling with concern and desire, making her wonder if this was it.

She held her breath.

Was he going to say it?

If he said he loved her . . .

Please, let him say he loved her . . .

Then everything would be okay.

He shifted his weight.

She clenched her jaw, biting back the coaxing words that stormed her brain. This was up to him. She couldn't prod him; she shouldn't intrude on whatever was going through his mind. She had to let him decide.

So . . .

What was he going to do?

What was he going to say?

She couldn't stand the suspense.

He bit his lower lip.

What the hell was taking him so long?

*Say it, Jace,* she begged silently. *Say it, damn it. For once, just come out with something that's on your mind. For once, just speak and act from your heart without weighing the consequences.*

"Patience," he said again, and took a deep breath. "I . . ."

She couldn't stand it another second. It was killing her. "What?" she blurted. "You *what*, Jace? Tell me!"

And in that moment, she realized that whatever he had been about to say was lost. Her own impulsiveness, her damned impatience, had shattered the moment.

His expression had changed. It wasn't angry, exactly. Or hurt. Just . . . bewildered, for a moment. And maybe disappointed.

And then he seemed to recover. He put his hands on her shoulders and said quietly, firmly, "Stay."

She stared at him. Waiting. Wondering if there were more. Needing there to be more, yet knowing it wasn't going to happen. Not here. Not now. Maybe not ever.

He cleared his throat.

"Jace," she said softly, her voice trembling as she searched his eyes.

"I want you to stay, Patience. Stay, okay? Please stay."

So there it was.

It wasn't *I love you.*

It didn't change everything.

But it changed enough to make her hand him her coat . . .

To make her look into his eyes and say, softly, "Okay."


After returning from their honeymoon, Ned and Anne had moved into a three-story brownstone on East Thirty-Seventh Street. Jace had seen it once, right before the wedding, when it was filled with painters' drop cloths and ladders instead of furniture and personal effects. With the high ceilings, tall windows, fireplaces, and old-world moldings, the place had charm even then.

Tonight, as he and Patience stepped into the foyer and handed their coats to the maid, he was even more impressed. The professional decorators Anne had hired had done incredible work.

"My God," Patience said under her breath, looking around. "What a showplace."

"They've done a nice job with it, haven't they?"

Jace took in the imported Oriental carpeting, the lush draperies, the polished antiques. The color scheme was made up of jewel tones—ruby and sapphire and emerald—and the fabrics covering the windows and upholstery were silk and velvet brocades.

"It's gorgeous," she admitted, "but it looks like a museum. I mean . . . it doesn't feel homey, does it?"

"For them it probably does. Have you ever seen Ned's parents' place in Newport?"

"No, but I can just imagine."

The maid directed them into a drawing room where the others waited, sipping drinks by the fire. Ned and Anne looked relaxed and happy as they greeted Patience and Jace.

Jace wondered if their clothes had been precoordinated or just happened to be strikingly similar. Ned wore black corduroys with a white roll-neck sweater; Anne had on a black velvet skirt and a white silk blouse, Jace couldn't quite imagine them planning matching outfits—it had probably just worked out that way. That sort of thing seemed to happen often with Ned and Anne.

He was shocked when he found himself envious.

It was so obvious that they belonged together—that

they were a perfect fit; that their marriage would be a success.

He wanted to be in a relationship like that. He wanted the kind of certainty that came from being with the right person.

And he wanted it with Patience. He wanted Patience to be the right person.

But when he was with her, no matter how contented he was feeling, he couldn't seem to let go of the nagging doubt. Sure, things might be fine now, but how long could a relationship last when the participants fundamentally disagreed about—well, basically everything?

Even what to wear to tonight's dinner party. She had on jeans and a thick, wooly cardigan; he was wearing dress slacks and a button-down shirt. He realized, looking around, that although nobody else was wearing jeans, Patience somehow managed not to be out of place. Most of it was attitude. If Jace had brought Sue to a party with his friends, she would have asked him what to wear. And if she had turned up in denim when everyone else was in silk and cashmere, she would have been horrified.

Not Patience. Breezy as ever, she had hooked her thumbs in the back pockets of her jeans as she chatted with Beth, who wore a black cocktail dress.

She was just so comfortable with her own choices.

A woman like Patience wasn't ever going to be reined in.

She was a free spirit and she wasn't about to give up her freedom. She intended to live her life on her own terms.

Jace admired her fierce independence. And he resented it.

"Does everyone know you two are together?" Anne asked in a low voice, pulling him aside slightly.

Jace shrugged, feigning a casual attitude he didn't feel. "They do now."

He greeted Beth with a polite hug and gave the obligatory handshakes to Bryan and Henry. He met a pretty blonde named Meg, who introduced herself as Bryan's girlfriend, and he didn't miss the way Bryan rolled his eyes at Henry behind her back when she said it. Then he watched as Patience joked easily in response to their teasing about the fact that she and Jace had arrived together.

"I know, can you believe it? Me and Jace, of all people." She tossed her curls and linked her arm through Jace's as he gratefully accepted a beer from Ned.

"Hey, who wants to set up a pool?" Bryan asked. "I've got a hundred bucks that says they won't make it till New Year's."

Jace felt Patience's grip grow tense on his arm.

"New Year's?" Henry said. "I give them until tomorrow morning, tops."

"You guys don't know what you're talking about," Patience scoffed lightly as Ned handed her the bourbon and water she'd requested. "Jace and I get along really well, don't we, sweetie?"

*Sweetie?*

She had never called him that. She never called him anything but Jace.

He nodded, doing his best not to seem stiff as he quipped, "We've only come to blows once or twice so far."

He hadn't missed the strain in Patience's voice despite her swagger. She was acting as though it didn't matter in the least that nobody thought they were going to last as a couple, but she, too, had her doubts.

*Just as you do,* Jace reminded himself.

He tried to be good-natured about the ribbing, but he was grateful when Anne, ever the conscientious hostess, subtly changed the subject, offering to show them the wedding album proofs and leading them over to the couch.

"Oh, come on, Anne. Hey, you don't have to look at wedding pictures, Jace," Ned said.

"Ned!" Anne protested. "Jace was in the wedding. Maybe he wants to see the pictures."

"Right," Beth put in, and gestured at Henry and Bryan. "Just because these two buffoons could care less doesn't mean that Jace isn't interested."

Jace was anything but interested in looking at a bunch of pictures of someone else's wedding, but the alternatives—hanging out with Henry and Bryan or going to the "powder room" with Beth and Meg—weren't any more appealing.

"It's okay, Ned," he said, and smiled at Anne. "Of course I want to see the pictures."

He pretended to be completely engaged in photo after photo of Anne in her wedding gown before the ceremony, and he listened to Patience gush about what a beautiful bride she had been, seeming to be absorbed in every detail of the gown, the veil, the flowers.

There was a hint of longing in her voice, Jace realized with a shock. Was Patience Magee secretly interested in becoming a bride?

A vision invaded his mind—Patience floating toward him in white silk and illusion, her expression serene.

He quickly dismissed it. If Patience ever got married, she would probably do it in black leather, or while skydiving.

Still . . .

"Oh, Anne, I never noticed your shoes," she bubbled as Anne flipped to a photo of herself holding up her gown to reveal a blue wisp of garter just above her knee. "I love the satin bows."

"They're nice," Jace murmured, feeling as though he had to say something.

"Thank you. Look, here's one of you two," Anne said, turning the page again.

Jace was startled by the image.

He had never seen a picture of himself with Patience. They had been together for over a month now, he realized, but this was the first time he had glimpsed an image of them as a couple.

In the photo, they were walking down the aisle. Her hand was gripping his arm. He looked taut; she looked restless. Neither of them looked comfortable.

*So? It's just a picture,* he reminded himself. *And it was taken long before you ever got together.*

Out of the corner of his eye, he saw Patience glance quickly at him, as if to gauge his reaction.

He pasted on a smile and said, "Hey, that's a great shot."

"You can order a copy if you want," Anne said. "I'm ordering pictures for everyone in the wedding party."

"That's all right," Jace said quickly as Patience simultaneously blurted, "No thanks."

Jace avoided Anne's searching look, gazing down at his beer as he took a sip.

"Oh, hey, look at that one of Beth," Patience said with forced amusement.

She and Anne bent their heads over the album once again, as Jace gave up pretending to be interested and wandered over to where the guys were discussing the Jets' chances of making it to the playoffs.

"What do you think, Jace?" Ned asked.

"I think they'll make the playoffs," he said, without giving it any thought. He was still distracted by an uneasy feeling about his relationship with Patience. It had been with him all week, ever since last Sunday night when they'd had that disagreement about coming here.

Something had been off between them ever since. It was as if they were being too careful with each other, tiptoeing around each other to avoid another flare-up.

"Don't listen to Jace," Bryan said. "Didn't he say the Mets were a shoo-in for the World Series this year?"

"They were one game away from making it," Jace told him, piqued. "And if it hadn't been for that bad call—"

"Just like a Mets fan, wanting to blame the ump," Henry said.

"I'm surprised Patience hasn't convinced you to switch your allegiance to the Yankees," Bryan said. "She actually tried to talk me out of rooting for the Red Sox when we went out."

"Yeah, well, that's because the Red Sox stink," Jace told him.

"Hey, Patience. Your boyfriend is picking on me," Bryan said as Patience wandered over with Anne.

"Now, Jace, that's not kind," she said in a mocking maternal tone. "Play nicely with the other boys. And Bryan, no tattling."

"Dinner should be ready," Anne said. "Let's go into the dining room."

Jace snuck a peek at his watch as they followed her down the hallway, wondering how long he and Patience had to stay. He couldn't wait to get out of here.

He should have known better than to give in and agree to come with her to the dinner party. She had even said she wouldn't mind if he skipped it. But he had felt funny bowing out if she were going to go. After all, Ned and Anne were his friends, too, and there was really no good reason for not wanting to be here.

He had told himself—and Patience—that he just

wasn't interested in an evening spent looking at wedding photos with a bunch of people with whom he had nothing in common. Of course he cared about Ned and Anne, and of course he wanted to see the wedding photos—well, sort of—but he didn't see the point in socializing with college acquaintances who had long since drifted from his life.

And that was true—more or less.

But the more overwhelming reason he hadn't wanted to come tonight was that he wasn't comfortable allowing the people who had known both him and Patience long before they ever got together to scrutinize their still-new-and-fragile relationship. He had known there would be a lot of teasing and curiosity. And he wasn't ready to have the rest of them analyzing the relationship when even he wasn't yet sure where they stood.

Just last week, when Patience was gone for Thanksgiving, he had been going crazy without her, wondering what he had ever done with himself before she came into his life. Nothing had felt right—not even the familiar, chaotic holiday dinner in Brooklyn, surrounded by all the aunts, uncles, and cousins.

Bubbe must have brought up the topic of Patience fifty times that day, telling everyone about Jace's new *friend*. She always elbowed the listener when she said the word, and emphasized it in a way that plainly revealed she didn't believe Jace and Patience were just *friends*.

Jace had been tempted to tell her she was right, just to get her off his back. But if he admitted that he and Patience were seeing each other, everyone would demand to know why she wasn't spending the holiday with him.

He had wondered that himself. He had invited her to come.

But she had already had a plane ticket home. She told him emphatically that she *always* went home for Thanksgiving; that nothing was as beautiful as November in New England—where, she had reminded him, the first Thanksgiving had taken place.

"Oh, really? And here my parents always told me the *Mayflower* landed in Brooklyn," he'd cracked, pretending to be good-natured about it.

But he wasn't.

He had sensed that she was trying to tell him something. That she wanted him to know she wasn't going to change her plans just because they were dating each other; that she didn't have any intention of spending the holiday with him. She was going to go ahead with her plans, and she was going to do what she wanted to do, for Thanksgiving . . . and always.

The message had come through loud and clear.

So Jace had spent three days missing her like crazy, and nothing had felt right until she walked over his threshold Saturday night. All he could think, from the moment she came back, was that he never wanted her to leave him again. Ever, for any reason. He wanted to be with her; he *needed* to be with her, because . . .

Because he loved her?

Because he loved her.

Though he thought that what he felt for Patience was the real thing had been flitting in and out of his consciousness for a while, it hadn't hit him full on until they had the argument about Ned and Anne's dinner party.

When Jace saw her walk to the closet to get her coat and heard her sniffling and hunting for her handkerchief, he knew he couldn't let her leave without telling her how much she mattered to him.

If she left, the fight would blow up into something

bigger than it really was, and he would never get the chance to tell her he was falling in love with her.

That was what he was trying to say—was *about* to say—when she cut in.

He had lost his nerve.

No, not just that.

He had seen something inscrutable in her eyes in the moment before she interrupted him. A frantic expression that could only be fear. Clearly, she had read his mind. She knew he was about to tell her he loved her, and for whatever reason, she didn't want him to say it. Either she wasn't ready or she didn't love him back or she was trying to spare him the tongue-tied soul-searching . . .

So he had swallowed the words.

Maybe it was better that way.

He realized later that he had been about to speak impulsively—that he hadn't really taken the time to truly consider whether what he felt really was love. For all he knew, he was simply infatuated with her.

After all, how did you know when you were in love with someone? Just because you wanted to be with them all the time, just because you were intensely attracted to someone didn't necessarily mean—

"Earth to Jace," Patience interrupted, tugging his sleeve.

He blinked, realizing they had arrived in Ned and Anne's candlelit formal dining room. The table was set with white linen, china, and crystal, and the sideboard was loaded with silver-covered platters.

"You're sitting there," Patience told him, gesturing at the chair next to the one she was about to pull out.

"Here, let me," Jace said, pulling out her chair for her.

"Thank you." She smiled up at him, sitting down.

"That's what I love about you, Jace. You're such a gentleman."

"So you're just with me for my manners? I knew you had an ulterior motive." He slid into the seat next to hers.

"I've got an ulterior motive, and it has nothing to do with proper behavior," she said in a low voice, letting her green eyes twinkle at him.

He grinned at her, wanting to lean over and kiss her.

*Then why don't you?* he asked himself. *Patience certainly would. If she wanted to kiss you, she would kiss you, no matter who was watching. She wouldn't think twice about it.*

But he couldn't do it. Spontaneity and public displays of affection just weren't his style.

"What's wrong, Jace?" Patience asked, her smile dimming.

"Nothing. What makes you think something's wrong?"

"You were just kidding around with me, and then you got this funny look on your face. As if something were wrong."

"Nothing's wrong," he repeated.

"Are you sure?"

"I'm sure," he said, and pretended to be fascinated with the sterling silver napkin ring in front of him.

He felt her eyes on him for a long time and was grateful when Ned tapped his glass with his fork and offered a toast.

"To friendship," Ned said, lifting his glass.

"To friendship." Jace clinked his goblet against Patience's.

"To friendship," she echoed, and met his gaze. She added in a low voice, "Friendship . . . and other things."

He smiled and nodded.

But he was wondering . . .
If they weren't friends . . .
And they weren't in love . . .
Just what, exactly, *were* they?


Six hours later, Patience lay awake staring at the ceiling in Jace's hushed bedroom as he slept peacefully beside her, his even breathing barely audible.

The least he could do was snore.

That way, she could wake him up, pretending he was keeping her awake. Then she could suggest that as long as they were both awake, they could have a little talk about their relationship.

But no, he slept silently. It figured.

*She* snored like a longshoreman.

She knew that because Jace had told her.

Luckily, he thought it was funny. He even said that he was surprised he didn't have a problem sleeping through it, because he usually had a problem sleeping through any kind of noise—the television, birds chirping. You name it; it kept him up.

But not her snoring.

Meanwhile, here she was, wide awake and restless, hours after they had made love and he had drifted off to dreamland as though he didn't have a care in the world.

She rolled over and snuggled against him.

He didn't stir.

She poked his back a little with her knee, wondering if she could accidentally-on-purpose jostle him awake.

He didn't stir.

Well, he'd told her that ever since they'd gotten together, he'd been sleeping more soundly than he ever had in his life.

Meanwhile, Patience, who had never had a problem

falling asleep, was no longer a stranger to tossing and turning.

Especially tonight.

She couldn't stop thinking about Ned and Anne's dinner party. It wasn't that anything earth-shattering had happened, because it had basically been uneventful. But there were so many little things, things that nagged at Patience's conscience long after Jace's tender lovemaking should have convinced her that everything was going to be all right.

Maybe she should have listened to him. Maybe they *should* have just stayed home and rented a movie.

That way, they wouldn't have had to listen to all those wisecracks about their relationship not lasting.

Sure, Henry and Bryan were jerks. And yes, they were just kidding around.

But their comments had hit a little too close to home.

The truth was, Patience didn't know if she and Jace would still be together at New Year's.

She didn't even know if they would still be together tomorrow.

It wasn't as if they had discussed it. It wasn't as if they were in a committed relationship. It wasn't as if they *loved* each other . . .

She flipped onto her stomach and bunched the pillow under her cheek, listening to Jace's even breathing.

*Love?*

Ha.

She had thought several times this past week that he might pick up where he had left off last Sunday night, but the only time he had mentioned the word *love* was when they were discussing the band Hole. Patience was a big fan, and Jace told her that even if he liked their music—which he didn't—he had no respect for the controversial lead singer, Courtney Love.

Which didn't surprise her.

Meanwhile, she kept waiting for him to turn to her with that look in his eyes that she'd glimpsed Sunday, kept praying that he would put into words how he felt about her—and that it would be the right three words.

Well, she hadn't exactly told him how she felt, either.

And the truth was, she honestly didn't know.

There were times when she thought she was falling in love with Jace.

But what about the times when they didn't get along? What about the fact that some things he did drove her absolutely crazy?

Like the way he wiped down the tile and shower doors after she took a shower in his bathroom. He said he didn't want to leave everything damp, explaining—almost apologetically—that he just had a thing about mildew.

Was he implying that she *liked* mildew?

Okay, of course he wasn't. But she sure didn't dislike it enough to blot away every water droplet every single time she took a shower. Even if she wanted to do it, she would never remember to do it. But Jace said he didn't mind doing it—that he actually did it automatically, without even thinking.

So why couldn't she just let him wipe down the damn shower doors with the damn towel after she took a shower?

Okay, she *did* let him do it. But every single time he did, she felt guilty about it.

As though he were making a point of proving that they just didn't have the same philosophy about housekeeping. As though he were making a point of reminding her that they didn't have the same philosophy about *anything*.

And maybe she did need that reminder. Because the way things were going lately, for the most part it was easy to forget that they were anything but meant for each other.

She was learning to get up earlier in the mornings; he was learning to hit the snooze alarm a couple of times. She had stopped salting her food before she tasted it; he had developed a penchant for cheese fries with ketchup and mustard.

Sometimes, it was almost as if they were more alike than different.

Almost as if the differences didn't matter.

Then reality would come crashing back in, the way it had tonight, and Patience would realize that it was hopeless. Whom were she and Jace trying to kid? They weren't going to be able to keep this thing going forever.

She sighed.

He stirred.

Rolled toward her.

"Jace," she said softly, swallowing over a sudden lump in her throat.

"Mmm . . ."

She snuggled against him. "Jace, hold me close. Please?"

He obliged, pulling her head onto his warm, solid chest, closing his strong arms around her.

She sighed.

"What's wrong?" he murmured drowsily.

"Nothing," she mumbled. "Bad dream."

*More like impossible dream*, she thought as he drifted easily back to sleep.

# Ten

"Jace, look . . . it's snowing!" Patience exclaimed as they emerged from a movie theater on Amsterdam Avenue late Sunday afternoon.

He grinned, watching her tilt her head back and open her mouth to catch a snowflake on her tongue. The frosty air swirled with fat white flakes, the wet, heavy kind that coated everything. Amazing. When they had gone into the theater almost three hours earlier, the sun had been shining brightly.

"Isn't it beautiful?" Patience asked, breathless and bouncing a little as they crossed the street and fell into step with the throngs of other pedestrians on the other side.

"Careful," he said, holding her hand. "The sidewalk is slippery."

"I know, it's sticking," she said blithely. "It hardly ever seems to snow like this here. Back home in New Hampshire, a foot or two is no big deal, but in New York, we're lucky if we get an inch. Beth said they're predicting a few inches, but I didn't think we'd get anything at all."

Jace knew by now that Beth was a secret Weather Channel addict. He also knew that she wore ridiculously expensive silk panties, that she had once eaten an entire one-pound box of Godiva chocolates in one sitting, and that she had every intention of landing a husband before her next birthday.

Patience talked about Beth a lot. Jace wondered how Beth would feel if she knew he was privy to her innermost secrets. Yet Patience was a fiercely loyal friend. She had insisted on keeping her standing brunch appointment with Beth today, even though, as Jace had pointed out, they had just seen each other last night at Ned and Anne's.

"That's why it's even more important for us to get together," Patience had said as he settled in on the couch with coffee and the *New York Times* and she bundled herself into a vintage men's overcoat for the trek to the midtown bistro where they were meeting. "We have a lot to talk about."

"You mean 'gossip about'?" Jace had asked, partly amused, partly annoyed at the realization that he might be among the gossip topics.

"Of course," Patience had said, throwing her arms around him and kissing him on the cheek. "I'll meet you at the movie theater at one."

"You'll be late," he had said.

And of course, she had been. But she only kept him waiting ten minutes this time. She was improving. They had missed the coming attractions, but not the opening credits.

Not that it had mattered to Jace either way this time. She had picked the movie, a subtitled art house period piece that didn't really appeal to him.

They had settled into a routine these past few weeks, taking turns picking movies, restaurants, even what kind of take-out cuisine to order. He had put up with some of her more bizarre choices, and to her credit, she had tolerated what she obviously considered mundane and predictable choices of his.

"Let's walk home through the park, Jace," Patience said, pretty much dancing along.

"The park? It's almost dark," he told her, glancing up at the stormy sky. "The park is dangerous after dark. Even you have to admit that."

"It won't be dark for another hour. We have plenty of time. Come on, Jace."

"Patience . . ."

"Jace, very few times in life are magical. This is one of them. It's Christmastime; it's snowing; it's the most exciting city in the world . . ." She let go of his hand and glided on the icy sidewalk, squealing, "Wheeee!"

"You're going to fall," he called after her, but he knew she wouldn't. Even if she did, she would just pick herself up—refusing assistance from him, of course—dust herself off, do it again.

"Come on, Jace . . . it's fun! It's like skating!"

He watched as oncoming pedestrians turned their heads to watch her. She slid past a group of teenagers, an elderly couple, a nanny clutching the hands of two young charges. He was amazed to see the teenagers—an ominous-looking bunch—break into grins, shaking their heads in amusement. The elderly couple smiled, too.

And he overheard one of the children asking the nanny why he couldn't skate on the sidewalk, too.

"Because it's dangerous," she was saying in a thick Jamaican accent. "You could fall and hurt yourself."

"But that lady is doing it."

"Well, that lady is silly," the nanny said sternly.

But Jace saw, as she passed him, that her eyes were twinkling.

He smiled. She was right. The lady certainly was silly. The lady was wonderful. And the lady belonged to him.

"Jace, come on," Patience called to him, and almost

lost her balance on the slick sidewalk. Her arms whirled like propellers at her side, and he rushed forward to catch her.

She regained her balance before he reached her. He was the one sprawled on the sidewalk.

"Jace, are you all right?" she asked, above him.

"I'm fine," he grunted.

"I take it back. You'd better stick to walking," she said with a giggle.

"I wasn't gliding. You were falling. I was trying to catch you."

"I didn't need you to catch me. And I didn't fall."

"No kidding," he grumbled, getting back to his feet and rubbing his butt.

"There's the park entrance," she said, gesturing across the street. "And the light is green." She pulled him along and they stepped off the curb as the white Walk sign became a flashing orange Don't Walk sign.

He could tell her it was dangerous to cross when the sign was flashing.

He could tell her he didn't want to walk through the park so close to dusk.

Or he could tell her he loved her.

That, he realized, was what he wanted to do. He wanted to pull her into his arms right here, right now, in the middle of Central Park West, with traffic honking and snow falling and people watching, and he wanted to tell her he loved her.

Because right here, right now, he was as close to being certain about that as he had ever been. *But not one hundred percent,* a little voice intruded. No. Not one hundred percent.

"Hey, let's sing Christmas carols, Jace," Patience said as they reached the park entrance. "Wait . . . you're Jewish. Are there any Hanukkah carols?"

He had to laugh at her eager, yet earnest expression.

"Let's sing 'Jingle Bells,' " he told her, shoving aside his inner turmoil.

Once again, the moment had been lost. Once again, he couldn't bring himself to say the words he was ninety-nine-point-nine percent certain were true.

When he opened his mouth, instead of I *love you,* what came out was a semimelodic, "Oh what fun it is to ride . . ."

A bum walking along in front of them joined in. So did a giggly group of middle school girls. And a family carrying ice skates. Jace listened in wonder as Patience Magee led them into an off-key "Deck the Halls," watched her *fa-la-la-la-la-ing* at the top of her lungs.

She was right, he thought as pure, giddy happiness took hold in his gut—or someplace a few inches above and to the left.

He sang out with all his heart. And it *was* magical. *She* was magical.

Right here, right now, all was right in the world. And he boldly dared believe it could last.

"Hey, what do you want for Christmas?"

Startled, Patience looked at Jace. 'The Odd Couple' had just gone to a commercial and she had almost started to doze on the couch, cozily wrapped in his arms.

"What do I want for Christmas?" she repeated.

"I want it to be something special," he told her. "But also, something you need."

*All I need is you,* she thought blissfully.

She smiled. "If you want it to be special, then it has to be a surprise."

"But I have no idea what to get you."

"Come on, Jace," she said, trying to ignore a flicker of disappointment that he hadn't already bought her the perfect gift—and the fact that she had no idea what to get him, either. "Use your imagination. I'm sure you can come up with something."

"Yeah, but at least give me a hint. Do you want something to wear? Or a new VCR?"

Her VCR *was* broken. But she had spent so little time at her apartment lately that it didn't really seem to matter.

Lately, she simply dashed down there on her lunch hours or after work to feed Rufus, who clearly resented the amount of time she was spending at Jace's place. She couldn't help feeling guilty about the reproachful expression in his amber feline eyes whenever she popped in and out.

Yet what was the alternative? She had tried explaining to Rufus that she couldn't stand spending nights apart from Jace; that his king-sized bed with the pillow-top mattress and down comforter was far more comfortable than her pull-out futon.

Rufus, clearly feeling spurned, gave her the silent treatment.

She tried promising him that she would bring him to Jace's one of these days, so that the three of them could spend some time together. He seemed to perk up a bit at that. He even rubbed against her legs, purring, when she left that day.

But Jace had flatly vetoed that idea, saying his co-op board absolutely didn't allow pets in the building. Being a fine, upstanding citizen, he wasn't the least bit amused by Patience's half serious suggestion that she wheel Rufus in disguised as a baby in a carriage.

"Not a new VCR," she told him now. "I'll get one eventually."

"You sure?"

"Jace, trust me, there is nothing romantic about consumer electronics."

He pulled her closer. "So you want something romantic?" he murmured, his mouth close to her ear.

"It would be nice."

"Jewelry?"

She considered that. Jewelry was romantic.

Except . . .

Jace would probably get her a string of pearls or diamond-stud earrings.

Not that there was anything wrong with a string of pearls or diamond-stud earrings, but . . .

Well, her taste ran more to silver bangles and ear cuffs. And, call her intuitive, but she just didn't think that was the kind of jewelry Mr. Traditional had in mind.

"I was thinking maybe a watch," he said. "Yours is never working right."

"It works fine," she told him, adding sweetly, "I just tell you it's not working right when I'm late, so that you won't hold it against me."

"I see," he said good-naturedly. "Okay, then, since you have a perfectly good watch that you'd just prefer not to consult, what would you like instead?"

"I'm not that crazy about jewelry, actually," she told him.

"What should I get you then?"

"I can't tell you. You're supposed to decide."

She was doing her best to keep exasperation from creeping into her voice, but it wasn't easy. Didn't he get it? You weren't supposed to *discuss* gift-giving, the way you discussed whether you were in the mood for Chinese or pizza. But practical-minded Jace apparently hadn't considered just buying her something on a whim. He had to plan in advance, to interview her on her preferences, to carefully deliberate before making his choice.

*Yeah, well . . . surprise, surprise.*

She noticed that 'The Odd Couple' had returned to the screen.

"Shh, I love this part," she cut in when he started to say something else about a gift.

The truth was, she had been wondering what to get him, too.

Jace was the quintessential man who had everything, and she had yet to come up with a suitable gift, despite several recent shopping excursions for that very purpose. In fact, she had discussed her dilemma with Beth at brunch earlier, vetoing Beth's suggestions of cologne (not a big enough gift), a cashmere robe (not within her budget), and a sweater (too boring). Jewelry was also out—she couldn't afford the kind that would suit him.

"Well, gee, why don't you just sell your hair to buy him a chain for his gold pocket watch?" Beth had finally suggested.

"Ooh, I'm impressed," Patience had said. "A reference to O. Henry."

"And I wasn't even an English major like *some* people who consider themselves literary intellects."

"Hey, my literary intellect days are over. I work at *She* magazine, remember?"

But despite their banter, her problem was a serious one. As Patience had told Beth, the trouble with a mutual exchange was that you were vulnerable to being seen by the other person as too cheap—which was humiliating—or too serious about the relationship—even more humiliating.

Beth had been wholly sympathetic.

Like any woman, she understood that the first gift exchange in a newly established relationship was highly significant. With any luck, one of you would have a birthday before the holidays arrived—preferably the female. That way, the male would have to buy the first gift, setting the tone for future gift-giving. For example, if he got you a paperback book, you would know not to buy him a small plane for *his* birthday.

Patience zoomed back to the present and tried to focus her attention on Tony Randall and Jack Klugman in a horse suit. But she was too distracted by the upcoming holidays to follow even this, the hilarious *Let's Make a Deal* episode.

Getting Jace a present wasn't the extent of her dilemma. There was something else, something even more pressing. She was planning to wait until the next commercial to bring it up, using the well-rehearsed speech she had devised this morning in the shower.

But she suddenly heard herself blurt out, "Jace, want to come to New Hampshire?" He snapped his attention from the TV screen to her face, his eyes searching. "Sure," he said slowly, looking vaguely confused. "Sometime. That would be fun."

"I mean, for Christmas."

He appeared startled. "Oh."

Seized by a sudden, desperate fear of rejection, she plunged on, telling him how her parents decked the farmhouse from top to bottom in evergreen boughs and lights, how her mother's homemade gingerbread scented the air, how there was ice skating on the pond behind the house and tobogganing on the steep slopes above it.

She even told him, breathlessly, that her family wasn't particularly religious so he wouldn't feel uncomfortable, that they did go to the candlelight midnight service on Christmas Eve, but nobody would think anything of it if he didn't come along—or maybe he would want to come along because the choir singing was really beautiful and nobody would ever realize he was Jewish anyway . . .

"Patience," he cut in the first time she paused to regroup, "I'm sure it's wonderful. It sounds great, and I would love to be there with you. But I'm planning on going home to Brooklyn on Christmas."

"But you're Jewish," she protested, as if he had somehow overlooked that relevant fact. "You don't celebrate Christmas . . . do you?" she added, suddenly filled with uncertainty. This wasn't going the way she had planned.

Not that she had planned for much longer than it took her to lather, rinse, and repeat. She probably should have given it more thought.

"No," Jace said, "but we celebrate Hanukkah."

"I know, but . . . doesn't it last eight days?"

He nodded. "One of them falls on Christmas this year. Your holiday and mine don't always coincide. Sometimes Hanukkah is earlier in the month, sometimes in the middle of December, but this year—"

"But, Jace," she interrupted, unable to believe he couldn't see the simple solution, "You can go home to Brooklyn to celebrate Hanukkah either before or after you come to New Hampshire with me. I wasn't planning on staying there more than a few days. I have to get back to work—I don't have any more vacation time left."

"Don't remind me," he said, rolling his eyes.

His tone was joking, but her defenses went up.

She pulled herself out of his embrace, took a brief moment to check her temper, and said reasonably, "I just don't see why you have to specifically celebrate Hanukkah with your family on Christmas Eve and Christmas Day when it lasts for eight days and nights."

"Because that's when we're doing it this year. Everybody is off from work. My brother-in-law's store is closed. It's when we're getting together. And I was hoping you would be able to come," he added mildly.

"You were hoping I would be able to come?" She bit her lower lip, doing her best to fight back sarcasm before asking, "When were you going to talk to me about it?"

He seemed to hesitate. "I just thought of it tonight. While we were eating dinner. When we were talking about different foods, and you said you had never tasted homemade potato pancakes."

She remembered. He had said they were called *latkes,* and that his father made them every year for Hanukkah, peeling and grating umpteen pounds of potatoes by hand. He had told her that the pancakes were eaten with sour cream and Bubbe's still-warm homemade applesauce.

"Come with me to Brooklyn, Patience," he said, reaching out and clasping her fingers in his own. "You've never celebrated Hanukkah before. You'd love it."

"Come with me to New Hampshire, Jace. You've never celebrated Christmas before," she returned. "You'd love it."

He stared at her for a minute.

Her heart was racing. She had a sick feeling inside.

"I can't," he said, and shook his head.

"No. You *can,* but you *won't.*"

"I can't," he repeated, dropping her hand. "I've already made my plans."

"And I've already made mine."

"But you were just in New Hampshire for Thanksgiving."

"And you were just in Brooklyn for Thanksgiving, too. Besides, you can go whenever you feel like it." She hated herself for being so petty, but she was unable to help it. "You're only twenty minutes away from home, Jace."

"That doesn't mean it isn't important to me to celebrate holidays with my family." He rose and paced across the room, then turned to face her. "Look, all I did was invite you to spend Hanukkah with me. I didn't mean to start a huge argument."

"Well, I asked you to come with me for Christmas before you turned the tables and asked me, and then made it into this huge thing," she told him, folding her arms across her chest.

"*I* made it into a huge thing?" he echoed. "That's completely untrue. You were the one who—"

"No, I wasn't!"

"Patience, don't pin this one on me. All I did was say that I already had plans."

"That's not 'all' you did, Jace." She glared at him. "You completely refused to compromise.

"Compromise? How can I possibly compromise? I can't be in two places at once."

"No, but your holiday lasts eight days. Mine lasts two. You're being unreasonable."

"*You're* being unreasonable," he snapped, striding over to stand angrily above her.

Was she? Maybe. But she couldn't help it. This wasn't just about the holiday. It went much, much deeper.

She stood and faced him, looking him squarely in the eye. "I already have my plane ticket to New Hampshire—"

"That's what you said when I asked you about Thanksgiving."

"So? It was true then, too. Is it 'unreasonable' for me not to want to waste hundreds of nonrefundable dollars? You, of all people, should understand the value of money. You're the financial expert, remember?"

She saw the muscles working in his neck. She realized it was taking every ounce of self-control he possessed for him to say, without shouting, "Let's just drop it."

She didn't want to drop it. She wanted to have it out. She wanted to vent every frustration that had been nagging at her for months. She wanted to have this screaming fight, and then she wanted to hear him utter the words that would mean it didn't matter—that even though they were at each other's throats, even though their relationship wasn't perfect, everything was okay, because he loved her, and he wasn't going anywhere. They could work it out.

But . . .

He hadn't said that.

"Fine," she agreed with a shrug. "Let's drop it. We can discuss it another time."

"There's nothing to discuss," he said, his eyes flaring dangerously.

"Yes, there is, Jace. We can discuss a compromise about the holidays."

"I told you that I can't—"

"And I'm telling you you're wrong. There *is* a way to compromise. I will go with you to Brooklyn to celebrate Hanukkah and eat latkes and light candles on one or two—or even six—nights of Hanukkah. You can come with me to New Hampshire for Christmas Eve and Christmas Day. Then we'll both be happy."

"I won't be happy. I just told you, my family is celebrating Hanukkah on Christmas Eve and Christmas Day!"

"Don't shout at me!"

"I wasn't shouting," he said, lowering his voice.

"Yes, you were."

"Look," he said, suddenly sounding weary, "this is stupid. It's late. We're both tired. Let's just forget about this and go to bed. Okay?"

"Fine. But I'm going to bed in my own apartment," she said, starting toward the closet.

He caught her shoulders. "It's late. Don't go."

"Don't worry. I'll take a cab instead of the subway," she said sarcastically. "I wouldn't want to get mugged and give you the satisfaction of saying 'I told you so.' "

"Patience, stop. I don't want to do this with you." He turned her around. "Look at me."

She stared stubbornly at the middle of his sweat-shirted chest.

"Look at me," he repeated, and tilted her chin upward with his hand.

She looked at him, thinking maybe this was it. Maybe he was going to tell her now . . .

But the expression in his eyes wasn't exactly tender and loving.

She told herself not to falter. Not to give in. He wanted her to tell him that everything was okay, that it was no big deal if she celebrated her holiday with her family and he celebrated his holiday with his family.

But it was a big deal. It was a huge deal.

Suddenly, everything—namely her future with Jace—depended on whether they were going to spend the holidays together.

He turned off the television. They took turns in the bathroom. Silently, they went to the bedroom and climbed into bed. He turned out the light.

"Good night," he said, after a moment.

"Good night," she answered politely.

The minutes ticked by. She lay stiffly awake on her side, knowing that he was awake on his, too.

They had never gone to bed without making love.

Nor had they ever gone to bed angry.

She tried telling herself that this issue wasn't as important as it seemed right now. That it would blow over. That they would even laugh about it in the morning.

But when morning came, she wasn't laughing.

What she wanted to do was cry.

She had spent the night thinking about what had happened, and what it meant. She had realized what she had to do when the sun came up. For once, she was going to be rational. She was going to act according to what her head told her, and not according to her heart. She was going to use common sense, and she was going to face the undeniable truth.

She got up before the alarm went off, without having slept a wink. She left Jace lying silently in bed, turned away from her. She was uncertain whether he had slept or not.

Armed with her well-thought-out plan, and determined to avoid looking at or talking to Jace, lest she impulsively change her mind, she went directly into the bathroom and took a shower.

When she was finished, she wiped down the tile and the shower doors with a towel, careful to blot every stray water droplet.

"Morning," Jace mumbled when he passed her on his way into the bathroom as she was coming out.

"Morning," she replied, reminding herself to stay detached.

She couldn't waver. For once, she had a plan, and she was going to stick to it.

She waited until she heard him running the water for his shower.

Then she grabbed a couple of the paper shopping bags he kept neatly folded in his pantry cupboard. She crammed them with every last one of her possessions that had found its way over to Jace's apartment. She took her coat from the closet and swallowed hard over the lump that had risen in her throat.

The shower was still running when she walked out the door.

Jace emerged from the steamy bathroom, a towel wrapped around his waist. Normally he dried off and put on a robe before returning to the bedroom, but today, he was in a hurry.

He wanted to tell Patience about the decision he had made while he was in the shower.

And he wanted to do it before he took the time to think about it, in case he changed his mind.

For once, he was going to be impulsive.

For once, he was going to act directly from his heart.

And his heart had told him, as he scrubbed his elbows, that he should give in and spend Christmas with her in New Hampshire.

She was right. He could celebrate Hanukkah with his family another time.

Granted, the big get-together with all the relatives was going to take place on the twenty-fifth; but as much as he always looked forward to it, he knew that it wouldn't kill him to miss it. If he couldn't be there that day, his father would make latkes and Bubbe would make applesauce and his mother would give him his gifts on a different day.

If only Patience hadn't made him so angry with her attitude last night, he would have conceded then.

But there was something about the way she had just assumed that it would be so easy for him to give in, to change *his* plans . . .

Well, he just couldn't let himself do it.

Not then.

Not when she was so unwilling to change hers.

Now, after spending a sleepless night in a chilly bed,

and realizing just how serious an issue this was, he knew he had to do something. She hadn't even looked his way when he'd greeted her on his way into the bathroom.

So. If it was the only way to save their relationship, then, despite his misgivings, he was going to tell her he would come with her to New Hampshire.

He smiled to himself, looking forward to it already. Not just to the trip itself—he had always been a little wistful about missing out on Christmas, so he had to admit he was enthusiastic about experiencing it—but mostly, he was looking forward to telling her.

He pictured her face lighting up, and wondered if they had time to tumble back into bed for a romantic make-up session before they both had to hurry off to work.

"Patience," he said, stepping into the bedroom, "I've got news for you."

He paused just inside the door, looking around.

She wasn't here.

She must be in the other room.

But . . .

Everything was just as he had left it here in the bedroom. The bed was still rumpled, the shades still closed.

But something was different.

Belatedly, he remembered something.

The shower walls and doors had been dry when he'd gone in. She had actually taken the time to wipe them down.

He knew, before he had opened the empty dresser drawer he had given her, before he had walked through the rest of the empty apartment, that she was gone, and so were her things.

And he knew what it meant.

She wasn't coming back.

# Eleven

"I'm not going to mince any words," Camisha Thompson said, steepling her fingers and eying Patience across her desk. "Something is up with you, Ms. Magee, and I want you to tell me what it is, because it's severely affecting your job performance. You've been moping around the office for weeks."

"I'm really sorry, Camisha," Patience said glumly. When her boss had summoned her into her office, she had thought she was about to get a holiday bonus. Instead, she'd been nabbed. What a pleasant surprise.

"What's going on, Patience? You've been miserable. And it shows in this article for the July issue." She slid the manuscript across her desk.

Patience didn't pick it up. She knew which one it was without looking at the title.

"Your assignment, if I recall, was to do a piece on—"

"I know, I know," Patience interrupted. "It was supposed to be 'Ten Ways To Show Him Fourth of July Fireworks Without Leaving the Bedroom.'"

"Instead, I get one called . . ." Camisha turned the manuscript toward her and read the title, "'Men— Who Needs 'Em?'"

"Sorry," Patience said, taking a candy cane from the basketful on Camisha's desk. "I guess I just haven't been in a very romantic mood."

"I guess not," Camisha said, flashing a sympathetic smile. "Man trouble?"

"More or less. I mean, there *is* no man—but there *was* . . . which is the trouble."

"Nasty breakup?"

Patience unwrapped the candy cane and bit off the hook, crunching dismally. "I don't think 'nasty' is the right word. We had a fight; I walked out, and he never called. That was just . . . the end. Except . . . somehow I didn't think it really would be."

"You were the one who walked out? And you haven't called him, either?"

She shook her head and exhaled her pepperminty breath heavily. "I can't. It's better this way. We just weren't suited for each other. We were too different."

Camisha tilted her head thoughtfully. "Sometimes opposites—"

"Attract," Patience cut in. "I know. Sorry to interrupt," she added, "but believe me, I've heard it all before."

She launched into her woeful tale, spilling her guts to Camisha about Jace. She told her everything that had happened, aware that she wasn't exactly being professional, but needing to purge her sorrowful soul on a sympathetic ear.

"Do you mind if I tell you something about relationships, Patience?" Camisha asked when she had finished her account—as well as most of the candy canes.

Patience wanted to tell her that she'd really rather not hear it, whatever it was, but Camisha *was* the boss here. Besides, she had been happily married for years. Maybe she really did have some new insight that would make Patience feel better. Not that belated advice could change things now. Jace was gone. It was over. What she had to do was accept that and move on.

"Relationships don't come easy," Camisha told her.

"You have to work at them every minute. My husband and I clicked from the moment we met—believe me, we thought we had *everything* in common—but, Patience, nobody has everything in common. No relationship is perfect. You can't expect to mesh your life with another person's life and not run into some bumps along the way."

"These weren't exactly 'bumps,' Camisha. Our problems made the potholes on lower Broadway look like hairline cracks."

"Ever hear of the saying that love conquers all?"

"Ever hear of the words 'I love you'?" Patience returned. "Well, guess what? *I haven't,*" she said significantly, reaching for the last candy cane in the basket.

"He never said he loves you? Did you say it to him?"

"No, but . . ." She took a deep breath. "I wasn't ever sure whether I loved him. I kept wondering how I could love somebody who had the ability to make me feel so bad."

"Patience, *only* the people you love most in this world are capable of tangling your emotions and making you feel truly terrible," Camisha said in a how-could-you-possibly-not-have-known-that tone. "People who don't matter—well, they just don't matter. Besides—how long did you say you were together?"

"About six weeks."

"Six weeks? After six weeks, my husband hadn't even come right out and said he liked me—even though I was pretty certain at that point that I loved him."

"When were you a hundred percent certain?"

Camisha smiled, a faraway look in her eyes. "When he got down on his knee and he told me he loved me and asked me to marry him. That was when everything fell into place."

Patience nodded, crumpling the last empty cellophane candy cane wrapper and shoving it into her pocket. "Well, your story had a happy ending, Camisha. You are incredibly blessed, and I swear I don't resent you—well, maybe I do a little. But not in an evil way."

Camisha grinned.

Patience went on, "But Jace and I can't get married. He doesn't love me. The relationship is totally over, and I'm going to figure out how to deal with it—but I promise I won't let it intrude on my work ever again. So I'll do the fireworks story and—"

"It's okay," Camisha cut in. "I kind of liked the 'Men—Who Needs 'Em?' piece. It had a certain bite to it. I'm going to run it in the July issue."

"You are?" Patience brightened.

Camisha nodded. "And listen, Patience, why don't you take tomorrow off? It's the day before we break for the Christmas holiday anyway, and I think you could use some time."

"But I don't have any more sick days or vacation days to use."

"I know. This is just between you and me. I won't even mark it on your time sheet for personnel. Consider it a Christmas gift from me."

"But you already gave me that Saks gift certificate," Patience protested. And she had already spent it on a sexy black satin-and-lace nightie that Jace would never see, damn it.

"Well, this is another gift. One you really deserve— and need. Maybe you'll use the day to track down Jace."

"Do I have to?" Patience asked. "Because if that's the condition, then I'd better come to work instead. As I said, Jace and I are finished."

"Use the day however you like, Patience," Camisha said, coming around from behind the desk and giving her a squeeze. "But I have a funny feeling you and Jace aren't quite over."

For such a wise woman, Camisha didn't always know what she was talking about, Patience thought as she walked out of the office. She went straight to her desk and phoned the airline to see if she could fly to New Hampshire a day earlier.

The sooner she got out of New York—with its perpetual reminders of Jace—the better.

"Talked to Patience lately?" Ned asked Jace as they waited for their racquetball court.

"Patience? No, not lately," Jace said as nonchalantly as possible.

"No?"

Jace shook his head and checked his watch. Five minutes to seven. The court wouldn't open up until seven. He was stuck, for now, with Ned and his questions, and assumed that the seemingly casual "No?" hadn't been the last of them. He was right.

"Is something going on with you two?" Ned wanted to know.

"Basically, nothing's going on with us anymore," Jace said squarely, giving his racquet a practice swing.

"Look, I actually knew that," Ned said, looking uncomfortable.

"You knew?" Jace stopped swinging. "How'd you know?"

"Patience mentioned it to Beth, and Beth told Anne. Anne told me to ask you about it when I mentioned to her that we were playing racquetball this morning."

"And being a dutiful husband . . ."

"Hey, I'm not prying for gossip, Jace. We just want to make sure everything's okay."

"If you mean am I okay with the breakup, then the answer is yes," Jace lied.

There were a few awkward moments of silence. Both Jace and Ned swung their racquets.

"What else did Beth tell Anne Patience said?" Jace finally had to ask.

"That you had a big blowup about where to spend the holidays. Wasn't that it?"

"That was it . . . for the most part."

Ned nodded and bent over to untie and retie his shoelace.

Jace wished he would ask about the part that had nothing to do with the holidays. The part that had everything to do with the fact that when push came to shove, he and Patience just couldn't make their relationship work, no matter how much they wanted it to.

Or rather, *he* had wanted it to.

*She*, on the other hand, had seemed to be doing everything in her power to sabotage it.

But Ned didn't ask, and Jace didn't tell. Guys just weren't comfortable talking about this kind of thing—especially with other guys.

Which was probably why, when Ned straightened and his eyes met Jace's, Jace quickly bent to untie and retie his own shoe.

When he stood up, Ned started talking about a case he was trying. Grateful, Jace did his best to listen. But his mind was on Patience. And the fact that tomorrow was Christmas Eve. They would be spending it apart. In fact, they would be spending the rest of their lives apart.

Well, it was better this way. It really was.

Sooner or later, maybe he would actually start believing that.

\* \* \*

"Surprise!" Patience called, stepping into the warm, fragrant country kitchen.

Her mother looked up, startled, from the box she was wrapping at the kitchen table. Her blond hair was pulled back into a smooth ponytail, and lengths of curling ribbon were draped around her neck. "Patience! You're home!"

"Yup. Merry Christmas!" She set her bulging duffel bag on the floor and stomped the snow from her boots, then found herself enveloped in her mother's arms. She fought back a sudden lump in her throat at how good it felt to be hugged.

*Oh, Mommy, I've been hurting,* she wanted to say.

"What are you doing here? We weren't expecting you until tomorrow."

"I caught an earlier flight," Patience said, dragging her mind away from the ever-present Jace. "My boss gave me an extra day off."

She looked around the kitchen. The counter was piled with round, colorful canisters that she knew were filled with decorated cookies. A tray of fudge cooled on a rack. The air was scented with chocolate and peppermint and, yes, gingerbread. The windowpanes above the sink were frosted over, and Bing Crosby's static-tinged voice sang "White Christmas" on the radio.

Home. She was home. *This* was home. Not—

*No,* she warned herself, *don't think about Jace. It's time to be happy.*

Moments later, the kitchen was filled with family. Dad in his plaid flannel shirt, his balding head concealed beneath the red-and-white fleece Santa hat he liked to wear around the house at Christmas. Brunette Hope looking rounder than she had at Thanksgiving, her pregnant belly protruding from her bright green maternity sweater. Her husband Jermaine, the proud papa-to-be, telling Patience that they'd had a sonagram and the baby would be a girl. Blond Faith, an elementary school teacher, decked out in a red Santa sweatshirt and a plastic Rudolph pin whose nose lit up when you tugged a little string. Her husband Gary pulling her back into the archway that led to the dining room and pointing slyly at the mistletoe overhead.

*Home,* Patience thought again, looking around at the faces she loved best in the world.

But she couldn't help feeling that someone was missing.

*"Baruch Atah Adonai . . ."*

Jace closed his eyes, listening as his father, holding the flickering *shamash* over the polished brass menorah, intoned the familiar Hebrew blessing. When the candles were lit, Bubbe began singing "Ma'oz Tzur," and the rest of the family joined in. Tonight it was just Lena, Paul, and the boys. Tomorrow, the house would be spilling over with aunts, uncles, and cousins. The children would gather on the floor to spin the dreidel, and later they would line up in front of Bubbe to collect their Hanukkah *gelt.*

Jace swallowed hard over a sudden lump in his throat as he looked across the table at his nephews. Their faces glowed and their eyes sparkled in the flickering candlelight as they stood on chairs on either side of his father, wearing their little yarmulkes.

When you were a child, everything was so simple. So joyous.

When you were a grown man, and your heart was breaking, there wasn't joy even in this season of celebration.

"Jason," Bubbe said, having finished the song, "come and help me bring in the platters."

"I'll help you, Ma," his mother said, starting to rise.

"No," Bubbe said firmly, "Jason will help me."

Jace obediently followed her to the kitchen, where an oval platter sat on top of the stove, heaped with just-fried, still-steaming golden latkes. He started to lift it.

"Wait," Bubbe said, touching his arm. "Not yet. First, we'll talk."

"We'll *talk*? About what?"

"About Patience Magee."

He glowered, picking up the platter. "What about her?"

"You're in love with her, Jason. And she isn't here. Why not?"

He almost dropped the platter. Bubbe took it out of his hands and set it firmly back onto the stove.

"I'm not in love with her, Bubbe," he protested, finding his voice. "How many times have I told you, we're just friends?"

"Plenty of times. But you aren't happy when I've seen you lately, Jason. And you were the happiest you've ever been the day you brought her here. I'm a smart old woman. I see things. I know things. You're in love with her. Admit it."

He looked at Bubbe, lifting his chin stubbornly.

She waited, her wrinkled old face set just as stubbornly.

And he realized that Bubbe really *was* a wise old woman.

"I'm in love with her, Bubbe. My God. You're right. I'm in love with her."

Bubbe nodded, satisfied. "Where is she?"

"In New Hampshire, with her family."

"Call her. Tell her."

"No." He wiped at his eyes with the sleeve of his

cashmere sweater. "I can't tell her over the phone. She probably won't even take my call."

"So go to New Hampshire," Bubbe said matter-of-factly.

As though he could just go to New Hampshire. Just like that. "Now?"

"News like this should wait?"

"But I can't," Jace protested. "It's Christmas Eve. I'll never get a flight."

"So you'll drive. It's New Hampshire, not Alaska."

"I'll drive to New Hampshire on the spur of the moment," he said incredulously, shaking his head—partly in wonder at what seemed like a preposterous—yet insanely perfect—whim. "On Christmas Eve. To tell Patience Magee I'm in love with her."

It was completely rash and impetuous to even consider doing something like that.

It was . . .

It was . . .

It was exactly the kind of thing Patience would do.


The bitter New England wind rattled the stained-glass windows of the small clapboard church. A winter storm had blown in late this afternoon, and the snow wasn't predicted to stop until morning.

Patience, clutching a lit white candle that dripped wax onto the cardboard collar at the base, listened as the choir sing "Silent Night." Tears were streaming down her face.

She always cried when they sang "Silent Night" at the midnight service.

But that wasn't entirely why she was crying at the moment.

Actually, it was what had set her off. A lump had promptly risen into her throat as she listened to the choir and gazed around at the beauty of the church. It was lit only by the candles held by the congregation, the white lights on the Christmas tree beside the pulpit, and the single spotlight shining down on the manger scene on the altar.

*Jace has never seen anything like this,* she thought, and that was when the tears spilled over. She longed to have Jace beside her.

She glanced at the row of faces in her pew—at her parents, Hope and Jermaine, and Faith and Gary. They were so serene, so contented, so sure of where they belonged. She had always thought she knew where she belonged, too. Here, with them. Now she wasn't so sure.

"Slee-eep in heavenly peace," the choir sang.

*Yeah, right.*

Patience hadn't slept in heavenly peace in weeks. She spent her restless nights thinking about Jace, wondering what she could have done to make things different. To make him love her.

*I love him,* she realized, reaching into her pocket for the handkerchief her mother had embroidered with holly leaves and berries. She wiped at her eyes, then blew her nose.

*I love Jace Hoffman . . . and he doesn't love me.*

If she had told him she loved him, would that have mattered? If she had told him she loved him, would he be standing beside her right now, instead of in Brooklyn with his family?

Or would she be there, in Brooklyn, with him?

*If you were there, you couldn't be here,* she reminded herself. *You would miss seeing the church decorated for Christmas and hearing "Silent Night" and going home to have omelets and eggnog before bed . . .*

But even those traditions couldn't fill the hollow

place in her soul. They weren't enough to make up for Jace not being at her side.

Nothing would ever make up for that.

Nothing, the rest of her life, would ever feel right again without him.

Nothing would ever make the hurt go away.

*I've got to tell him,* she told herself urgently. *I've got to tell him that I love him.*

And in that moment of truth, she wanted, more than anything, to rush out of the church and drive through the blinding snow all the way back to New York.

But that, she realized, would be dangerous. She'd have to wait till the weather cleared.

*But I don't want to wait,* she told herself. *I want to tell him now. This minute.*

She thought about what Jace would say. He would say, *"Patience, Patience."*

Maybe it was time she learned to listen. Not just to the things he had said . . .

But also, she realized, to the things she hadn't given him a chance to say.


Jace pulled his father's Buick into the newly plowed winding tree-lined lane of a driveway, checking the wrought-iron number hanging from the evergreen-and-red-ribbon-wrapped fence post once again.

This was the address Anne had given him when he'd tracked her down at Ned's parents' house in Newport last night.

"Are you going up there tonight, Jace?" she had asked in disbelief "I heard it's snowing like crazy north of here. Be careful."

"I will," he had said impatiently. And, tempted as

he was to speed through the blizzardlike conditions in his haste to reach Patience, he *had* been careful.

So careful that he had reduced his speed to roughly ten miles an hour and followed a plodding snowplow part of the way—and spent another few hours at a roadside rest stop when the state police temporarily closed the highway.

It had taken him all night to get here. It had stopped snowing somewhere around Worcester after daybreak. Now the sun shone brightly in a dazzling blue sky, and the world was white and frozen. *Magical*, Patience would call this frigid Christmas morning, he thought, steering carefully around a bend in the drive.

The farmhouse came into view, looking much as she had described it to him. It was white, with green shutters and a wide, spindled porch bedecked with greens and red bows. The chimney puffed wisps into the frosty air, and the front door was hung with the biggest wreath he had ever seen. In the picture window was a Christmas tree strung with colored lights that were illuminated at this early hour. Good. That meant somebody was awake.

He breathed deeply of mountain air tinged with wood smoke and evergreen as he stepped out of the car. His Gucci loafers disappeared into knee-high snowdrifts.

*Who cares?* he thought, anxiously plodding toward the porch. He'd left his coat in the car in his haste to get to the door, and the icy winter air seemed to blow right through him. He shivered and patted the back pocket of his corduroys to make sure it was still there—the gift he had brought to give to Patience, if she would accept it.

He held the ice-encrusted railing and edged his way up the steps. Somebody had already shoveled them and sprinkled them with rock salt. He could hear

Christmas carols playing inside even before he opened the storm door and knocked on the inner door.

As soon as he saw her, he was going to sweep her into his arms. He was going to tell her, right away, that he loved her, before she could get a word in. He was going to reach into his pocket and get down on his knee and—

A man in a Santa hat threw the door open. Behind him were five curious faces—three of them females whose pretty faces bore a resemblance to Patience's. But she wasn't among them.

"Let me guess. Jace Hoffman," the man said finally, a bemused expression in his green eyes that were an exact replica of Patience's. "Come in. You must be frozen out there."

"Is Patience here?" Jace managed to ask, his teeth chattering violently.

"Funny you should ask," her father said, rubbing his chin.

"Bubbe! I'm so glad you're the one who answered the door," Patience said, wiping her boots on the mat on the stoop as the yellow cab pulled away from the curb. "Happy Hanukkah."

"And Merry Christmas to you," Bubbe replied—looking a bit dazed, Patience noted. Maybe she wasn't a morning person.

"Um . . . can I come in?" Patience asked uncertainly, thrown off kilter by the strange expression in Bubbe's wrinkle-lined eyes. "I really need to talk to Jace."

"Is that so?" Bubbe held the door open wide.

"Is everyone else still sleeping?"

"Everyone is sleeping," Bubbe replied. "But Jace—"

"You mean he's up?"

"No, he's—"

"I smell coffee," Patience said, sniffing the air. "Do you mind if I have a cup while I wait?"

"How did you get here?" Bubbe asked, leading the way down the hall to the kitchen. An old-fashioned silver percolator sat on the counter, giving off a tantalizing aroma. A loaf of challah bread steamed on the counter in a pan that Bubbe had obviously just removed from the oven.

"I flew," Patience said, taking a seat at the table. "I got the first flight out this morning."

"You were in a hurry to surprise Jason, eh?" With a gleam in her eye, Bubbe set a steaming mug of coffee in front of Patience. "Cream and sugar?"

"Both," Patience said, and helped herself to a macaroon from the plateful on the table. There was something about Bubbe's expression—it was as if she were enjoying her own private little joke. Patience said around a mouthful of sweet, chewy coconut, "Yes, I was in a hurry. I mean, I'm in a hurry a lot, but this time, it was—well, can I tell you a secret, Bubbe?"

"Of course." The old woman's eyes twinkled down at her as she handed over the sugar bowl and a carton of cream.

"I'm in love with your grandson. And I'm going to tell him that, the minute he wakes up."

"That's wonderful news!" Bubbe said, giving her a squeeze.

Patience considered asking Bubbe if she could wake up Jace right this minute, so anxious was she to tell him. But she held back.

*Patience, Patience.* It was a refrain she had repeated to herself all night long, as she had packed her bags and waited for the snow to stop and the sky to grow light.

When Bubbe released her, she grabbed the spoon

and dumped three heaps of sugar into her coffee, then added a generous splash of cream.

"Patience," Bubbe said, watching her closely, "there's something you should know . . ."

*"New York?"* Jace echoed, staring at Patience's father in disbelief "What is she doing in New York?"

"She's in Brooklyn, actually," Patience's bathrobe-clad mother put in as her husband said, "She's looking for you."

"Looking for me?" Jace was stunned. "She went to Brooklyn looking for me?"

"I drove her to the airport first thing," said a tall man who had his arm around the pregnant Patience look-alike. He added, "I'm her brother-in-law Jermaine, by the way."

"And I'm her sister Hope," said his wife.

"I'm Faith," the blond woman next to her announced, and gestured at the man whose arms encircled her waist, "And this is Gary."

"It is really—" Jace, reeling, searched for the right words as he looked from one beaming face to the next. "—really incredible to meet you all. I've heard a lot about you. I'm just a little . . ."

"Surprised that Patience isn't here?" her father said helpfully.

"Exactly," he said, nodding, trying to digest the news. "So she went to Brooklyn."

"She didn't want to be away from you, Jace," Patience's mother spoke up. "She wanted to tell you—"

"Honey," Patience's father said in a warning voice.

"You're right," her mother said. "I'll let Patience tell you herself. It's just a shame that you missed her."

*'A shame' doesn't even begin to cover it,* Jace thought glumly.

* * *

*"New Hampshire?"* Patience echoed, gaping at Bubbe. "Jace went to New Hampshire? But—I mean—are you sure?"

"Positive."

"I can't believe it."

"Believe it," Bubbe said. "He drove all night. He called me from his car phone just before you knocked to tell me that he was almost at your parents' house."

"But . . . it was snowing," Patience protested, unable to fully grasp what Bubbe was telling her. "Jace wouldn't drive through snow. It's so dangerous, and he's so . . . well, you know."

"I know," Bubbe said with a nod. "But a man in love doesn't always stop to think. A man in love acts from the heart."

"A man . . . in *love?*" Patience echoed weakly.

Bubbe clamped a hand over her mouth.

"Bubbe," Patience said, her heart racing. "Are you saying—"

"I'm not saying anything else," Bubbe said, getting up and walking to the phone on the wall. She lifted the receiver and handed it to Patience. "I'll let my grandson do the talking from now on. Go on. Dial."


The telephone rang just as Jace was taking his first swallow of the rich, creamy, nutmeg-speckled eggnog Patience's mother had handed him. It was laced with rum that warmed his throat going down and his belly when it landed, warming him at last.

They were gathered around the big round oak table in the cozy kitchen with its blue-and-white-checked wallpaper. The house was just as Patience had described it, and so was her family. Comfortable and friendly and welcoming. He had been here only minutes, yet he knew it was the kind of place where he wanted to stay awhile. He wanted to fit in, to become one of them.

"I'll get it," Hope said, rising and going toward the phone on the wall behind the table.

"No," her father said, giving her a look. "Let Jace get it."

"Oh," Jace said, understanding. They thought it was Patience.

He lifted the receiver with a trembling hand. "Hello?"

"Jace!" Patience's voice exclaimed.

"Patience," he breathed, filled with longing so acute he sank into his chair again, shaking.

"You're there," she said, her voice choked with laughter—or tears—or both.

"I'm here," he said, conscious of her family listening. "And you're there."

"Happy Hanukkah, Jace."

"Merry Christmas, Patience." He took a deep breath and glanced around.

Her parents and sisters and brothers-in-law were watching him unabashedly.

It didn't matter. He didn't care who was watching, who was listening. His heart was brimming. He wanted her to know, he wanted her to know right now, that he really, truly—

"I love you, Jace," Patience said fervently.

"No!" he shouted, clutching the phone to his ear.

"Yes," she rushed on, "I do. I mean it, Jace. And even if you don't—I mean, I had hoped you—but if you—"

"I meant, *no, don't say it first,*" Jace said, dizzy with the emotions that careened through him. She loved him. She loved him! *"I* wanted to say it first. So you would know—So—oh, it doesn't matter. I love you, Patience Magee. I love you. I love you."

There. He had said it. Three times. He wanted to *keep* saying it, so he did.

"I love you!" He was exuberant.

"I love you!" Nothing had ever felt so wonderful in all of his life.

He loved her, and she . . .

Wow. She loved him.

"I love you, too," she was saying, laughing, crying, on the other end of the phone. "It doesn't matter who said it first, Jace. I love you and you love me and we belong together."

"Then how come we're not?" he asked, laughing, crying, too. "How am I supposed to give you your Christmas present over the phone?"

"You can give it to me later," she said. "It doesn't matter . . ."

And then he heard Bubbe's voice in the background. "Trust me, it matters. Don't wait, Jace," she was calling. "Give it to her." Jace reached into his pocket, and he looked around at Patience's family. They wore huge, delighted grins, all six of them.

"You guys have to help me out here," he said, and he handed her mother the phone.


"Patience?" her mother's voice asked in her ear.

"Mom! What are you doing on the line? Where's Jace?"

"Jace wants me to tell you what he's doing."

Patience frowned slightly as she wiped her eyes with the back of her hand, trying to compose herself.

"Why?" she asked. "What's he doing?"

Bubbe handed her a tissue.

# ASK ME AGAIN    251

"Thanks, Bubbe," she whispered, and blew her nose heartily, then asked, "Mom? What's he doing?"

"He . . . he's getting down on the floor." Her mother sounded concerned.

"Is he all right?" Patience asked, worried. "Jace?"

"He's . . . oh! He's on his knee, Patience. On one knee."

Patience's jaw dropped.

Bubbe was smiling at her.

"He's reaching into his pocket, Patience. He's taking something out."

"What . . . what is it, Mom?" Patience asked frantically. It couldn't be. It couldn't *be*.

"A ring!" her mother shrieked into the phone. "He has a ring, Patience, and it's . . . it's a beautiful antique ring. It looks like platinum, and diamonds."

"An antique ring," Patience told Bubbe in wonder. "He has an antique ring. But where did he——?"

And then she knew.

She took Bubbe's wrinkled old hand in her own and unfolded her fingers. The fourth one was bare. "Oh, Bubbe," she said on a sob, "your ring from Poppop."

"I want you to have it," Bubbe said, smiling through her own tears. "And someday, I want you to give it to your child. It belongs in the family . . . and so do you."

And then Patience heard Jace's voice on the line again, warm and sure as he said, "Patience, will you please do me the honor of becoming my wife?"

For a moment, the wind was knocked out of her.

"Ask me again," she whispered, then, pressing her hand against her heart.

"What?"

"Ask me again," she said, louder. "Those are the sweetest words I've ever heard, and I . . . I just never thought I'd hear you say them, and I want to hear them again. Please, Jace . . ."

"Patience," he said slowly, succinctly, with heartfelt emotion, "will you please do me the honor of becoming my wife?"

"Yes, Jace," she replied, her heart soaring. "Definitely. Yes, yes, yes."

"She said yes!" he shouted to her family, and Patience heard the other end of the line erupt into happy cheers.

"He asked me to marry him. Oh, Bubbe," she said, squeezing the old lady's ringless fingers.

"And you said yes." Bubbe nodded, satisfied. *"Mazeltov,* my dear."

"Patience?" Jace was calling over the phone. "Are you there?"

"I'm still here," she bubbled, giddy and breathless. Her head was spinning. "But, Jace, I can't stand being away from you. I need to come up there. I can rent a car—"

"No, I'll come back down there."

"That'll take too long. I know I'm working on having patience, and believe me, I'm doing a great job of it, but I don't want to wait for you to drive all the way here, Jace."

"Okay, then I have an idea," Jace said. "How about if we meet halfway?"

"That," Patience said with a grin, "is the best idea I've ever heard. I'll meet you halfway, Jace."

And she did.

# Epilogue

"Jace? Is that you?" Patience called, turning away from her computer screen when she heard a door slam. She was in her office—the smaller of two spare bedrooms in the spacious apartment she and Jace had leased just last week. Packed boxes were stacked all around her. She figured she'd get to them at some point. To his credit, Jace hadn't even bugged her about them.

"Yeah, it's me," Jace called back. She heard his keys jangling and knew he was hanging them on the hook beside the door. In theory, hers were supposed to be there, too, but as usual she had no idea where she'd left them.

She sighed. Maybe someday she'd learn to be as organized as Jace was. If not, oh well. She could certainly live with herself, and luckily, it had turned out Jace could, too. Especially since he had hired Aggie, their full-time housekeeper whose main purpose in life was to keep the apartment the way he liked it.

Jace appeared in the doorway, wearing a summer suit and tie and still holding his briefcase in one hand. "How's the last chapter going?"

"It's pretty much finished," she said, going over to him and stretching up to give him a kiss. "Mmm, you taste like lemonade."

"That's because I just drank about a gallon of it in the cab on the way uptown. You have no idea how hot it is out there."

"Yeah, well, July in Manhattan, Jace. What do you expect? Anyway, all you have to do is make it through another week, and then we'll be out of here until the middle of next month."

"Another whole week?" He groaned and tightened his arms around her. "I can't wait that long to marry you."

"I know." She kissed the soft hollow on his neck behind his ear. "I keep thinking we should scrap the whole wedding plan and go down to City Hall—like, *now*."

"You *would* think that," he said with a smile. "And it doesn't sound like a bad idea, except—"

"Everyone will be so disappointed," Patience said, nodding. "I know. After our parents went to so much trouble to line up a rabbi and a minister willing to collaborate—"

"And Bubbe made thirty dozen rugelach for the reception—"

"And my mother sewed all those tiny pearls on my headpiece—"

They sighed and touched their foreheads together.

"It's going to be a great wedding, you know," Patience said.

"Even if it's not barefoot on some beach?" Jace asked her, grinning.

She smiled back. "I'll live. I mean, who can complain about getting married at the Plaza Hotel? And then there's the European honeymoon . . ." She sighed blissfully.

"You're just marrying me for my money."

"Yup. It's the cold, hard truth—you were just my ticket out of the nine-to-five world, Jace. I wanted to live in this fabulous apartment—" Which happened to be located in the East Thirties, halfway between their former apartments, in a neighborhood that had character enough for Patience and was upscale enough for Jace—"and I wanted to sit at a computer all day in my pajamas and write romance novels—speaking of which, I have to print this out for you so you can read it and tell me what you think before I send to John."

"Who's John?"

"Camisha's book editor friend, remember? I've decided to use a pseudonym after all, though, because Patience Magee Hoffman is a real mouthful."

"What about a title? Did you come up with one yet?" Jace asked, as Patience returned to the keyboard and hit the Print command. The laser printer whirred to life.

"Yup." She grabbed a sheet of paper as it emerged from the printer, and handed it to him. "Here's the title page. What do you think?"

" *'Ask Me Again,'* " he read aloud, and smiled. "It's perfect."

"You think so?" She scrolled down the screen to the manuscript's last page. "What about the ending? I keep feeling like it needs something more. Maybe one more line."

"Allow me," Jace said. He reached past her to type, *"And they lived happily ever after."*

# BOOK YOUR PLACE ON OUR WEBSITE AND MAKE THE READING CONNECTION!

We've created a customized website just for our very special readers, where you can get the inside scoop on everything that's going on with Zebra, Pinnacle and Kensington books.

When you come online, you'll have the exciting opportunity to:

- View covers of upcoming books
- Read sample chapters
- Learn about our future publishing schedule (listed by publication month *and author*)
- Find out when your favorite authors will be visiting a city near you
- Search for and order backlist books from our online catalog
- Check out author bios and background information
- Send e-mail to your favorite authors
- Meet the Kensington staff online
- Join us in weekly chats with authors, readers and other guests
- Get writing guidelines
- AND MUCH MORE!

Visit our website at
http://www.zebrabooks.com